PRAISE FOR HÅKAN NESSER

THE INSPECTOR AND SILENCE

'The atmosphere of the small town, the mysterious fringes of the forest full of aspens and blueberries, are evocatively drawn . . . The clarity of Nesser's vision, the inner problems of good and evil with which Van Veeteren struggles, recall the films of Bergman'

Independent

'Satisfying novel from a rising Swedish star . . . Van Veeteren [the detective], disengaged, thinking of retirement and wonderfully enigmatic, makes an enjoyable change from all those fictional policemen who persist in taking their work home with disastrous consequences . . . an intense read'

Guardian Review

'Nesser works the slow pace skilfully and Van Veeteren is an appealing companion'

Metro Crime Books of the Year

WOMAN WITH A BIRTHMARK

'Håkan Nesser is in the front rank of Swedish crime writers . . . A novel with superior plot and characters'
The Times

'It's set to become Nesser's breakthrough novel in this country, and he is being favourably compared with Henning Mankell and Stieg Larsson'
Sunday Times

'Nesser is one of the best of the Swedish crime writers . . . a literate writing style, a brooding atmosphere and a plot that never wallows in the purely salacious . . . what might have been a routine serial-killer novel becomes a tense and subtle morality tale'
Mail on Sunday

THE MIND'S EYE

'Van Veeteren is a terrific character, and the courtroom scenes that begin this novel are cracking'
Daily Telegraph

'Håkan Nesser's Chief Inspector Van Veeteren has earned his place among the great Swedish detectives with a series of intriguing investigations . . . This is Van Veeteren at his quirkiest and most engaging'
Seven* magazine, *Sunday Telegraph

'A psychological thriller in a class of its own . . . This stunning novel by one of Sweden's foremost crime writers might have been written as a script for Alfred Hitchcock'
Sunday Times

THE RETURN

'Nesser made a strong impression with *Borkmann's Point*, the first of his novels published into English. *The Return* is just as tense and clever'

Marcel Berlins, *The Times*

'Nesser's insight into his main characters and gently humorous narrative raise his otherwise conventional police procedural to a higher level'

Sunday Telegraph

'This is splendid stuff: Scandinavian crime writing that is so rivetingly written it makes most contemporary crime fare – Nordic or otherwise – seem rather thin gruel'

Barry Forshaw, *Waterstone's Books Quarterly*

BORKMANN'S POINT

'An absorbing tale with an unexpected ending'
Sunday Telegraph

'The novel's prime asset is the mordant clarity of Nesser's voice. Its understatement is a pleasure in itself, as investigations pause for Van Veeteren to finish his beer'
Times Literary Supplement

'Van Veeteren is destined for a place amongst the great European detectives'
Colin Dexter

THE RETURN

Håkan Nesser is one of Sweden's most popular crime writers, receiving numerous awards for his novels featuring Inspector Van Veeteren, including the European Crime Fiction Star Award (Ripper Award) 2010/11, the Swedish Crime Writers' Academy Prize (three times) and Scandinavia's Glass Key Award. The Van Veeteren series is published in over 25 countries and has sold over 5 million copies worldwide. Håkan Nesser lives in Uppsala with his wife and two sons, and spends part of each year in the UK.

Also by Håkan Nesser

BORKMANN'S POINT

THE MIND'S EYE

WOMAN WITH A BIRTHMARK

THE INSPECTOR AND SILENCE

HÅKAN NESSER

THE RETURN

AN INSPECTOR VAN VEETEREN MYSTERY

Translated from the Swedish by
Laurie Thompson

PAN BOOKS

First published in Sweden 1995 as *Återkomsten*
by Albert Bonniers Forlag, Stockholm

First published in English 2007 by Pantheon books,
a division of Random House, Inc., New York

First published in Great Britain 2007 by Macmillan

This paperback edition published 2012 by Pan Books
an imprint of Pan Macmillan, a division of Macmillan Publishers Limited
Pan Macmillan, 20 New Wharf Road, London N1 9RR
Basingstoke and Oxford
Associated companies throughout the world
www.panmacmillan.com

ISBN 978-1-4472-2833-2

1 3 5 7 9 8 6 4 2

A CIP catalogue record for this book is available from
the British Library.

Typeset by Intype Libra Ltd, London
Printed and bound by CPI Group (UK) Ltd, Croydon CR0 4YY

You ask me how long life is,
and I shall tell you like it is.
Just as long as the distance
between two dates on a headstone.

W. F. Mahler, poet

ONE

24 AUGUST 1993

1

It was the first and the last day.

The steel door was locked behind him and the metallic click hovered for a while in the cool morning air. He took four paces, paused and put down his suitcase. Closed his eyes, then opened them again.

A thin morning mist hung over the deserted car park, the sun was just rising over the nearby town and the only sign of life was the flocks of birds swooping over the fields that surrounded the cluster of buildings. He stood there for a few seconds and indulged his senses. The scent of newly harvested corn wafted into his nostrils. The dazzling light quivered over the asphalt. In the distance, a mile or so to the west, he could hear the persistent hum of traffic on the motorway that carved a path through the open countryside. The sudden realization of the world's true dimensions gave him a moment of vertigo. He had not set foot outside these walls for twelve years; his cell had been seven feet by ten, and it dawned on him that it was a long way to the town and the railway station. An incredibly long way, perhaps impossibly far on a day like this.

He had been offered a taxi, that was normal practice, but he declined. Didn't want to take a shortcut into the world at this early stage. Wanted to feel the burden and the pain and the freedom in every step he took this morning. If he were to have a chance of succeeding in the task he had set himself, he understood what he needed to overcome. Overcome and get the better of.

He picked up his suitcase and started walking. It didn't weigh much. A few changes of underwear. A pair of shoes, a shirt, pants and a toiletry bag. Four or five books and a letter. He had tried on the clothes he was wearing and signed for them at the equipment store the previous day. Typical prison clothing. Black synthetic-leather shoes. Blue trousers. Pale grey cotton shirt and a thin windcheater. As far as the locals were concerned he would be as easily identifiable as a Roman Catholic priest or a chimney sweep. One of the many who wandered into the railway station carrying a cardboard suitcase, eager to leave. Having spent time out here in the Big Grey between the municipal forest and the motorway. Having been so near and yet so far away. One of them. The easily identifiable.

The Big Grey. That's what they called it around here. For him it was nameless – just a brief stretch of time and hardly any space. And it was a long time since he'd been worried about other people staring at him; a long time since he'd been forced to turn his back on that kind of superficial and pointless contact. He had left his former life without hesitation; there was no alternative, and he'd never longed to return. Never.

You could say he had never really been a part of it.

The sun rose. He had to stop again after a hundred yards. Wriggled out of his jacket and slung it over his shoulder. Two cars overtook him. A couple of warders, presumably, or some other staff. Prison people in any case. Nobody else ventured out here. There was only the Big Grey here.

He set off once more. Tried to whistle but couldn't hit upon a tune. It occurred to him that he ought to have sunglasses: Maybe he could buy a pair when he got to town. He shaded his eyes with his hand, squinted and scrutinized the townscape through the dazzling haze. At that very moment church bells started ringing.

He glanced at his wristwatch. Eight. He wouldn't be able to catch the first train. There again, he hadn't really wanted to: better to sit in the station café over a decent breakfast and today's paper. No rush. Not this first day, at least. He would carry out the task he'd set himself, but the precise timing depended on factors he knew nothing about as yet, naturally enough.

Tomorrow, perhaps. Or the day after. If all these years had taught him anything, anything at all, it was precisely this. To be patient.

Patience.

He continued walking purposefully towards town. Took possession of the deserted, sun-drenched streets. The shady alleys leading from the square. The worn cobbles. Strolled slowly along the path by the brown, muddy river where listless ducks drifted in a state of timeless inertia. This was in itself something remarkable – walking and walking without coming up against a wall or a fence. He paused on one of the bridges and watched a family of swans huddled together on a muddy islet, in the shade cast by chestnut trees on the riverbank. Observed the trees as well, their branches that seemed to stretch down as much as upwards. Towards the water as well as the sky.

The world, he thought. Life.

A spotty youth stamped his ticket with obvious distaste. Single ticket, yes, of course. He gave him a look, then headed for the news-stand. Bought two newspapers and some men's magazine or other featuring large, naked breasts, without displaying the slightest embarrassment.

Next, a pot of coffee in the café, freshly made sandwiches with jam and cheese. A cigarette or two. Another hour to go before the train, and it was still morning.

The first morning of his second return, and the whole world was full of time. Innocence and time.

Hours later he was nearly there. He'd been alone in the carriage for the last few miles. Looked out through the scratched, dirty window; watched fields, forests, towns and people marching past – and suddenly everything fell into place. Took on their own specific significance. Buildings, roads, the subtle interplay of the countryside. The old water tower. The soccer fields. The factory chimneys and people's back gardens. Gahn's Furniture Manufacturers. The square. The high school. The viaduct and the houses along Main Street. The train ground to a halt.

As he disembarked he noticed that the platform had a new roof of pale yellow plastic. The station building had been renovated. New signs as well.

Apart from that it was just as before.

He took a cab. Left the town behind. A quarter of an hour's drive with nothing said, following the shore of the lake that sometimes vanished, sometimes glittered beyond cornfields and copses of deciduous trees, and then he was there.

'You can stop after the church. I'll walk the last bit.'

He paid and got out. There was something vaguely familiar about the driver's wave as he drove off. He waited until the car had made a U-turn and disappeared behind the dairy. Then he picked up his suitcase and the plastic carrier bag of groceries and set out on the last lap.

The sun was high in the sky now. Sweat was running down his face and between his shoulder blades. It was farther than he remembered, and more uphill.

But then, it was twelve years since the last time.

The house was also twelve years older, but it was still there. She had cleared a path as far as the steps, as promised, but no more. The borderline between garden and forest seemed to be blurred, birch saplings had invaded, grass and undergrowth were three or four feet high along the house walls. The roof of the barn was sagging, the roof tiles seemed to be rotting away, an upstairs windowpane was broken, but it didn't bother him. Insofar as he had expected anything, it all came more or less up to expectations.

The key was hanging under the gutter, as it should have

been. He unlocked the door. Had to give it a heave with his shoulder in order to open it. It seemed to have swelled a bit.

It smelled stuffy, but not excessively so. No rot, no mice, apparently. There was a note on the kitchen table.

She wished him all the best, it said. That was all.

He put his suitcase and the plastic carrier on the sofa under the clock and looked around. Started to walk round the house and open windows. He paused in front of the mirror in the bedroom and examined his own image.

He had aged. His face was grey and hollow. His lips thinner and more severe. His neck looked puffy and wrinkled. His shoulders lopsided and somehow dejected.

Fifty-seven years old, he thought. Twenty-four behind bars. No wonder.

He turned his back on himself and started looking for a gun. He had to have a gun, no matter what, so he'd better find one right away. Before he started having second thoughts.

As evening approached he sat in the kitchen with the letter. Read it through one more time, his cup of coffee standing on the flowery tablecloth.

It wasn't long. One and a half pages, almost. He closed his eyes and tried to see her in his mind's eye.

Her dark eyes, marked already by death, on the other side of the grille. Her hands wringing.

And her story.

No, there was no other way.

TWO

20 APRIL TO 5 MAY 1994

2

It was one of those outings.

There should have been four adults, of course. Or at least three. That had been the intention, but half an hour before they were due to leave Henriette had phoned to report yet another less than convincing indisposition. Shortly afterwards it became clear that Hertl ought to stay behind and assist the nurse, who was due that afternoon to vaccinate the two-year-olds.

Which meant that only Elisabeth and Moira were left. It could be taken for granted that Moira would feel a migraine coming on sooner or later. So in practice Elisabeth would be in sole charge of the whole flock. But so what? It wouldn't be the first time.

Fourteen of them. Varying in age between three and six. Eunice, six, set the ball rolling by throwing up in the bus after a mere five hundred yards. Paul, three, peed himself copiously at about the same time. Shortly afterwards Ellen and Judith, four and five, attempted to scratch each other's eyes out over a green scarf with pink rabbits. Emile, three and a half, started yelling for his mother so loudly that the whole bus shook, and Christophe, six, had a toothache.

They were well behaved as they got off the bus when it stopped at the edge of the woods. She counted them quickly. All present and correct. Fourteen, fifteen with Moira. She took a deep breath. Three hours of walking through the trees, grilling sausages, a treasure hunt and various botanical excursions lay in store. She could just about see the sky getting darker through the crowns of the trees, and she wondered how long it would be before it started pouring down.

It took barely twenty-five minutes, in fact, but they were quite a long way into the woods by then. Moira had started to feel a throbbing in her forehead and was keeping fifty yards ahead of the main group so as not to make it any worse. Erich and Wally had been teasing Eunice so much that the fat little girl refused to stay with the others: She was walking by herself in among the trees and undergrowth instead of sticking to the path, but Elisabeth kept shouting to her to maintain contact. One of the Jümpers twins had fallen and hit his head on a tree root, so she had to carry him. The other one was playing around behind her, clinging to her belt with grubby fingers.

'It's started raining!' yelled Bartje, four.

'I want to go home!' squealed Heinrich, five.

'Stupid bastards,' declared Erich and Wally. 'Clear off home and screw your mum.'

'Screw her,' squeaked an anonymous three-year-old.

'Shut up, Wally and Erich,' hissed Elisabeth. 'If you don't I'll cut your ears off.'

Moira had stopped at one of the volunteer corps huts where they were going to have lunch.

'We're in luck,' she whispered when the main group had caught up with her. As usual she felt obliged to whisper to prevent the migraine from bursting out into full bloom. 'Hurry up now and come in out of the rain!'

Even before Wally had got as far as the door it had dawned on Elisabeth that it was locked, and the key was in Hertl's purse in the staff room.

'It's locked, for fuck's sake!' yelled Erich. 'Hand over the damn key!'

Moira looked uncomprehendingly at Elisabeth, who sighed. Closed her eyes and counted up to three. It was raining cats and dogs, and she could feel her heels slowly sinking into the soaking wet grass.

'I'm cold,' piped the Jümpers brat in her arms, shivering.

'I'm hungry,' said the other one.

'Don't say you've forgotten the key, you stupid bitches!' yelled Erich, hurling a lump of mud at the wall.

Elisabeth thought for three more seconds. Then she thrust her injured patient into Moira's arms, went around to the back of the hut and smashed a window.

It stopped raining after about an hour. All the packed lunches had been eaten, Elisabeth had read eighteen fairy tales that she'd read eighteen hundred times before, some of the five- and six-year-olds had gone off exploring on their own and were so caked in mud that she doubted whether the bus driver would allow them on board again. Moira had managed to snatch some sleep in an upstairs room and felt a little bit better, but not much. Gerard, three years old and allergic, had come out in an angry rash on his face and around the crook of his arms, thanks to a candy with nuts that some as-yet-unidentified friend had tricked him into eating. One of the four-year-olds and a three-year-old had peed themselves.

Apart from that, everything was under control. She decided to assemble the children on the steps outside and prepare for the walk back to the bus stop.

Thirteen. There were only thirteen of them. Fourteen with Moira.

'Who's missing?' she asked.

It turned out to be Eunice.

Preliminary cross-questioning revealed that she had vanished about twenty or maybe even thirty-five minutes ago. Nobody was exactly championship class when it came to timing, and the reason for her disappearance was not all that clear either – Wally or Erich, or possibly both of them, might have hit her with a lump of wood, Marissa could perhaps have called her a fatty-face. Or maybe she had a stomach ache.

Most likely a combination of all those things.

After a few minutes of vague shouting and screeching, Elisabeth decided that a search party was called for.

Moira would have to look after the three- and four-year-olds inside the hut, while she would take the older children with her into the woods.

Older? she thought. Five and six years old. Seven of them.

'We'll walk in a line at ten-yard intervals,' she explained. 'We'll keep shouting all the time, and keep in sight of each other. Is that clear?'

'Yes, boss!' yelled Wally, giving her a salute.

*

It was Wally who eventually found her.

'She's sitting in a goddamn ditch, hiccupping,' he said. 'Over there. She says she's found a dead body without a head.'

Elisabeth knew right away that this was the truth. The time was ripe for the day's highlight.

In fact it wasn't only the head that was missing. The body – what was left of it – had been wrapped up in a thick carpet, and there was no time to extract from Eunice an explanation of why on earth she had wanted to investigate it. Perhaps a bone had been sticking out. In any case, the well-built and strong little girl had managed to drag it far enough out of the ditch for her to be able to unroll it. The carpet was soaked through . . . and covered in mould and fungi and every imaginable kind of decay, it seemed to Elisabeth. It was falling to pieces in some parts, and the body in the middle of it was no doubt in just as bad a state.

No head, then. No hands, no feet.

'Back to the hut!' she bellowed, clutching the shivering Eunice tightly in her arms.

She suddenly felt violently sick, and it struck her that what she had just been staring at was one of those visions that would turn up faithfully in her mind's eye every dark night for the rest of her life.

3

'Report, please,' said Hiller, clasping his hands.

Reinhart gazed up at the ceiling. Münster dutifully performed the throat-clearing ritual and Van Veeteren yawned.

'Well?' said Hiller.

'Let me see,' said Münster, leafing through his notebook.

'Come on now, get a grip!' said the chief of police, checking his rolled-gold wristwatch. 'I have a meeting in twenty-five minutes from now, an outline report will suffice.'

Münster cleared his throat again.

'Well, we're dealing with the body of a man,' he began. 'Found at about one yesterday afternoon in some woods on the outskirts of Behren, about twenty miles from here. Found by a six-year-old girl . . . she was on an outing organized by the day nursery she attends. The body was wrapped up inside a carpet in a ditch about forty yards from the nearest passable road, and it had been lying there for a long time.'

'How long?'

'A good question,' said Reinhart. 'A year, perhaps. Maybe more, maybe less.'

'Can't that be established accurately?' Hiller asked.

'Not yet,' Van Veeteren said. 'Meusse is working flat out on it. But at least six months in any case.'

'Hmm,' said Hiller. 'Go on.'

'Well,' said Münster, 'it hasn't been possible to identify the body as the murderer cut off his head, his hands and his feet . . .'

'Can we be certain that it was a murder?' asked the chief of police. Reinhart sighed.

'No,' he said. 'Obviously, it could be a straightforward natural death. Somebody who couldn't afford a proper funeral, though. It's an expensive business nowadays . . . The widow no doubt donated his head and the rest to medical research, in accordance with the wishes of the deceased.'

Van Veeteren coughed.

'It'll presumably take a while to pin down the cause of death,' he said, inserting a toothpick into his lower teeth. 'It seems there are no signs of fatal injuries on what's left of the body – although people generally do die if you cut their head off, of course.'

'Meusse isn't exactly thrilled by this corpse,' said Reinhart. 'You can see his point. It's been lying in that rotting carpet all winter, maybe longer. Freezing, then thawing out, freezing again, thawing again. The odd animal has had a nibble here and there, but they evidently didn't think much of him either. I suppose he was a bit hard to get at as well. He's been lying half submerged, and that's helped to preserve him or there wouldn't have been much left apart from the skeleton. He looks a bit of a mess, to be honest.'

Hiller hesitated.

'Why are . . . Why are these parts of the body missing, do we know that?'

We? Münster thought. Do we know that? What is this damn place, a police station or a hospital? Or a madhouse, like Reinhart usually suggests? Sometimes it was hard to say.

'Hard to say,' said Van Veeteren, reading his thoughts. 'We do occasionally come across a bit of butchery in this line of business, but the point must surely be to make identification difficult.'

'You have no idea who it is?'

Van Veeteren shook his head.

'Obviously, we're going over the area with a fine-tooth comb,' Münster said. 'But then, you ordered that yourself. Twenty officers have been searching the woods since yesterday afternoon – not during the night, though, of course.'

'Waste of time,' said Reinhart, taking his pipe from his jacket pocket.

'You can smoke when we've finished,' said the police chief, checking his watch again. 'Why is it a waste of time?'

Reinhart put his pipe away and clasped his hands behind his head.

'Because they won't find anything,' he explained. 'If I kill somebody and take time to cut off his head and hands and feet, I'm not going to be damned stupid enough to leave them lying around where the rest of the body is. The fact is that there's only one place in the whole wide world where we can be absolutely certain of not finding them, and that's where we're looking. Clever stuff, you have to admit.'

'All right,' said Hiller. 'Van Veeteren wasn't here yesterday, and I thought . . .'

'OK,' said Van Veeteren. 'I suppose there's no harm in taking a close look at the place where the body was found, but I think we'll put a stop to that this evening. Not many clues are going to survive a whole winter, no matter what, and I think we can be pretty sure he wasn't killed there anyway.'

Hiller hesitated again.

'How are we going to set up the investigation, then?' he asked. 'I'm a bit short of time . . .'

Van Veeteren made no attempt to hurry.

'Well,' he said, 'I suppose we'd better think that over. How many officers do you want to give us?'

'There're those damned robberies,' said Hiller, rising to his feet. 'And that blackmailer . . .'

'And those racists,' said Reinhart.

'This blackmailer . . .' said Hiller.

'Racist bastards,' said Reinhart.

'Oh, what the hell,' said Hiller. 'Stop by tomorrow, VV, and let's see where we've got to. Is Heinemann still off sick?'

'Back on Monday,' said Münster.

He didn't mention that he was intending to take a few days off when Heinemann came back. Something told him that now wasn't the right moment to apply for leave.

'OK, you'd better get on with it,' said Hiller, starting to usher everybody towards the door. 'The quicker we sort this one out, the better. It shouldn't be too difficult to find out who the poor sod is, in any case. Don't you think?'

'Nothing is impossible,' said Reinhart.

'Well, what do you reckon, Münster?' said Van Veeteren, handing over the photographs.

Münster examined the pictures of the mutilated body, covered in brown stains, and of the spot where it was found: quite a good hiding place by the look of it, with thick undergrowth and an overgrown ditch. Hardly surprising that the body had been undetected for so long. On the contrary, its unexpected discovery by the poor little six-year-old girl surely had to be classified as pure coincidence.

'I don't know,' he said. 'Seems to have been pretty carefully planned, in any case.'

Van Veeteren muttered something.

'Carefully planned, you can say that again. We can take that for granted. What do you say to the mutilation?'

Münster thought for a moment.

'Identification, obviously.'

'Do you usually recognize people by their feet?'

Münster shook his head.

'Not unless there's something special about them. Tattoos or something of that sort. How old was he?'

'Between fifty and sixty, Meusse thought, but we'll have to wait until tonight. It's not a very nice body, as we've already established. It'll probably be you and Rooth who have to look after it.'

Münster looked up.

'Why? What are you . . . ?'

Van Veeteren raised a warning finger.

'I'm up to the neck in it with this damned robber. And no doubt Reinhart will want to wrap up his terrorists as quickly as possible. And then, well, I'll be going in soon to have my stomach cut up. First week in May. You might as well take charge of everything from the start.'

Münster could feel himself blushing.

'Obviously, I'll be at your service when you find yourself in a corner,' Van Veeteren said.

When, Münster thought. Not if.

'I'd better find a corner where I can get stuck first,' he said. 'Has Rooth checked missing persons yet?'

Van Veeteren switched on the intercom and five minutes later Detective Inspector Rooth appeared with a sheaf of computer printouts in his hand. He flopped down onto the empty chair and scratched his beard. It was straggly and recent and made him look like a homeless dosser, it seemed to Münster. But so what? It could be an advantage to have colleagues who couldn't be picked out as the filth from a hundred yards away.

'Thirty-two missing persons reported in our area over the last couple of years,' he announced. 'Who haven't been found, that is. Sixteen locals. I've been weeding them out a bit. If we assume that he's been lying out there for at least six months and at most a year, he ought to have been reported as missing between April and December last year. We'll have to see if that's right when we get Meusse's report, of course . . .'

'How can as many people as that go missing?' wondered Münster. 'Can that really be right?'

Rooth shrugged.

'Most of them go abroad. Mainly young people. I doubt if there's any kind of crime involved in more than fifteen or twenty per cent of the cases. That's what Stauff claims, anyway, and he knows what he's talking about. I assume he's not including minor misdemeanours. Quite a lot of druggies go missing. Clear off to Thailand and India and places like that.'

Van Veeteren nodded.

'How many candidates does that leave you with?'

Rooth thumbed through the lists. Münster could see that he had circled round some names, put a question mark against others, crossed some out, but there didn't seem to be many hot tips.

'Not a lot,' said Rooth. 'If we're looking for a man in his fifties, about five feet ten, including his head and his feet – well, I reckon there are only a couple to choose from. Maybe three.'

Van Veeteren studied his toothpick.

'One will be enough,' he said. 'As long as it's the right one.'

'He doesn't need to be a local either,' said Münster. 'There's nothing to suggest that he was killed in the Behren area. It could have been anywhere, as far as I can see.'

Rooth nodded.

'If we consider the list from the country as a whole,

we've got seven or eight to choose from. In any case, I suppose we'd better wait for the post-mortem report before we start looking for possible widows?'

'Yes indeed,' said Van Veeteren. 'The fewer that need to look at him, the better.'

'OK,' said Münster after a pause, 'what do we do in the meantime, then?'

Van Veeteren leaned back, making his desk chair creak.

'I suggest you two clear off somewhere and draw up an outline plan. I'll tell Hiller you're sorting everything out. But as I say, I'm at your disposal.'

'Well then,' said Rooth when they had settled down in the canteen with their mugs of coffee. 'Do you reckon we can sort this out within a week?'

'I hope so,' said Münster. 'When does Meusse expect to be ready?'

Rooth checked his watch.

'In about an hour, I think. We'd better go and see him together, don't you think?'

Münster agreed.

'What about a response from the general public?' he asked. 'There's been quite a bit in the papers.'

Rooth shook his head as he washed down half a Danish pastry.

'Nothing that makes sense so far. Krause is keeping an eye on that side of things. There'll be an appeal on the news tonight, both on the telly and on radio. But I'll be damned if it isn't one of these.'

He tapped the computer printouts with his spoon. Münster picked up the lists and considered Rooth's notes. He'd drawn a double circle round three of the names: they seemed to be the hottest candidates.

Candidates for having been murdered, mutilated and dumped in an overgrown ditch just outside Behren, that is. He ran through them:

Claus Menhevern
Drouhtens vej 4, Blochberg
born 1937
reported missing 1/6/1993

Pierre Kohler
Armastenstraat 42, Maardam
born 1936
reported missing 27/8/1993

Piit Choulenz
Hagmerlaan 11, Maardam
born 1945
reported missing 16/10/1993

'Yep,' he said, sliding the lists back over the table. 'It's got to be one of them.'

'Sure,' said Rooth. 'In that case, we'll crack it within a week. I can feel it in my bones . . .'

4

He left the police station an hour earlier than usual and drove straight home. The letter was still where he'd left it, on the bookshelf in the hall. He opened it and read it once more. The text was still the same:

> We are pleased to inform you herewith that a time has been reserved for the operation on your Cancer Adenocarcinoma Coli on Tuesday, May 5.
>
> You are requested to confirm this date by mail or telephone by April 25 at the latest, and to present yourself at Ward 46B no later than 9 p.m. on Wednesday, May 4.
>
> After the operation a further two to three weeks in the hospital will probably be necessary; we mention this in order to assist you in planning your domestic and working life accordingly.
>
> Yours faithfully,
> Marike Fischer, Appointments Secretary,
> Gemejnte Hospitaal, Maardam

Oh, hell! he thought. Then he checked the data at the bottom of the page, dialled the number and waited.

A young girl's voice answered. Twenty-five at most, he decided. Like his own daughter, more or less.

'I suppose I'd better turn up then,' he said.

'Excuse me? Who's that speaking?' she asked.

'Detective Chief Inspector Van Veeteren, of course. I have cancer of the large intestine, and I'm going to let this Dr Moewenroedhe cut it out, and . . .'

'One moment.'

He waited. She picked the phone up again.

'May fifth, that's right. I'll make a note. We look forward to seeing you the day before. I'll reserve a bed for you in Ward forty-six B. Have you got any questions?'

Will it hurt? he thought. Will I survive? What percentage never come around from the anaesthetic?

'No,' he said. 'I'll get back to you if I change my mind.'

He could hear the surprise in her silence.

'Why should you change your mind?'

'I might be busy with something else. You never know.'

She hesitated.

'Are you worried about the operation, Mr Van Veeteren?'

'Worried? Me?'

He tried to laugh, but even he could hear that it sounded

more like a dying dog. He had some experience of dying dogs.

'That's all right, then,' she said cheerfully. 'I can assure you that Dr Moewenroedhe is one of our most skilful surgeons, and it's not all that complicated an operation after all.'

No, but it's my stomach, Van Veeteren thought. And my intestine. I've had it for a long time and I've grown quite fond of it.

'You're welcome to call and ask questions if you like,' she added. 'We're here to help.'

'Thank you very much,' he said with a sigh. 'OK, I'll probably call you beforehand, in any case. Goodbye.'

'We look forward to seeing you, Mr Van Veeteren.'

He stood for a few seconds with the letter in his hand. Then he tore it into four pieces and threw it into the waste-paper basket.

Less than an hour later he had eaten two bratwurst sausages with potato salad on his balcony. Drunk a glass of dark beer with it and started to wonder if he ought to go to the corner shop and buy a pack of cigarettes. He had run out of toothpicks and it was a pleasant evening.

I'm going to die, in any case, he thought.

He heard the clock striking six in Keymer. In his bedside

cupboard he had two half-read novels tucked away, but he accepted that they would have to remain half read for some time yet. He wasn't sufficiently at peace with himself. On the contrary, restlessness was lurking inside him, sharpening its claws, and of course there was no mystery about why.

No secret at all. The air was mild; he could feel that. A gentle, warm breeze wafted over the balcony rail, the sun was a red disc over the brewery roof on the other side of Kloisterlaan. Small birds were twittering away in the lilac bushes behind the cycle shed.

Here I am, he thought. The notorious Chief Inspector Van Veeteren. A fifty-seven-year-old, 195-pound cop with cancer of the large intestine. Two weeks from now I shall lie down on the operating table of my own free will and allow some totally inexperienced butcher's apprentice to cut out four inches of my body. Hell.

He could feel a vague turmoil in the lower part of his stomach, but that was always the same after eating nowadays. No pain as such. Just this little irritation. Something to be grateful for, of course. It was true that bratwurst was not on the diet sheet he'd been presented with when they did the tests in February, but what the hell? The main thing was to last until the day of the operation with his mind still working. If all turned out well, then it might be time to consider a new lifestyle. Healthy living and all that.

There's a time for everything.

He cleared the table. Went to the kitchen and piled the dirty dishes in the sink. Continued into the living room and sorted absentmindedly through his collection of CDs and tapes.

Four inches of my body, he thought, and then was struck by the photographs he'd seen that morning.

The headless man out at Behren.

Missing a head, two hands and two feet.

Could have been worse, he thought.

Between fifty and sixty, Meusse had judged.

That matched. Perhaps the two of them were the same age, in fact? Fifty-seven. Why not?

It could have been much worse.

Ten minutes later he was in his car with a Monteverdi choral piece rattling the loudspeakers. Another hour and a half before it got dark. He had plenty of time.

He only wanted to take a look, that's all. He didn't have anything else to do . . .

There's a time for everything, as he'd already established.

5

'How's the love life going?' asked Münster as he eased himself into Rooth's old Citroën. They ought to talk about something that had nothing to do with work, after all.

'Not very well,' said Rooth. 'I sometimes wish they could give you an injection that would cure you of any urges once and for all.'

'Oh dear,' said Münster, wishing he'd never broached the subject.

'There's something odd about women,' said Rooth. 'The ones I meet, at least. I took a lady out last week – a red-headed broad from Oosterbrügge who was attending some nursing course or other here in Maardam. We went to the movies and saw Krause, and then when I invited her up to my place for a glass of port wine and a bite of cheese, do you know what she said?'

'No idea,' said Münster.

'That she had to get back home to the boyfriend. He'd

come to visit her and was waiting for her at the hostel she was staying at. Or so she said.'

'Hard cheese,' said Münster.

'A real cock-up,' said Rooth. 'No, I think I'm getting too old to go running after women. Maybe I ought to try putting an ad in the newspapers instead. Kurmann in Missing Persons has found himself a very nice bit of stuff that way . . . But you have to have the luck of the devil, of course.'

He concentrated on overtaking a blue removal van before finding himself nose to nose with a No. 12 tram. Münster closed his eyes, and on opening them again was able to establish that they had made it.

'What about you?' asked Rooth. 'Still no snags with the most beautiful policeman's wife in the world?'

'Pure paradise,' said Münster; and when he came to think about it, that wasn't so far from the truth. But Synn was Synn. The only thing that worried him now and again was what a woman like her could see in him – a badly paid detective ten years older than she was, who worked so hard that he hardly ever had time for her or the children. It was easy to convince himself that he had something more than he deserved. That sooner or later he would be punished for it.

But why worry? He was happily married, had two children; perhaps he should just be grateful and accept whatever came his way, for once. In any case, that was not something he had any desire to discuss with Detective Inspector Rooth.

'You should get rid of that beard,' he said instead. 'If I were a woman, I'd run a mile from that fuzz.'

Rooth ran his hand over his chin and examined his face in the rear-view mirror.

'I don't know, damn it all,' he said. 'Doesn't look all that bad, I reckon. I'm not sure you understand the way women think.'

'OK,' said Münster. 'You do what you like. How are we going to deal with Meusse?'

'I suppose we'd better buy him a drink, as usual,' said Rooth as he pulled up outside the forensic clinic. 'Or what do you say?'

'Yep, no doubt that will be the simplest way,' said Münster.

Meusse was not yet finished with today's quota of dead bodies, and rather than interrupt him, Münster and Rooth decided to wait for him in his office.

He turned up twenty minutes late, and Münster could see that he'd had a rough day. His thin, bird-like body seemed skinnier than ever, his face was ashen and behind his thick glasses his eyes seemed to have sunk deep into their sockets – after having seen enough, and no doubt more than enough, of the evil and perversity this world has to offer, one could safely assume. As far as Münster was concerned, looking at the butchered body for five seconds would have been enough, or ten seconds examining the photographs. He guessed that the forensic specialist must have been poking around in the rotten flesh for at least ten or twelve hours.

Meusse nodded a greeting without saying a word and hung his stained white coat on a hook next to the door. Washed his hands and wriggled his way into the jacket that had been lying on his desk. Stroked his completely bald head a few times and sighed.

'Well, what can I do for you gentlemen?'

'Maybe we'd find it a bit easier to talk over a glass of something tasty in the bar?' Rooth suggested.

The Fix bar was just over the road from the forensic laboratories – if you left by the back door, that is, and there seemed to be no reason to take any other exit but the usual one today either.

Meusse led the way, hands in pockets and shoulders hunched, and it wasn't until he had a double gin and a beer chaser on the table in front of him that he seemed up to discussing his findings. Both Münster and Rooth had been through this many times before and knew there was no point in trying to speed him up – or in interrupting him once he'd got going, come to that. He would answer any questions when he'd said what he had to say; it was as simple as that.

'Well, gentlemen,' he began. 'I note that Chief Inspector Van Veeteren is conspicuous by his absence on this occasion. Can't say I'm surprised. This body you've come across is a pretty nasty object. If a mere pathologist might be allowed to express a wish, it would be that you would make an effort to dig them out a bit sooner in future. We are not exactly inspired by dead bodies that have been rotting away for an age . . . Three months, four at most, that's where the limit ought to be set. The fact is that one of my assistants couldn't cope and let me down this afternoon. Hmm.'

'How old is this one, then?' asked Rooth, trying to put his oar in while Meusse was busy exploring the depths of his beer glass.

'As I said,' he went on, 'it's an unusually unsavoury body.'

Unsavoury? Münster thought, and recalled how Meusse had once told him how his life had been changed and made more miserable by his less-than-uplifting profession. How he had been impotent by the age of thirty, how his wife had left him when he was thirty-five, how he'd turned vegetarian at forty, and how he'd more or less stopped eating solid food by the time he was fifty . . . His own body and its functions had become more and more repulsive as the years went by. Something he could only feel disgust and aversion for, he had confessed to Münster and Van Veeteren one afternoon when, for whatever reason, the drinks had become more numerous than usual.

Perhaps that was nothing to be surprised by, Münster thought. Merely a natural development?

'It is difficult to be specific about the time,' said Meusse, lighting a cigarillo. 'I would guess about eight months, but I could easily be wrong by a month or two in either direction. We'll have the lab report in a week or so. Cause of death will be just as hard to pin down, I fear. The only thing that's obvious, of course, is that he died some considerable time earlier . . . Before he was dumped in the ditch, that is. At least twelve hours, no doubt about that. Maybe as much as twenty-four hours. There is no blood on the carpet, and not much in the body either, come to that. The decapitation and mutilation took place at an earlier stage. The blood had drained away, to put it in simple terms.'

'How did the butchery take place?' Münster asked.

'In an amateurish way,' said Meusse. 'An axe, presumably. It doesn't seem to have been all that sharp, so it probably took quite a while.'

He emptied his glass. Rooth went to get him a refill.

*

'What I can say about the cause of death is that it was in his head.'

'In his head?' said Rooth.

'In his head, yes,' said Meusse, pointing at his own bald pate to make his meaning clearer. 'He might have been shot through the head or killed by that axe, or something else. But the cause of death was a blow to the head. Apart from the mutilations and natural decay, the body is uninjured. Well, I'm ignoring certain secondary effects caused by hungry foxes and crows who managed to get at it in a few places, but even they haven't caused all that much damage. The carpet and the water in the ditch have had a certain amount of embalming effect. Or delayed the onset of decay at least.'

Münster had picked up his beer glass, but put it back down on the scratched table.

'As for age and distinctive features,' said Meusse, who was unstoppable once he was in his stride, 'we can assume he was between fifty-five and sixty, or thereabouts. He would have been five foot nine or five foot ten, slimly built. Well proportioned, I think I can say. No broken arms or legs, no surgical scars. There might have been some other superficial scars, but they have either rotted away or stuck to the carpet. Things were made a bit more difficult by what you might call a symbiosis of death between the body and the carpet. They have sort of fused together here and there, or do you say fused into each other?'

'Holy shit!' said Rooth.

'Precisely,' said Meusse. 'Any questions?'

'Are there any distinctive features at all?' Münster asked.

Meusse smiled. His thin lips parted and revealed two rows of unexpectedly white and healthy teeth.

'There is one,' he said, and it was obvious that he was enjoying this. The pleasure of being able to keep them on tenterhooks at least for a second or two. Satisfying his professional honour, Münster thought.

'If the murderer was in fact trying to remove things that would make identification possible,' said Meusse, 'he missed one.'

'What was that, then?' wondered Rooth.

'A testicle.'

'Eh?' said Münster.

'He had only one testicle,' explained Meusse.

'Einstein?' said Rooth, looking foolish.

'Hmm,' said Münster. 'That will need following up, of course.'

He realized immediately that he had offended the little pathologist by his irony. He coughed and raised his glass, but it was too late.

'As far as the carpet is concerned,' said Meusse curtly, 'you'll have to speak to Van Impe tomorrow. I think I'll have to go now. Obviously, you will have a written report on your well-polished desks tomorrow morning.'

He emptied his glass and stood up.

'Thank you,' said Rooth.

'Good evening, gentlemen,' said Meusse. 'It would be appreciated if you didn't call in with another old torso during the next few days.'

He paused in the doorway.

'But if you come across the remaining parts of the one we already have, we shall naturally help you to match them up. We're always pleased to be of assistance.'

Münster and Rooth stayed put for a few more minutes and finished their beer.

'Why has he only one testicle?' asked Rooth.

'No idea,' said Münster. 'Mind you, one's enough when all's said and done. I suppose he must have injured the other one. An operation, maybe?'

'Could some animal or other have eaten it? While the body was in the ditch, I mean.'

Münster shrugged.

'Search me. But if Meusse maintains it was missing from the start, no doubt it was.'

Rooth nodded.

'A damned good clue,' he said.

'Yes,' said Münster. 'It's the kind of thing that's bound

to be in all the databases. NB, only has one ball! Do you still think we'll clear this up inside a week?'

'No,' said Rooth. 'Inside a year maybe. Let's be off.'

They didn't speak much during the drive back to the police station. One thing was obvious, however: the third man on the list of possible candidates, Piit Choulenz from Hagmerlaan, was presumably on the young side. According to the information they had, he had not yet reached fifty, and even if Meusse was careful to say that he was only guessing, Rooth and Münster both knew that he was rarely wrong. Not even when he was only speculating.

But both Claus Menhevern and Pierre Kohler were possibilities, it seemed. And naturally, they would take one each. They didn't even need to discuss that.

'Which one would you like?' asked Rooth.

Münster looked at the names.

'Pierre Kohler,' he said. 'I suppose we might as well get that sorted out this evening?'

Rooth looked at his watch.

'Absolutely,' he said. 'It's only just turning seven. No self-respecting cop should turn up at home before nine.'

6

When he got there, they were busy packing stuff into the patrol wagons.

'Good evening, Chief Inspector,' said Inspector le Houde. 'Is there anything special you want?'

Van Veeteren shook his head.

'I just thought I'd take a look. Have you abandoned the fingertip search now?'

'Yes,' said le Houde. 'We had orders to that effect. Seems fair enough. Not much hope of anything turning up, I don't suppose.'

'Have you found anything?'

Le Houde gave a laugh. Took out a handkerchief and wiped his brow.

'Quite a lot,' he said, pointing at a collection of black plastic sacks in the patrol wagon with the back doors open. 'Six of those. We've collected everything that didn't ought to be in a forest . . . from an area equal to about twenty soccer fields. It'll be fun going through it all.'

'Hmm,' said Van Veeteren.

'We'll be sending a bill to Behren's Public Cleansing Department. It's their job after all.'

'Do that,' said Van Veeteren. 'Anyway, I'll have a scout around.'

'Good luck,' said le Houde, closing the doors. 'We'll be in touch.'

He followed the path. That was where the group from the day nursery had walked, if he understood it rightly. It wasn't much of a path, mind you, not more than a couple of feet wide, full of roots and sharp stones and all kinds of bumps and pot-holes. The local police were doubtless right: the murderer had come from a different direction. The probability was that he'd parked on the bridle path on the other side of the little ridge that ran right through the woods – then he must have carried, or dragged, his load fifty or sixty yards through the undergrowth, uphill. The woods were not very well maintained, it was fair to say – so it was quite a task. Unless there had been more than one person involved, the murderer must have been pretty big and strong. Hardly a woman, nor an elderly man: surely that was a reasonable conclusion to draw?

He reached the spot. The red and white tape still cordoned off the relevant stretch of ditch, but there were no longer any guards on duty. He stopped three or four yards short of the tape and spent half a minute studying the grim plot, wishing he had a cigarette.

Then he stepped over the ditch and made his way towards the bridle path. The murderer's route, in all probability. It took him seven or eight minutes and resulted in several scratches on his face and hands.

If we'd found him right away, he thought, we could have followed his route inch by inch.

That was impossible now, of course.

Impossible, and not of much interest either, presumably. If they ever did get to the bottom of this, a few broken twigs weren't going to make any difference. There was no doubt at all that as things stood now, this crime and its perpetrator were far, far away from their grasp. In both time and space.

Not to mention the victim.

He started walking towards the village again.

It suddenly struck him: what if nobody misses him? What if nobody has noticed that he's disappeared?

Nobody at all.

The thought stayed with him. And if that little fat girl hadn't happened to see him, years could have passed by without anybody missing him. Or finding him. It could have been an eternity. And meanwhile the process of decay and all the rest of it would have wiped out all trace of him. Why not?

Apart from the odd bone, of course. And a grinning skull. Yorick, where are those hanging lips . . . No, come to think of it, there was no head.

And nobody would have needed to lift a finger.

A totally unnoticed death.

It was not a pleasant thought. He tried to dismiss it, but the only thing that replaced it was the clinically lit operating table and a limp, anaesthetized body – his own.

And the stranger dressed in green, brandishing razor-sharp knives over his stomach.

He quickened his pace. Darkness had started to fall, and twenty minutes later, as he stood outside the railway station buying a pack of cigarettes, he also felt the first drop of rain on his hand.

7

After some deliberation Rooth decided to phone rather than call round in person. It was more than ten miles to Blochberg and it was nearly half past seven.

Afterwards, when he replaced the receiver, he was relieved to think that at least the woman at the other end of the line didn't know what he looked like. With a bit of luck, she wouldn't be sure of his name either: he hoped that he had managed to mumble it so indistinctly that she hadn't picked it up.

It had not been a successful telephone call.

'Hello?'

'Mrs Menhevern?'

'Marie-Louise Menhevern, yes.'

The voice was shrill and discouraging.

'My name is Rooth, from the Maardam police. I'm calling in connection with a missing person. You telephoned us last June to inform us that, unfortunately, your husband seemed to have vanished, is that right?'

'No. I never said anything about it being unfortunate. I merely said he'd disappeared.'

'In June 1993?'

'Precisely.'

'Has he come back home?'

'No.'

'You haven't had any sign of life from him?'

'No. If I had, I'd have informed the police, of course.'

'And you have no idea what's become of him?'

'Well, I assume he's run off with another woman and is hidden away somewhere. That's the type he is.'

'Really? Where might he be, do you think?'

'How the hell should I know? I'm sitting here watching the telly, constable. Are you sure you're from the police, come to that?'

'Of course.'

'What do you want, then? Have you found him?'

'That depends,' said Rooth. 'How many testicles did he have?'

'What the hell was that you said?'

'Er, well, I mean, most men have two, obviously . . . He hasn't had an operation and lost one, or something like that?'

'Hang on, I'm going to have this call traced.'

'But Mrs Menhevern, please, it's not what you think . . .'

'You are the worst sort, do you know that? You don't even dare to come and look me in the eye. Telephone pig! If I could lay my hands on you I'd . . .'

Rooth terminated the call in horror. Sat there for half a minute without moving. As if the slightest careless move might give him away. Stared out of the window as darkness began to fall over the town.

No, he thought, I'm no good with women. That's all there is to it.

Then he decided to remove Claus Menhevern from the list of possible victims. Which meant there was only one left.

Münster parked outside the dilapidated apartment block on Armastenstraat. Lingered in the car before walking over the street and venturing in through the outside door. An unmistakable stench of cat piss hovered over the stairs, and large lumps of plaster had given up all hope of clinging on to the walls, leaving gaping holes. There was no mention of a Pierre Kohler on the list of tenants in the hallway, but that seemed to be as unreliable as the rest of the building and so he decided to investigate what it said on the doors.

He hit the jackpot on the fourth floor.

Pierre Kohler
Margite Delling
Jürg Eschenmaa
Dolomite Kazaj

it said on a handwritten scrap of paper pinned above the letter slot.

He rang the bell. Nothing happened – presumably it wasn't working. He knocked several times instead. After almost a minute he heard footsteps and the door was opened by a woman in her fifties. She had a mauve dressing gown wrapped loosely round her overweight body, and she eyed Münster critically up and down.

She was evidently unimpressed by what she saw.

So was Münster.

'I'm from the Maardam police,' he said, flashing his ID for a tenth of a second. 'It's about a missing person. May I come in?'

'Not without a warrant,' said the woman.

'Thank you,' said Münster. 'We've found a dead body in some woods not far from here, and it seems possible that it might be Pierre Kohler, who was reported missing in August last year.'

'Why should it be him?' the woman wondered, tightening the belt of her robe.

'Well, we don't know for certain, of course,' said Münster. 'We're just checking everybody who's been reported missing. The age seems to fit, and his height; but this is purely a routine check. There's nothing else to suggest that it could be him.'

Why am I being so polite to this damned bitch? he wondered. It's obvious I should have clamped down on her right from the start.

'Well?' she said, lighting a cigarette.

'There is one detail,' said Münster.

'One detail?'

'Yes, something that will enable us to make a positive identification. You see, the body we found didn't have a head. That's what's making it so difficult for us to establish who it is.'

'You don't say?'

A man had appeared in the hall behind her. Nodded brusquely at Münster and put his hand on the woman's shoulder.

'What kind of a detail?' he asked.

'Er,' said Münster. 'Well, our victim is missing a testicle. Presumably it was operated on some considerable time ago. Do you happen to know . . . ?'

The man started coughing, and Münster broke off. When the attack was over, Münster realized that it had been more of an outburst of laughter. He was grinning. The woman as well.

'Well, mister fucking chief of police,' said the man, hammering his clenched fist against his forehead. 'This is my head. If you want to count my balls, you'd better step inside. My name is Pierre Kohler.'

Why the hell didn't I telephone instead? thought Münster.

When Münster'd got back home and read the bedtime stories for the kids, Rooth rang.

'How did you get on?' he asked.

'It's not him,' said Münster. 'He's alive and kicking. They'd forgotten to inform the police.'

'Oh dear,' said Rooth.

'What about yours?'

'Same thing, presumably,' sighed Rooth. 'Doesn't seem to be missing a testicle, in any case. Nor does his wife. The fact is, he's probably done a runner.'

'Huh,' said Münster. 'What do we do now, then?'

'I had a bright idea,' said Rooth. 'About that butchery job. Either there must have been some kind of distinguishing feature on his hands or feet, or there might be a simpler explanation.'

'Simpler?' wondered Münster.

'Fingerprints,' said Rooth.

Münster thought for a moment.

'You don't get rid of fingerprints by cutting a man's feet off,' he said.

'True,' said Rooth. 'But he probably did that to confuse us. Do you see what I'm getting at?'

Münster thought for another couple of seconds.

'Of course,' he said. 'We've got his fingerprints. He's on our crime register.'

'There's a clever boy,' said Rooth. 'Yes, we've got his fingerprints somewhere in the archives; I'll bet my damned life on it. Do you know how many we have, by the way?'

'Three hundred thousand, I think,' said Münster.

'Just over, yes. Ah well, given the way things are we can't pin him down that way, in any case, but at least it's a lead. See you tomorrow.'

'Yes, see you,' said Münster, putting the phone down.

'What's keeping you so busy?' asked Synn when they had switched the light off and he'd put his left arm around her.

'Oh, nothing special,' said Münster. 'We're looking for an old lag who disappeared sometime last year, that's all. He's between fifty-five and sixty, and only has one testicle.'

'How fascinating,' said Synn. 'How are you going to find him?'

'We have done already,' said Münster. 'He's dead, of course.'

'Ah,' said Synn. 'I'm with you. Could you cuddle me a bit more tightly, please?'

8

It was true that Münster won all three sets, but there was no doubt that this was the closest match they had played for many a long year. The final scores were 15–10, 15–13, 15–12 – not that anybody bothered to record them – and Van Veeteren had been leading for much of the time, in both the second and the final set. In the latter by as much as 12–8.

'If I hadn't mishit that crappy serve, you'd have bitten the dust,' he maintained as they strolled back to the changing rooms. 'I want you to be quite clear about that.'

'An unusually good game,' said Münster. 'You seem to be on song.'

'On song!' snorted Van Veeteren. 'I'm just going through the death throes. I shall be under the surgeon's knife tomorrow, let me remind you.'

'Oh yes, so you will,' said Münster, as if it wasn't a fact that everybody at the police station knew all about it. 'When exactly will it happen?'

'I'll go in this evening. The operation is set for eleven o'clock tomorrow morning. Ah well, it happens to all of us sooner or later.'

'An uncle of mine has had cancer of the intestine,' said Münster. 'They've operated on him twice. He's fighting fit now.'

'How old is he?'

'Seventy, I think,' said Münster.

Van Veeteren muttered something and flopped down on the bench.

'Let's have a glass at Adenaar's when we've been in the shower,' he said. 'I want to hear about how you're getting on.'

'OK,' said Münster. 'I'll have to ring Synn first, though.'

'By all means,' said Van Veeteren. 'Give her my regards.'

He doesn't think he's going to pull through, Münster thought, and it occurred to him that he felt sorry for his boss. This was very definitely the first time ever, and it was a surprising feeling. He ducked under the shower and allowed the hot water to rinse away the smile it brought on.

But at Adenaar's the detective chief inspector was his usual self again. He complained peevishly that there was water in his beer, and had his glass changed twice. Sent Münster to buy him some cigarettes. Knocked ash into the flower-pots.

'As I said, you'd better make the most of it while I'm still available. You're not getting anywhere, I gather?'

Münster sighed, took a deep drink and started to explain the position.

No, he had to admit that Van Veeteren was quite right in his assumption. The unidentified body in Behren was still just as unidentified as ever. Two weeks had gone by, and they had made no progress.

Not that the effort being put in by everybody left anything to be desired; it was simply that it wasn't producing any results. They had made several appeals, in the press, on the radio and on television. There was no doubt that the case fascinated the whole country, even if the interest of the mass media had waned after the first week. Every missing-person case nationwide (males between forty and seventy, just to cover the unlikely possibility that Meusse had made a mistake) had been investigated, but none of them tallied: if it wasn't the testicle business, it was something else. Rooth had contacted several hospitals and established that between nine thousand and ten thousand men in that age group were missing one testicle, for one reason or another. Considerably more than one might have guessed, but it was virtually impossible to follow all of them up via case notes and similar data, not least because of the secrecy oath applying to the medical profession. Münster had also been in touch with three or four prison governors, but found that checks on prisoners' genitalia were regrettably not a priority as far as looking after criminals was concerned.

'It seems pretty pointless bothering about prisons,' Münster said. 'That business of fingerprints was only a guess, after all.'

Van Veeteren nodded.

'What about the carpet?' he asked.

'Well,' said Münster, 'we know quite a lot about it, of course. Do you want to hear it all?'

'In outline, please.'

'A cow-hair carpet. Fairly low quality, blue and green once upon a time. Five foot six by six foot six. Between thirty and forty years old, apparently. No manufacturers' labels or similar stuff, quite worn even before it was used as a . . . shroud.'

'Hmm,' said Van Veeteren.

'There are traces of dog hair and about fifty other things you find in every household. Brown paper string as well. Used to tie around the bundle, of course. A double strand wound around several times. The commonest kind. They sell about 250,000 yards of it every year. Nationwide, that is.'

Van Veeteren lit a cigarette.

'Anything more from Meusse?'

'Oh yes,' said Münster. 'They've done a DNA analysis and produced the full genetic code, if I understand it rightly. The problem is that we don't have anything to compare it with. No registers.'

'Thank God,' said Van Veeteren.

'I agree,' said Münster. 'Anyway, we know more or less everything there is to know about this damned body . . .'

'Apart from who it belonged to,' said Van Veeteren.

'Apart from that, yes,' sighed Münster.

'Have you tried floating the testicle story in the media? I haven't seen anything.'

'No,' said Münster. 'We thought it best to keep quiet about that. So that we can be sure when the right identification turns up, but I think that a whisper has been going around.'

Van Veeteren pondered for a while.

'He must have been a lonely bastard,' he said eventually. 'Incredibly lonely.'

'I've read about people lying dead for two or three years without being missed,' said Münster.

Van Veeteren nodded gloomily. Beckoned to the waitress and ordered two more beers.

'I don't know if I should . . .' Münster began.

'I'll pay,' said Van Veeteren, and the matter was closed.

'Do you really think he's been reported as missing? Anywhere?'

Münster gazed out of the window and thought it over.

'No,' he said. 'I have been thinking about that, and I don't think he has.'

'He could be a foreigner, of course,' Van Veeteren pointed out. 'The borders are so open nowadays that anybody can drive into the country with a dead body in the boot.'

Münster agreed.

'What are you planning to do next, then?'

Münster hesitated.

'I don't know, put it on ice, I suppose. Rooth has already started working on something else. I suspect Hiller wants me to join Reinhart's group from the day after tomorrow onwards. Our body will probably have to lie in the deep freeze waiting for the next coincidence, I guess.'

Van Veeteren nodded in appreciation.

'Good, Münster,' he said. 'I couldn't have put it better myself! Lie in the deep freeze waiting for the next coincidence – I don't think that's what they had in mind, though, that business of life after death. But cheers in any case!'

'Cheers,' said Münster.

*

'So you don't have any good advice to offer?' he asked as they were on their way out.

Van Veeteren scratched the back of his head.

'No,' he said. 'You've said all there is to say. You have to be able to show a bit of patience after all. Hens don't lay eggs any quicker if you stand watching them.'

'Where do you get all your expressions from?'

'No idea,' Van Veeteren said, feeling quite pleased with himself. 'That's the way it is with us poets. They just come.'

9

She'd failed to catch on from the first indication. A few lines she'd read in one of the evening papers while travelling from the airport in a taxi. Anybody might have overlooked it.

Then it became more worrying. When she'd finished unpacking and taken her two tablets, she turned her attention to the daily papers that Mrs Pudecka had left in two neat piles on the kitchen table, as usual. She lay back in the Biedermeier armchair in front of the fire and started to work her way slowly through them, one by one; that was when the suspicion began to nag at her. Of course, it was pure fantasy at the moment – a whimsical idea, something of that sort, prompted and set in motion by her bad conscience, no doubt. The vague feeling of guilt that naturally had no justification but was nevertheless always with her, deep down, more or less insistent, but never totally absent. She wished it had been otherwise. That it could have made up its mind to be completely – absolutely and very definitely – absent. Once and for all.

But that was not how it was, of course.

She went to the kitchen. Made another cup of tea, took some of the newspapers to the bedroom and started working through them more systematically. Stretched herself out under the blanket and read, letting her mind wander back through time as she tried to recall dates and events. Dozed off for a few minutes when dusk crept up on her, but was thrust out of a dream in which his face had suddenly appeared before her, in sharp detail.

His totally silent and expressionless face with those unfathomable eyes.

She stretched out a hand and switched on the lamp.

Could it be him?

She looked at the clock. Half past six. In any event it was too late to set off in the car this evening. The flight had tired her out, as usual. Nobody could expect her to sort things out immediately, but she was also aware that it was not something she could sweep under the carpet and hope it would stay there. There were some things you simply couldn't skirt around. There was such a thing as duty.

She took a shower and spent a few hours in front of the television. Phoned Liesen to tell her that she was back home, but didn't say a word about her misgivings. Of course not. Liesen was one of the people who knew nothing about it; there had never been any reason to tell her.

No compelling reason.

They didn't mention a word about it on the news. That wasn't so odd, when you came to think about it; over two weeks had passed, and of course there were other more important things to keep citizens informed about. Presumably it had all begun to fade away and disappear from people's minds, and she suspected that if she didn't intervene, the whole business would soon be forgotten.

She sighed uneasily. Wouldn't that be best? For it to be forgotten? Surely there was no rhyme or reason why the past should be raked over again? Think of the unpleasantness that might be stirred up. Would he never tire of following her like a . . . like a, what is it they say nowadays? A poltergeist? Something like that, in any case.

But there was that vague stirring of conscience. That slight, nagging feeling of guilt. That is what it was really about, and would she ever be rid of it if she kept out of it this time as well? A good question, to be sure. Even if she looked on the positive side she could hardly have more than ten or twelve years left, and sooner or later she would find herself standing in front of that wall.

Facing her maker, that is. In which case it might be a good idea to be on solid ground.

Yes, indeed. She sighed, stood up and switched off the television. She would have to follow this up.

But there again, there was nothing, nothing at all, in fact, to suggest that it really might be him. Not the slightest detail.

No doubt it was just her nerves getting the better of her.

She set off early the next morning. She had woken up at half past five, another of those inevitable curses that old age brings with it. Got up, had breakfast and driven the car out of the garage before seven.

There was not much traffic; once she had wriggled her way out of town and reached the hills, she was more or less alone on the road. It was a lovely morning, with a thin layer of mist that slowly dispersed as the sun broke through. She stopped at the picturesque inn between Geerlach and Würpatz and drank a cup of coffee. Pulled herself together and tried to keep her thoughts and the nagging worry under control as she leafed through the morning papers. There wasn't a word. Not in any of them.

She drove straight through Linzhuisen without stopping and arrived at the house soon after half past nine. Got out and walked up to the door. Managed to open it with a little difficulty, and then it was not many minutes before she realized that her worst fears could very well be true.

It was far from certain, of course, but having come this far she clearly had no alternative but to contact the police.

She did that shortly afterwards; from the telegraph station in Linzhuisen, to be exact, and the call was logged in to Maardam at 10:03 by the duty officer, Police Constable Pieter Willock.

Ten minutes later Detective Inspector Rooth marched into Inspector Münster's office without knocking and announced with ill-concealed excitement:

'I think we've got him.'

10

Sleep, he thought. That's all I want.

The hours before he had been admitted were not the orgy of solitude he had imagined, and perhaps it was those telephone calls just as much as What Is In Store that were hounding him and keeping him awake long into the early hours.

Not that they had phoned to bid him farewell – or at least, it hadn't sounded like that. But if something unexpected were to happen, they would naturally feel better, having spoken to him that final evening.

Renate was first. Beating about the bush as usual: talking about the holiday cottage they had once owned; about books she hadn't read, but had seen; about her brother and sister-in-law (that awful brother of hers: for some unknown reason he got on rather well with the sister-in-law – in the old days, that is); and it was not until after a quarter of an hour or more that she came around to mentioning the operation.

Was he worried?

Worried? Of course not. No, needless to say she hadn't expected him to be. Perhaps he could give her a ring when it was all over, in any case?

He had half promised. Anything to prevent her from going on about how they ought to get together again. They had been living apart for almost three years now, and if there was one thing in this life that he didn't regret, it was the separation from Renate.

Maybe that was sufficient reason to claim that their marriage hadn't been such a bad thing after all, it suddenly struck him. As a means to an end, that is.

Depressive people should be wary of one another, Reinhart had announced on some occasion or other. The sum often becomes greater than the parts. Much greater.

Then there was Mahler. No sooner had he put the phone down after the first call than he had the old poet on the line.

He must have let slip something about what was in store for him at the club, of course. Presumably while playing chess last Saturday, or the Saturday before. In any case, it was a surprise. Mahler was not exactly a close friend – whatever that means – but it could be that there was more to their companionship in the smoke-filled vaults than he had imagined. Or dared to imagine. He hadn't thought very deeply about it, needless to say, but the call was a genuine surprise.

'I suppose you'll have to miss a few matches,' he said. Mahler, that is.

'I'll soon be back,' Van Veeteren had countered. 'Nothing boosts your potency better than a few weeks' abstinence.'

And Mahler had laughed in that deep voice of his and wished him the best of luck.

Last of all, Jess, of course.

She gave him a big daughterly hug over the miles, but promised to visit him in a few days with grapes, chocolate and grandchildren.

'Not on your life,' he protested. 'Drag the kids a couple of hundred miles to gape at a doddery old bastard? I'd frighten the life out of them!'

'Balderdash,' said Jess. 'I'll treat them to an ice cream afterwards and they'll get over it. I know you're frightened to death of this operation even if you flatly deny it when anybody says so.'

'I flatly deny it,' said Van Veeteren.

She laughed, just like Mahler had done, and then he'd spoken to two three-year-olds in his schoolboy French, and they also threatened to come and gape at him shortly. If he'd understood them rightly. And they seemed to know all about it, he had to admit.

'You'll get an injection; then you'll fall asleep,' said one of them.

'They put the dead bodies in the basement,' added the other.

When he had survived that call, it was high time to set off. He left a key with Mrs Grambowska, two floors down, as usual, and tonight even this white-haired, faithful old servant seemed to exude a strange sort of glow full of sympathy and reconciliation. She took his hand and stroked it tenderly, a gesture the likes of which he had never seen from her in all the years he had known her.

'Goodbye,' she said. 'Take care.'

I'll disappoint them all if I pull through this, he thought as he got into the taxi. Not a bad tip to send him on his way, in fact. Take care! When he was lying on the table, drugged and carved up, he should avoid getting carried away and doing something silly. He must remember that.

He was aware that the only one who hadn't been in touch was Erich, but of course it was possible that he'd tried earlier in the afternoon. The match with Münster and the visit to Adenaar's had taken a lot of time, and he'd been at home for only a couple of hours or so. No doubt there were restrictions even on such things as telephone calls when you were in prison.

There were two beds in the pale yellow room that the nurse ushered him into, but the other one was empty and so he was able to lie alone and think his thoughts without distraction.

And they were many and varied. And sufficiently urgent to keep sleep at bay. He used the phone calls to grope his way back through time: it was not a mapped-out journey, but his thoughts dragged him along in their wake and before long he had started to remember all the pains and delights his life had afforded him, and he tried to understand what had made him what he had become, and what he was . . . If he could be excused such an infantile way of putting it. But in any case, the time seemed to be ripe for reflection; like writing his own epitaph, it struck him – his own obituary, written in advance, with authentic facts. Or questions.

From memory, not in.

Ex memoria.

Who am I? Who have I been?

Needless to say, no answers came to him, apart from a realization that quite a lot seemed to have followed a pattern. Piloted him in the same inexorable direction in some mysterious way.

His father: that deeply tragic figure (but children are blind to great tragedies, of course), who had such a significant influence on him. Unswervingly and inexorably he had inculcated into his son a certainty that we can never expect the least favour from life. Nothing is permanent; all is transient, arbitrary, coincidental and obscure.

Well, something like that, if he'd understood his father rightly.

His marriage: twenty-five years with Renate. To be sure, it had produced two children and that was the important outcome. One of them was in prison and likely to continue along that path; but there again, Jess and the grandchildren were an unexpectedly healthy branch on the old, sickly tree. There was no denying that.

They put the dead bodies in the basement!

His job: if nothing else had pointed in that direction, thirty-five years of Sisyphean labour in the shady side of life and society must have presented him with the occasional indication that something positive can be achieved.

Yes, there was after all a trace of a pattern.

He thrust his hand down under the stiff blanket and fingered his stomach. There . . . Somewhere around there is where it was, to the right of his navel, if he had understood it rightly. That was where they were going to cut into him.

He squeezed tentatively. Suddenly felt hungry, as if he had been pressing a button. He had been forbidden to eat anything after six p.m., and it struck him that in fact he hadn't eaten since twelve. At this very moment his intestine was doubtless locked in a vain struggle to suck the last drop of nutrition from the beer he had drunk at Adenaar's . . . He tried to conjure up the process in his mind's eye, but the images that shimmered into view were blurred and abstract, way beyond the limits of comprehension.

It must have been at some point in this flickering sequence of incomprehensible images that he lost consciousness. No doubt the dim film show emanating from his intestines lasted for a while longer, but soon things started to become clearer. All at once the images sharpened. The stage was well lit and crystal clear. The operating theatre peopled with mysterious figures in green, flitting around without a sound, their concentration hypnotic in its intensity. Only the faint, shrill clang of sharp instruments being whetted or dropped into metal dishes occasionally disturbed the dense, conspiratorial silence.

He lay there, naked and exposed on the cold marble table, and it struck him that it was all over. This wasn't an operation. This was taking place in the familiar and rather chilly autopsy theatre at the forensic clinic, where he'd watched Meusse and his colleagues at work many a time.

He approached the table and the group of enthusiastically cutting and carving figures, and it occurred to him that he couldn't be the one lying there, that it must be some other poor, unfortunate and totally unknown soul. But there again, maybe not so unknown . . . There was something familiar about that headless body. It didn't seem to have any hands either, and no feet, and when he finally managed to force his way past Meusse and that pale, fat assistant whose name he could never remember, it dawned on him that it wasn't a table they were working at, but a piece of very ordinary woodland, a ditch in fact; and what they were busy with was not an operation or an autopsy – they had just rolled up the body in a big, dirty piece of carpet and were hurrying to force it down into the overgrown ditch where it belonged. Where everything belonged. Now and for evermore.

And then he was the one rolled up inside the carpet, after all. He couldn't make a sound, could hardly breathe, but he could hear their excited whispers even so. This is a good place to put him! Nobody will ever find him here. He's a totally unnecessary person. Why should we worry about anybody like that?

And he yelled at them, to bear in mind their moral responsibilities. Yes, that is exactly what he yelled, but of course it didn't do much good, the carpet was too thick and they were already leaving, and it was extremely difficult to make yourself heard when you didn't have a head.

The woman shook his arm. He opened his eyes and was just going to yell once more that they should bear in mind their moral responsibilities when he realized that he had woken up.

She said something, and he had the impression that her eyes were full of sympathy. Or something like that, at least.

Am I dead? Van Veeteren wondered. She looked quite angelic, in fact. It was not an impossibility.

But she was holding a telephone receiver. Everything seemed to be bordering on the profane, and then the penny dropped: he hadn't even been operated on yet. It was morning, and everything was still in store.

'Telephone,' she said again. 'A call for the chief inspector.'

She handed him the receiver and walked away. He cleared his throat and tried to sit up.

'Hello?'

'DCI Van Veeteren?'

It was Münster.

'Speaking.'

'Please excuse me for troubling you at the hospital, but you did say that the operation wasn't until eleven . . .'

'What time is it now, then?' He searched for a clock on the empty walls, but couldn't see one.

'Twenty past ten.'

'Oh.'

'I thought I ought to tell you that we know who it is . . . You did seem to be a bit interested.'

'You mean the body in the carpet?'

For a fraction of a second he thought he was dreaming again.

'Yes. We're all quite sure it must be Leopold Verhaven.'

'What?'

For a couple of seconds Van Veeteren's mind was a blank. A minute expanse of stainless steel from which everything bounced off and had no chance of penetrating.

'What the hell was that you said?'

'Yes, Leopold Verhaven. He's the one. I take it that you remember him?'

Three seconds passed. The steel melted and allowed the information to penetrate.

'Do nothing!' said Van Veeteren. 'I'm on my way.'

He started to climb out of bed, but at that very moment the doors opened and in marched an unexpectedly large squad of personnel dressed in green.

*

The receiver was left dangling.

'Hello?' said Münster. 'Are you still there?'

The nurse picked it up.

'Mr Van Veeteren has just left for the operating theatre,' she explained and replaced the receiver.

THREE

24 AUGUST 1993

11

There were two good vantage points and two possible trains.

The first wasn't due until 12:37, but even so he had taken up his position at about 11:00. It was important that he should get the right seat: at one of the window tables on the veranda. He had scouted it out a few days beforehand: the view over the square in front of the station was excellent, especially the area between the taxi rank and the news-stand. It was at the centre of his field of vision, and all newly arrived passengers were bound to end up there sooner or later.

Unless they took the prohibited route over the railway tracks, of course; but why would he do that? His house was in this direction; there was no reason for him to head northwards; so if he intended to come straight home, he would pass by here. Sooner or later, as already stated. Most likely round about a quarter to one.

An hour and a half from now.

What he would do next was an open question; but the probability was that he would take a cab for the remaining ten miles or so. That was of minor significance. The main thing was that he came.

Then everything would work out, no doubt. Somehow or other.

He ordered lunch – cold cuts with salad; bread, butter and cheese. But he hardly touched the food during the two hours he sat there. Instead he smoked about fifteen cigarettes, occasionally turning the pages of the book he had propped up to the right of his plate – without reading more than the occasional line here and there and without having the slightest idea of the content. If this was camouflage, it was a poor effort. Anybody taking a closer look at him would doubtless have noticed that something fishy was going on. He was well aware of that, but there was no risk.

Who on earth would want to take a closer look at him?

Nobody, he had decided; and that was, of course, a perfectly correct conclusion to reach. Between eleven and two, some 200 to 250 customers would have lunch at the railway restaurant. Most of them were regulars; but there would be a large number of chance diners, making it highly unlikely that anybody would pay any attention to this ordinary-looking man in corduroy trousers and greyish-green pullover by the window, minding his own business.

Especially if you bore the time factor in mind. He couldn't help smiling to himself at the thought. If everything went to plan, an awful lot of time would pass. Months. With any luck, years. Masses of time. Ideally what was going to happen would never be discovered.

Needless to say, that would be the optimal solution – nothing ever seeing the light of day – but he realized that it would be stupid to bank on that. It was better and smarter to be prepared for all eventualities. Better to sit here quietly and do nothing to draw attention to himself. An unknown diner among a lot of unknown diners. Noticed by nobody, forgotten by everybody.

At about twelve, when the place was at its busiest, some of the customers tried to take the seat opposite him at the little table, but he turned them away. Explained politely that unfortunately it was reserved, he was waiting for a friend.

Later, during the critical moments around a quarter to one, he became tense. That was inevitable. When he saw the first of the newly alighted passengers, he moved his chair closer to the window and ignored everything else. It was essential to concentrate hard: identifying him might well be the weakest link in the whole chain. A long time had passed, and who could tell how much he might have changed during all those years? Obviously, in no circumstances must he miss him.

He must not let him pass unnoticed.

When he did eventually see him, he was emerging from the café on the other side of the square an hour and a half later. It was obvious there was no need to have worried.

Of course, it was him. That was immediately clear when he was still thirty yards away – the same energetic, wiry little figure; slightly hunched, perhaps, but not much. His hair thinner and paler in colour. Receding at the temples. Movements a bit stiffer.

A bit greyer, a bit older.

But definitely him.

He left his table and went out into the street. The man was standing at the taxi rank. Just as expected. Number three in the line, searching for something in his pockets. Cigarettes, money, could be anything.

Nothing to do but wait, then. Wait, go and sit in the car, then follow him. There was no hurry. He knew where the cab would take him.

Knew that everything was going to happen according to plan.

For one brief moment he felt slightly dizzy as blood

rushed to his head, but he soon regained control of himself.

The taxi pulled away. Drove round the square, and as it passed him outside the café, he could see the familiar profile through the back window less than six feet away, and he knew at that moment that there would be no problem.

No problem at all.

FOUR

5–10 MAY 1994

12

'What do you think?' Rooth asked.

Münster shrugged.

'I don't know. But he's probably our man. We'll have to wait and see what the forensic officers say.'

'It's not exactly a cheerful place.'

'No. That's certainly what strikes you, somehow. Shall we take a walk to the village? We're not doing any good here. We'll have to talk to the neighbours sooner or later anyway.'

Rooth nodded and they set off in silence down the winding path through the woods. After a few hundred yards the countryside opened up, with low farmhouses on each side, and only a stone's throw farther on was the village of Kaustin. They continued as far as the church and the main road.

'How many souls live in this place, do you know?' asked Rooth.

Münster glanced at the churchyard, but assumed the question referred to those who had not yet been laid to rest.

'A couple of hundred, I would guess. There's a store and a school, in any case.'

He pointed down the road ahead of them.

'What do you reckon?' said Rooth. 'Shall we do a bit of sounding out?'

'Might as well,' said Münster. 'If the shopkeeper doesn't know anything, nobody else will.'

There were two old ladies sitting on chairs inside the store, and it was obvious to Münster that they had no intention of leaving. While Rooth took a careful look at the range of chocolate bars and bags of candy, he steered the slimly built shopkeeper into the storeroom. Perhaps that was unnecessary. Their arrival in the village, five or six cars one after the other on a forest track that was normally quiet, could hardly have passed unnoticed. Even so, there was plenty of reason to keep in the background as far as possible. The link was not yet confirmed, when all was said and done.

'My name's Münster,' he said, producing his ID.

'Hoorne. Janis Hoorne,' said the shopkeeper with a nervous smile.

Münster decided to get straight to the point.

'Do you know who owns that house in the forest up there? The turnoff by the church, I mean.'

The man nodded.

'Who, then?'

'It's Verhaven's.'

His voice is hoarse, Münster thought, his eyes shifty. What's he worried about?

'Have you had this store for long?'

'Thirty years. My father ran it before I did.'

'You know the story, then?'

He nodded again. Münster waited for a few seconds.

'Has something happened?'

'We don't know yet,' Münster explained. 'Possibly. Have you noticed anything?'

'No . . . no, what should I have noticed?'

His nervousness was like an aura around him, but there might be a good reason for that. Münster eyed him up and down before continuing.

'Leopold Verhaven was released from prison in August last year. The twenty-fourth, to be exact. We think he came back to his house round about then. Do you know anything about that?'

The man hesitated, rubbing his thumbs nervously against his index fingers.

'You must know about most of what goes on here in Kaustin, surely?'

'Yes . . .'

'Well? Do you know if he came back here? Then, in August, or at some other time?'

'They say . . .'

'Yes?'

'Somebody saw him round about that time, yes.'

He produced a handkerchief from his pocket and wiped his upper lip.

'When was that?'

'Er, one day in August last year.'

'But there's been no sign of him since then?'

'Not that I know of.'

'So it was just one day, is that right? He was seen on one or possibly several occasions, was he?'

'I don't know. I think so.'

'By whom?'

'Excuse me?'

'Who saw him?'

'Maertens, if I remember rightly . . . Maybe Mrs Wilkerson as well, I can't really remember.'

Münster made notes.

'And where can I find Maertens and Mrs Wilkerson?'

'Maertens lives with the Niedermanns, the other side of the school, but he works in the churchyard. You're bound to find him there now, if you . . .'

He didn't know how to go on.

'And Mrs Wilkerson?'

The shopkeeper coughed and popped a couple of tablets into his mouth.

'She lives in the house just before you get to the forest. On the right-hand side. On the way up to Verhaven's, that is.'

Münster nodded and closed his notebook. As they were leaving the store Hoorne plucked up enough courage to ask a question.

'Has he done it again?'

It was hardly more than a whisper. Münster shook his head.

'No,' he said. 'Hardly.'

'Would you like a piece?'

Rooth held out a half-eaten bar of chocolate.

'No thank you,' said Münster. 'Did you interrogate the old ladies?'

'Hmm,' said Rooth, his mouth full. 'Shrewd characters. Refused to open their false teeth even an eighth of an inch unless they had a lawyer present. Where are we headed for now?'

'The church. The verger is supposed to have seen him.'

'Good,' said Rooth.

*

Maertens was busy digging a grave as Münster and Rooth approached, and Münster was reminded how he had once played a very immature Horatio while at school. He smiled briefly at the thought. Perhaps what the enthusiastic little drama teacher had claimed really was true, and that *Hamlet* was a play that contained something for every single phase of one's life.

He didn't dare to develop the thought any further and never asked whose grave it was.

'Do you mind if we ask you a few questions?' Rooth said instead. 'You are Mr Maertens, aren't you?'

The powerfully built man took off his cap and slowly straightened his back.

'I am indeed that gentleman,' he said. 'Always delighted to assist the police.'

'Hmm,' said Münster. 'It's about Leopold Verhaven. We wonder if you've seen him around lately?'

'Lately? What do you mean by lately?'

'The last year or so,' said Rooth.

'I saw him when he came back last summer . . . Let's see now, that would have been August, I think. But he hasn't been around here since then.'

'Tell us about it,' said Münster.

Mr Maertens replaced his headgear and clambered out of the as-yet shallow grave.

'Well,' he began, 'it was just the once. I was raking the

gravel here in the churchyard. He came by taxi, got out just outside the gate. Er, then he started walking up the hill towards the woods. Went home, in other words.'

'When exactly was it?' Rooth asked.

Maertens thought for a moment.

'August, as I said. End of the month, if I remember rightly.'

'And that's the only time you saw him?'

'Just the once, yes. God only knows where he went after that. They'd let him out again, of course. We talked about it in the village, it seemed to be about the right time, and so . . .'

'Do you know if anybody else saw him?'

He nodded.

'Mrs Wilkerson. Her husband as well, I think. They live up there.'

He pointed to the greyish-white house on the edge of the forest.

'Thank you,' said Rooth. 'We might need to come back with more questions.'

'What's he done now?' said Maertens.

'Nothing,' said Münster. 'Did you know him?'

Maertens scratched the back of his head.

'In the old days, I suppose. He sort of dropped out of circulation.'

'I'd more or less gathered that,' said Rooth.

*

The Wilkersons appeared to have been expecting them, and that probably wasn't surprising. The road was only about ten yards from the kitchen table where Mr Wilkerson was now sitting with a cup of coffee and a tray of cookies in front of him, trying to look as if he was reading the newspaper. His wife produced two extra cups, and Münster and Rooth sat down.

'Thank you,' Rooth said. 'I'm looking forward to this.'

'I've retired,' said the man, somewhat abruptly. 'It's my son who runs the farm nowadays. My back couldn't cope, I'm afraid.'

'Backs always cause lots of trouble,' Rooth said.

'Lots.'

'Anyway,' said Münster, 'we'd like to ask you a few little questions, if we may. About Leopold Verhaven.'

'Fire away,' said Mrs Wilkerson, sitting down beside her husband. She slid the tray of cookies towards them.

'We understand he came back here in August last year,' said Rooth, taking a cookie.

'Yes,' said Mrs Wilkerson. 'I saw him coming. Going past.'

She pointed at the road.

'Can you tell us exactly what you saw?' said Münster.

She took a sip of coffee.

'Well, I saw him walking up the hill, that's all there was to it. I didn't recognize him at first, but then I saw . . .'

'You're quite certain?'

'Who else could it have been?'

'I suppose there can't be many people using this track?' said Rooth, taking another cookie.

'Hardly a soul,' said Mr Wilkerson. 'Only the Czermaks opposite, but there's hardly ever anybody up in the forest.'

'Are there any other houses?' Münster wondered.

'No,' said Wilkerson. 'The track peters out fifty yards or so past Verhaven's. I suppose we might get the occasional hunting party shooting hares or pheasants, but that's not very often.'

'Did you see him as well, Mr Wilkerson?'

Mrs Wilkerson nodded.

'I shouted to him, of course. Yes, we both saw him all right. The twenty-fourth of August it was. Three o'clock, maybe just after. He had a suitcase and a plastic carrier bag, that's all. He looked just like he always did. I must say I thought he'd have changed more than he had.'

'Really?' said Rooth. 'Then what?'

'What do you mean?'

'Well, you must have seen him several times?'

'No,' said Wilkerson emphatically. 'We didn't.'

Rooth took another cookie and chewed thoughtfully.

'What you are saying,' said Münster, 'is that you saw

Leopold Verhaven walking past here on August twenty-fourth last year – the same day that he was released from prison – but that you haven't seen him since?'

'Yes.'

'Don't you think that's odd?'

Mrs Wilkerson pursed her lips.

'There's a lot about Leopold Verhaven that's odd,' she said. 'Don't you agree? What's happened?'

'We don't know yet,' said Rooth. 'Was there anybody in the village who mixed with him at all?'

'No,' said Wilkerson. 'Nobody.'

'You must have gathered that,' said his wife.

Yes, I've started to, thought Münster. He was beginning to feel cooped up in this over-elaborately furnished and decorated little kitchen, and was coming around to the view that it would probably be best to save other questions for a later occasion. Until they had a bit of flesh on the skeleton, as it were. At the very least until they were certain that Leopold Verhaven really was their man.

Their dead body. It would be damned annoying if he suddenly crawled out from under a stone and disproved his own demise, as it were.

Although Münster was becoming more and more convinced with every hour that passed. It couldn't very well be anybody else. There are signs and there are signs, as Van Veeteren always said.

Rooth seemed to have read his thoughts. And in any case, the tray of cookies was empty.

'We might have to come back to you,' he said. 'Many thanks for the coffee.'

'It's a pleasure,' said Mrs Wilkerson.

As they were leaving, Münster asked a question out of nowhere.

'We spoke to the storekeeper,' he said. 'He seemed to be . . . uncomfortable, to say the least. Have you any idea why?'

'Of course,' said Mrs Wilkerson curtly. 'Beatrice was his cousin, after all.'

'Beatrice,' said Rooth as they were walking back to the house. 'She was the first one. Nineteen sixty-two, was it?'

'Yes,' said Münster. 'Beatrice in 1962 and Marlene in 1981. Nearly twenty years between them. It's a very peculiar story, this one is – have you realized that?'

'I know,' said Rooth. 'I had the impression that it was all cut and dried, but I have to say that I'm not so sure about that now.'

'What do you mean by that, Inspector?' asked Münster.

'Nothing,' said Rooth. 'Let's see what the technical guys have come up with. Kluisters and Berben have been hard at work, by the looks of things.'

13

'Welcome to the gang,' said Rooth.

DeBries flopped down onto the chair and lit a cigarette. The smoke immediately started to irritate Rooth's eyes, but he decided to put a brave face on it.

'I would be grateful if my good friend the inspector would be so kind as to put me in the picture,' said deBries. 'Slowly and clearly, if you don't mind. I was sitting wide awake in a car all night, keeping an eye on a house.'

'Did anything come of it?' Rooth wondered.

'I should say so,' said deBries. 'The house is still there. How long have you been growing that thing, by the way?'

'What thing?'

'That thing you have on your face . . . It reminds me of something, but I can't put my finger on it. Oh yes, that's it! Pat Boone!'

'What the hell are you on about?'

'My guinea pig, of course. That I had when I was a boy.

He caught some virus or other and his fur fell out. He looked a bit like that just before he died.'

Rooth sighed.

'Very funny,' he said. 'How old are you?'

'Forty, feel like eighty. Why?'

Rooth scratched his armpits thoughtfully.

'I'm just wondering if you remember the Beatrice murder . . . Or if you were too little and gormless even then.'

DeBries shook his head.

'Sorry,' he said. 'Maybe we should get started. No, I don't remember the Beatrice murder.'

'I remember it only too darned well,' said Rooth. 'I was ten or eleven. Nineteen sixty-two it was. Read about it in the papers every single day for months while it was going on. Well, a month at least. We used to talk about it at school, in the lessons and during the breaks. Oh yes, I'll be damned if it isn't one of the clearest memories I have of my childhood.'

'I was only eight,' said deBries. 'There's a big difference between eight and ten . . . I didn't live here then either. But I read about it afterwards, of course.'

'Mm,' muttered Rooth, blowing back a cloud of smoke. 'There was something about the whole mood. I remember my father going on about that Leopold Verhaven at our kitchen table, when we were having dinner. It wasn't exactly usual for him to talk about such things, so we knew that it must be something very special. Everybody was interested in that murder. Every man jack. Believe you me!'

'I've gathered,' said deBries. 'A bit of a witch hunt, wasn't it?'

'Not just a bit,' said Rooth.

DeBries got up and stubbed out his cigarette in the washbasin.

'Start at the beginning,' he said.

'The athletics business, you mean? You know he was a leading sprinter in the fifties?'

'Yes,' said deBries. 'But start with the murders.'

Rooth went back a few pages in the notepad on the desk in front of him.

'All right,' he said. 'We'll start on April sixteenth, 1962. That's the day when Leopold Verhaven tells the police that his fiancée has disappeared. Beatrice Holden. In fact she's been missing for nearly ten days by that time. They've been living together for a year and a half, or thereabouts . . . living together in that house in Kaustin. Without getting married, I should make clear, perhaps.'

'Go on,' said deBries.

'About a week later she's found murdered in the forest a few miles from there. The police put a lot of resources into it, of course, and before long the suspicion is that

Verhaven himself might have something to do with it. There are plenty of pointers in that direction, and at the end of the month he's arrested and charged with murder. The trial gets under way.'

'His name was in the papers right from the start, isn't that right?'

'Yes, indeed. They'd named him in connection with the disappearance of the girl – he was a bit of a celebrity after all – and now they saw no reason to hold back. Unless I'm much mistaken it's the first time in our country that a man who was only a suspect has been named in print. Maybe that's what blows it up to such proportions. I think the papers published every word uttered in court . . . All those reporters – from all parts of the country – they were staying at Konger's Palatz, the whole crowd, and they would hold court every night . . . The defence counsel was there as well, incidentally. Quenterran, he was called, an odd name. I suppose you could say it was the first mass-media murder. It must have been hellish for any thinking person, but I didn't understand that at the time. I was only eleven after all.'

'Hmm,' said deBries. 'And he was found guilty.'

'Yes. Although he denied it. June twentieth it was. I remember it was the week before the holidays began, and we heard it on the wireless at school.'

'Incredible,' said deBries. 'How long did he get?'

'Twelve years,' said Rooth.

DeBries nodded.

'Got out in 1974. And when did it start all over again?'

'Nineteen eighty-one. He'd gone back home and re-opened his chicken farm.'

'Chicken farm?'

'Yes. Or egg farm, or what the devil you want to call it. They hadn't broken him, not in the least. He'd started his feathery farm before the Beatrice affair happened. He was a bit of a pioneer, I think, with artificial lighting in the henhouse, so that they thought it was day when it was night and all that sort of thing. That shortened the day by two hours and made them lay more quickly, or something of the sort . . .'

'Who'd have thought it?' said deBries. 'Clever devil.'

'Oh yes,' said Rooth. 'Used to sell his eggs in Linzhuisen and here in Maardam as well. The Covered Market mainly, if I remember rightly. He got back on his feet again; he always did.'

'Strong?' said deBries.

'Yes,' said Rooth, pausing to think for a moment. 'That was just it. Superhumanly strong, in a way.'

He paused again and deBries lit another cigarette.

'What about the Marlene murder?' he asked, blowing a thin wisp of smoke over the desk. Rooth coughed.

'Goddamn chimney,' he said. 'Well, they found another

woman's body in the same bit of forest. Almost the very same place, in fact. And a few months later he was inside again. That was twenty years after the first occasion.'

'Did he confess this time?'

'Confess? Did he hell! Didn't give an inch. He'd had it off with the girl a few times, that was all, he claimed. There was another show trial, but we'll take that another time. He's a one-off, in any case . . . Was a one-off, I should say.'

'Meaning what?'

'Nobody else in this country has ever been found guilty of first degree twice, despite denying it. Totally unique.'

DeBries pondered.

'Psychiatric report?' he asked.

'Both times,' said Rooth. 'Fit as a fiddle, they reckoned. No doubt about it.'

'Did he rape them as well?'

Rooth shrugged.

'I don't know. No traces of sperm at all events. But they were both naked when found. Strangled, by the way, both times. Same method, more or less.'

'Hmm,' said deBries, clasping his hands behind his head. 'And now he's bought it as well. Something fishy there, I can't help thinking. Where's Münster, to jump from one thing to another?'

Rooth sighed.

'At the hospital,' he said. 'Surely you don't think our detective chief inspector can resist a goody like this.'

'A goody?' said deBries. 'For fuck's sake.'

14

Münster removed the paper from around the yellow roses and stuffed it into his jacket pocket. The nurse was waiting for him with a guarded smile, and as she opened the door for him, she whispered, 'Good luck.'

I'll no doubt need it, Münster thought as he entered the room. The bed immediately to the left was empty. Lying in the bed to the right, next to the window, was Van Veeteren, and the first thing to come into Münster's head was an old, not very funny story about why the inhabitants of the city of Neubadenberg were so incorrigibly stupid.

Because they do things the wrong way round in their maternity wards.

They throw away the babies and raise the afterbirth.

Van Veeteren an afterbirth? Perhaps it wasn't quite as bad as that, but as he tentatively approached the bed it was clear to him that he wouldn't be called upon to play badminton in the immediate future.

'Hmm,' he said hesitantly, standing by the foot of the bed.

Van Veeteren opened his eyes, one at a time. A few seconds passed. Then he also opened his mouth.

'Shit.'

'How are you?' Münster asked.

'Pull me up,' snarled Van Veeteren.

Münster put the flowers on the bedcover and managed to raise the patient into a half-sitting position, more or less – with the aid of a few pillows and the chief inspector's wheezing instructions. The colour of his face reminded Münster of strawberries that have been marinating in spirits overnight, and there was nothing to suggest that that wasn't how Van Veeteren felt as well. He repeated his welcoming speech.

'Shit.'

Münster picked up the roses again.

'These are from all of us,' he said. 'The others send greetings.'

He found a vase and filled it with water from the wash-basin in the corner. Van Veeteren watched proceedings suspiciously.

'Huh,' he said. 'Give me some as well.'

Münster poured him a glass from the jug on the bedside table, and after a second one, Van Veeteren appeared to be capable of conversation at least.

'I must have dozed off,' he said.

'You get extremely tired after an operation,' said Münster. 'It's normal.'

'You don't say.'

'Reinhart sends his special regards and says he'd like you to remember that pain drives out evil.'

'Thank you. Well?'

Raring to go again already? Münster thought and sat down on the visitor's chair. He opened his briefcase. Took out the envelope and propped it up against the vase of flowers.

'I'll put the photocopies here. They're only from the newspapers. It will take a bit of time to dig out the records of the trial, but I'll pop in with them tomorrow.'

'Good,' said Van Veeteren. 'I'll look through them after you've gone.'

'Don't you think you ought to have a good rest first, when . . . ?'

'Hold your tongue,' snapped Van Veeteren. 'Don't talk such a lot of crap. I'm feeling better by the second. And there's never been anything wrong with my head, for Christ's sake. Tell me what you've all been doing!'

Münster sighed and launched into an account of the visit to Kaustin and the search of Verhaven's house.

'The forensic team hasn't finished yet, of course, but everything points to him being our man. He only seems to have been at home for one day. In August last year. There was a newspaper, some food marked with a use-by date and a few other things. It appears to have been the twenty-fourth, the same day as he was released. A few witnesses saw him arriving – in the village, that is. Maybe he stayed the night; some things suggest that. He went to bed in any case. The clothes he was given on leaving prison are still there.'

'Hmm?' said Van Veeteren. 'Hang on a moment . . . No, carry on; it's OK!'

'They haven't found anything startling. Nothing to suggest that he died there. No bloodstains, no weapon, no sign of violence. But over eight months have passed since then, of course.'

'Time doesn't heal all wounds,' said Van Veeteren, rubbing his hand gingerly over his stomach.

'No,' said Münster. 'That's possible. We shall see. It's possible that he was murdered there the same day. Or night. The butchery might have been done there or somewhere else. It could have been anywhere.'

'Hmm,' said Van Veeteren again. Münster stood up, leaned back against the wall and waited.

'Pull me up!' said Van Veeteren after a while, and Münster repeated the procedure with the pillows. Van Veeteren pulled a face as he worked himself into a slightly better position.

'It hurts,' he said, nodding towards his stomach.

'What did you expect?' Münster asked.

Van Veeteren muttered something and took another drink of water.

'Heidelbluum,' he said eventually.

'Eh?' said Münster.

'He was the judge,' said Van Veeteren. 'In both trials. He must be eighty now, but you'll have to go and see him.'

Münster made a note.

'I have the impression that he's good,' Van Veeteren added. 'A pity Mort's dead.'

Detective Chief Inspector Mort was Van Veeteren's predecessor, and Münster gathered that he must have been involved in the second of the cases at least. Probably in both. What was clear was that Van Veeteren did not play a major role in either; Rooth had already checked that.

'Then there's the motive, of course.'

'Motive?'

Van Veeteren nodded.

'I'm tired,' he said. 'Give me your views on the motive, please.'

Münster thought for a few moments. Leaned his head back against the wall and contemplated the meaningless pattern of squares formed on the ceiling by the lamps.

'Well, I think there are several possibilities,' he said.

'Such as?' Van Veeteren asked.

'I suppose an inside job is the first obvious one. Something to do with prison, that is. Some sort of settling of accounts.'

Van Veeteren nodded.

'Right,' he said. 'You'd better look into what he got up to while he was locked up. Where was he, by the way?'

'Ulmentahl,' said Münster. 'Rooth's on his way there now.'

'Good,' said Van Veeteren. 'Next? Another motive, that is!'

Münster cleared his throat. Pondered again.

'Well, if it isn't anything to do with what happened in prison, it could have something to do with what happened in the past.'

'It could indeed, certainly,' said Van Veeteren, and it seemed to Münster that the pale grey colour vanished briefly from his face.

'How?' said Van Veeteren. 'For hell's sake, Inspector, don't try and tell me you haven't given a thought to this! It's over a day since you received the damned tip-off.'

'Only half a day since we were sure,' said Münster apologetically.

Van Veeteren snorted.

'Motive!' he said again. 'Come on!'

'Somebody who didn't think the prison sentence was long enough,' said Münster.

'Possibly,' said Van Veeteren.

'Somebody who hated him. One of those women's friends who had been waiting for revenge, perhaps. It's a bit hard to get inside a prison and kill a man, after all.'

'Very hard,' said Van Veeteren. 'Unless you get another prisoner to take on a contract, that is. There could well be the odd one who wouldn't be too hard to persuade. Have you any other suggestions?'

Münster paused for a moment.

'It's not exactly a suggestion,' he said.

'Out with it even so,' said Van Veeteren.

'There's no evidence for it.'

'I want to hear it nevertheless.'

His facial colour had intensified again. Münster cleared his throat.

'All right,' he said. 'There's a slight possibility that he was innocent.'

'Who?'

'Verhaven, of course.'

'Really?'

'Of one of the murders at least, and it could have something to do with that . . . somehow or other.'

Van Veeteren said nothing.

'But it's pure speculation, naturally . . .'

The door opened a few inches and a tired nurse stuck her head round it.

'Could I remind you that visiting time is over. Dr Ratenau will be doing his rounds in a couple of minutes.'

Van Veeteren gave her a dirty look, and she withdrew her head and closed the door.

'Speculation, ah yes. Don't you think I can allow myself a bit of speculation while I am residing here in the dwelling of the condemned?'

'Of course,' said Münster, getting to his feet. 'Goes without saying.'

'And if,' Van Veeteren continued, 'if it turns out that this poor bastard has spent twenty-four years in prison for something he hasn't done, then . . .'

'Then?'

'Then damn me if this isn't the biggest legal scandal to hit this country in a hundred years. No, the biggest ever!'

'There is no evidence to support it,' said Münster, as he headed for the door.

'Calpurnia,' said Van Veeteren.

'Excuse me?' said Münster.

'Caesar's wife,' explained Van Veeteren. 'Suspicion is enough. And there is suspicion in here,' he added, tapping his forehead with his index finger.

'I'm with you,' said Münster. 'Goodbye for now, then. I'll call in tomorrow afternoon, as I said.'

'I'll phone this evening or tomorrow morning and tell

you what I need,' said Van Veeteren to round things off. 'Tell Hiller that I'm in charge of this from here on in.'

'Will do,' said Münster as he slunk through the door.

Ah well, he thought as he waited for the lift. He doesn't seem to have changed fundamentally.

15

PC Jung looked at his watch and sighed. He had arranged to meet Madeleine Hoegstraa at her home at four o'clock, and rather than arrive too early he had decided to spend three-quarters of an hour in a bar in her neighbourhood in the outskirts of Groenstadt. The drive there had gone much faster than he'd expected, and needless to say he was well aware that the key was his deep-seated fear of arriving too late for anything at all.

He sat down at one of the window tables with a large cup of Bernadine. The curtains were semi-transparent, and he could see blurred images of passers-by: just for a moment he had the impression of watching an old surrealistic movie. He shook his head. Movie? Good God, no! Exhaustion, that's what it was. The usual set-up: cops too shattered to keep awake.

He stirred his hot chocolate and started sketching out questions in his notebook instead. Now that he started examining it more closely, it dawned on him that it was really a vocabulary book full of French verbs, and he realized that he must have put it in his briefcase after testing Sophie on her homework the other night.

Sophie was thirteen, getting on for fourteen, and the daughter of Maureen, whose company he'd been keeping for some time now.

Quite a long time, to be honest, even if opportunities to be together were few and far between. And as he sat there waiting for time to pass by, he started to wonder a bit vaguely if anything serious would ever come of it. Of him and Maureen, that is. Tried to work out if that was really what he wanted.

And above all: did Maureen want it?

Maybe it was better if she didn't. Better to leave the cake uncut and just pick off a currant here and there when he felt like it. As usual, in other words. The same old routine.

He sighed once more and took another sip.

But he liked Maureen and liked being together with Sophie in the evenings and helping her with her maths lessons. Or French, or whatever it happened to be. It had only happened three or four times so far, but it had struck him that for the first time in his life, he had been playing the role of father.

And he liked it. It had a sort of dimension he hadn't experienced before. That gave him a feeling of equilibrium and security and stability, things that hadn't exactly featured prominently in his life hitherto.

Not clear precisely what that meant, but even so.

Sure is, he muttered to himself – and at the same time, he wondered where on earth he had picked up such a silly expression.

But when he thought about those unassuming evenings, the simple and yet awe-inspiring task of taking on a bit of responsibility for a growing child – well, he had to admit that he hoped that one of these days Maureen would pop the question.

Ask him to stay on. Throw his hat into the ring. Move in and make a family of them.

On other days the same idea could frighten him to death. He was well aware of that and would never dream of raising the matter himself. But the thought was there all right. A sort of secret wish, something close to his heart whose delicacy or frailty was so sensitive that he never dared to pick it up and examine it in detail. Never really come to grips with it.

The fact was that life had its cul-de-sacs; and needless to say, it wasn't always possible to turn back and retreat.

What the hell am I on about, he thought.

He checked his watch once more and lit a cigarette. Another quarter of an hour. He wasn't exactly looking forward to interviewing Mrs Hoegstraa. As far as he could make out, he was required to cross-question an upper-class lady of the old school. A privileged and spoiled woman with an abundance of rights but no corresponding obligations. That's the impression she had given on the telephone, at least. Mind you, it wasn't at all clear how this fitted in with Verhaven.

Verhaven had never been a member of the upper classes, surely.

No doubt she would pin him down, no matter what. Note his characteristic young man's smell of tobacco and cheap aftershave lotion. Stained trousers and dandruff on his shoulders. Sum him up, then make sure to keep him at arm's length. Imply that people of her social standing regarded the police as servants. That was something they had committed themselves to and thrown their weight behind – aspects of society that had to be maintained: money, the fine arts, the right to dispose of one's wealth as one sees fit – and so on.

Fuck it all, he thought. I'll never get over this. I'll always be standing here with my dirty cap in my hand, and I'll keep on bowing to my superiors as long as I live.

I'm so sorry to impose on you. So sorry that I have to ask you a few questions. So sorry that my dad was sacked by the printing works and drank himself to death.

Oh dear, I'm so sorry, your ladyship, I must have got it

wrong. Of course, I want to be buried in the pet cemetery with all the dogs. That's where I belong!

He emptied his mug of hot chocolate and stood up.

I worry too much, he thought. That's my problem.

I hope she doesn't serve up camomile tea, he thought.

Mrs Hoegstraa kept the safety chain on and examined his ID through the narrow crack.

'Sorry about that; I try to be very careful,' she said as she opened the door wide.

'You can never be too careful,' Jung said.

'Please come in.'

She led him into a living room overfilled with furniture. Invited him to sit in one of the pair of plush armchairs, like thrones in front of the fire. There was also a glass-topped table teeming with cups and saucers, scones, cookies, butter, cheese and jam.

'I always drink camomile tea myself,' she said. 'For my stomach's sake. But I don't suppose that would appeal to a man. Would you like coffee or a beer?'

Jung sat down feeling relieved. He had evidently misjudged this plump little woman somewhat. His worries had been exaggerated and originated from inside himself. As usual, perhaps.

This lady was human, no doubt about that. She exuded warmth.

'I wouldn't say no to a beer,' he said.

Perhaps there was something else about her, he thought as he watched her head for the kitchen. Something he was well acquainted with.

A bad conscience, no less?

'Fire away,' he said. His notebook with the questions he'd planned to ask could wait a bit. He might not even need to produce them at all.

'Where shall I start?' she asked.

'At the beginning, perhaps,' he suggested.

'Yes, I suppose that would be best.'

She took a deep breath and settled down in her chair.

'We have never been in close touch,' she said. 'You will obviously have gathered that we severed all connections after these . . . this murder business. But to tell you the truth there wasn't much contact before that either.'

She took a sip of tea. Jung put a slice of cheese on a cracker and waited.

'There were three of us siblings. My elder brother died two years ago, and I'll be seventy-five this autumn. Leopold was an afterthought, as they say. I was seventeen when he was born. Both Jacques and I had left home by the time he started school.'

Jung nodded.

'Then my mother died. He was only eight. He and Dad were the only ones left.'

'In Kaustin?'

'Yes. Dad was a blacksmith. But at that time he was away fighting the war, of course. They gave him special dispensation to go home six months before it was all over, to look after Leo. I helped out a bit, but I was married and had my own children to look after. Lived in Switzerland, so it wasn't all that easy to drop everything and do one's bit. My husband ran a company in Switzerland, and I was needed to make a contribution there as well.'

Oh yes, Jung thought. A guilty conscience, as usual.

'But you didn't live in the house your brother eventually bought? Not then, when you were a child?'

'No, we lived in the village. The smithy has closed down, but the house is still there.'

Jung nodded.

'Leopold bought that smallholding when he moved back there. That was after the athletics scandal.'

'Tell me about it,' said Jung. 'I'm all ears.'

She sighed.

'Leo had a lot of problems when he was growing up,' she said. 'I think he was a very lonely child. He had a hard time at school, found it hard to get on with his schoolmates, if I've understood it rightly. But you can no doubt find out more about this from others. He left school at twelve, in any case. Helped Dad in the smithy for a while, but then moved out to Obern. Just packed up and moved out: I assume there was some kind of row between him and Dad, but we never knew any details. He must have been fifteen, sixteen. It was 1952, if I remember rightly.'

'But things went well for him in Obern?'

'Yes, they did. He wasn't afraid of work, and there were plenty of jobs at that time. Then he joined that athletics club and started running.'

'Middle distance,' added Jung, who was quite interested in athletics. 'He was a brilliant runner – I'm a bit too young to have seen him, but I've read about him. Middle distance and upwards.'

Mrs Hoegstraa nodded.

'Yes, they were good years, in the mid-fifties. Everything seemed to be going well.'

'He held several records, didn't he? National records, that is . . . For the fifteen hundred and three thousand metres, if my memory serves me correctly.'

She shrugged and looked apologetic.

'Forgive me, Inspector, but I'm not very good at sports. And in any case, he was stripped of them all afterwards.'

Jung nodded.

'It was an enormous scandal, obviously. Banned for life – that must have been a bitter blow for him . . . very bitter. Had you any contact with him during those years?'

Mrs Hoegstraa looked down.

'No,' she said. 'We didn't. Neither my brother nor I.'

Jung waited for a while.

'But we were not the only ones at fault. That's the way he wanted it. He was a loner, always preferred to be on his own. He was always like that. Obviously, we would have preferred it to be different, but what can we do about it now? What could we have done then?'

She suddenly sounded weary.

'I don't know,' said Jung. 'Can you bear to go on a bit longer?'

She took another sip of tea, then continued.

'He left everything and moved back to Kaustin. Bought that house – he'd evidently managed to save a bit of money, from his work and his running. He was found guilty of taking drugs, and for . . . what do they call it? Breach of amateur regulations?'

Jung nodded again.

'I've read about it,' he said. 'He collapsed during a five-thousand-metre race while going for the European record. He'd been promised a large sum of money if he broke it, on the quiet, of course . . . And they discovered the amphetamine and quite a few other things when they got him to hospital. He was one of the first athletes to be caught for drugs offences in the whole of Europe, I think. Ah well, please go on, Mrs Hoegstraa.'

'Well, he bought that house, as I said. The Big Shadow, as they used to call it when I was a child, I don't know why. It's a bit off the beaten track, of course. It had been empty for a few years, and he got it cheap, I suppose. And then he got going with his chickens. He'd been working in that line while he was in Obern and had no doubt seen the potential. He could be quite enterprising when he put his mind to it. Had a good business sense, that sort of thing.'

She paused. Jung took a swig of beer, then asked:

'And then there was Beatrice?'

She suddenly looked very dejected.

'Do we really have to take that as well, Inspector?'

I don't know, he thought. Besides, I'm not an inspector yet. Might never be, come to that.

'Just a few little questions?' he suggested.

She nodded and clasped her hands on her knees. He started to feel for the vocabulary book in his inside pocket, but decided yet again to do without it.

'Did you ever meet her?'

'Not when she was grown up. I knew her when she was a child in Kaustin. They were more or less the same age. In the same class at school.'

'But she hadn't stayed put in the village either, had she?'

'No. She came back a few months after Leopold. She'd been living in Ulming for a time, I think. Left a man behind there as well.'

Jung pondered. Didn't really know what he was trying to find out. What it was permissible to ask about, and what the point of it was. Surely this poor old lady couldn't have anything to do with it? What was the justification for his sitting here and plaguing her with memories she'd spent all her life trying to forget?

There again, one never knows.

'Was she pretty?' he asked eventually, when the silence was starting to become too much for him.

She hesitated.

'Yes,' she said. 'From a man's point of view, she must have been very beautiful.'

'But you never saw her.'

'No, only in photographs. In the newspapers.'

He changed track. Completely.

'Why did you wait so long before contacting the police, Mrs Hoegstraa?'

She swallowed.

'I didn't know anything. Believe me, Inspector. I had no idea that anything had happened to him. We had no contact, none at all; you have to understand that.'

'Don't you think it's odd that your brother could be dead for eight months without anybody missing him?'

'Yes, I'm so sorry . . . It's terrible.'

'You never visited him when he was in prison?'

'Once, that first time. He made it very clear that he didn't want any more visits.'

'And you respected that?'

'Yes, I respected that.'

'What about your brother?'

'Yes. He tried once after the second murder. Leo refused to see him.'

'Did you write to him?'

She shook her head.

'But you looked after the house for him?'

'No, not at all. I just looked after the key. We went there twice during the last twelve years. The second time was a week before he was due for release. He sent me a postcard asking me to leave the key there for him.'

'And that was all?' Jung asked.

'Yes,' she said, looking slightly embarrassed. 'That was all, I'm afraid.'

Huh, Jung thought as he crossed the street a quarter of an hour later. I must remember to phone my sister this evening. This is not what ought to happen.

I'd better call Maureen as well, come to that. About the vocabulary book if for nothing else.

He had already driven a few miles before it occurred to him that he'd forgotten to ask about the testicle business; but no matter how he looked at it, he couldn't see that it was significant. In any case, it would be easier to deal with that detail on the telephone.

And not to have to be so embarrassingly close, that is.

I suppose I'm a bit of a prude really, he thought, switching on the radio.

16

On the way to Ulmentahl, Inspector Rooth found himself sitting at the wheel while thinking about various geographical circumstances; in retrospect he realized that those thoughts must have been triggered when he drove through Linzhuisen and happened to see the place names Kaustin and Behren on the same signpost.

Kaustin 10. Behren 23.

In different directions, of course. Kaustin to the northwest. Behren almost due south. If his rudimentary knowledge of geometry had not let him down, that should mean that the distance between the two places was . . . thirty miles or more?

Why had the murderer chosen to place the dead body just there?

In Behren. A little town with, perhaps, twenty-five thousand inhabitants? No more than thirty, in any case.

Pure coincidence?

Very possible. If the murderer's intention had been no

more than to dump the body sufficiently far away from Kaustin for the link with Verhaven not to strike anybody, then yes, that was probably far enough. But on the other hand, a greater distance would have been even better for his purpose.

They could take it as read that Verhaven had been killed in his own house. Or could they? Nothing was absolutely certain yet, one way or the other, and perhaps he could have left the house without being seen by Mrs Wilkerson's hawklike eyes? Or anybody else's?

Of course he could. During the night, for instance. Or through the forest. It was only that road down to the village that had eyes. And the village itself.

So, yes, he probably could have gone to Behren. Or somewhere else. And met his killer there. No doubt about it.

He turned onto the motorway. Next question?

How? How, if that was what happened, could Verhaven have found his way to Behren? (Or somewhere else, as stated.)

He didn't have a car of his own any more. So bus or taxi, that seemed to be the only . . . And if that was the case, it ought not to be all that difficult to look into it.

Eventually, that is. So far they had managed to keep the mass media at arm's length; that was a blessing, to be sure, when it came to their working conditions and the atmosphere in which the investigation was conducted, but sooner or later, they would need help from the media. And obviously, it was only a matter of time before the echo of jungle drums in Kaustin was picked up a little farther away. Before long the news would be broadcast all over the country, and they would have to take the rough with the smooth. As usual.

Journalists are like cow shit, Reinhart used to say. I'm not especially keen on the stuff as such, but I understand that it has its uses.

So if there was a cab driver, Rooth thought, or a bus conductor who could recall a particular passenger setting out from Kaustin one evening in August . . . Or early morning, perhaps . . . To – why not Behren? Well, yes indeed, that would narrow things down quite a lot.

Concentrate minds a bit.

He increased speed and tapped his fingers on the steering wheel.

As things were at the moment, you could ask as many questions as you liked. And every damned question gave rise to another three. Or even more.

Like that Greek monster, whatever its name is.

No, better to worry about something else instead, he decided, and ran his hand through his beard.

No, not through. Over, rather.

What had deBries said? A dying hamster?

Whatever, another 130 miles to Ulmentahl. He would have to put some life into this case before very long, that was beyond discussion.

Mr Bortschmaa's office was light and airy and pleasantly cosy with framed sports certificates and crossed tennis racquets. The prison governor himself was a powerfully built man in his fifties, Rooth estimated, dressed in a light blue sports shirt, with tanned forearms and youthful, flaxen hair.

The group of furniture where visitors were entertained by the picture window – looking out onto the barbed-wire top of the prison wall and the peaceful flat countryside beyond – comprised thin steel chairs with eye-catching blue and yellow upholstery and a table made of red plastic. On one of the chairs sat an overweight man with receding hair and sweat stains under his arms. He did not look happy.

Rooth and the governor sat down.

'Meet Joppens, our welfare officer,' said the latter.

'Rooth,' said Rooth, shaking hands.

'The inspector would like to ask you some questions about Leopold Verhaven,' Bortschmaa explained in one direction. 'I thought it a good idea for Joppens to be present,' he explained in the other. 'Please fire away, Inspector.'

'Thank you,' said Rooth. 'Maybe you could describe him briefly.'

'Yes,' said the welfare officer. 'If there is anybody who can be described briefly, he's the one. You can have a comprehensive description in half a minute. Or on half a page handwritten.'

'Really?' said Rooth. 'What are you implying?'

'I had to do with him for eleven years, and I know as much about him now as I did when I first met him.'

'A hermit,' said Bortschmaa.

'He had no contact at all with anybody,' Joppens continued. 'No fellow prisoner, nobody outside prison, none of the warders. Not with me and not with the chaplain either.'

'Sounds remarkable,' said Rooth.

'He might as well have spent all his sentence in solitary confinement,' said Bortschmaa. 'It wouldn't have made much difference. An introspective type. Extremely introverted. But a model prisoner, of course.'

'He never misbehaved?' asked Rooth.

'Never,' said Joppens. 'Never smiled either.'

'Did he take part in any activities?'

The welfare officer shook his head.

'Went swimming once a week. Went to the library twice a week. Read newspapers and borrowed a book occasionally. I don't know if you would call that activities.'

'But you must have spoken with him, surely?'

'No,' said the welfare officer.

'Did he answer if you addressed him?'

'Oh yes. Good morning and goodnight and thank you.'

Rooth thought that over. What the devil was the point of sitting in a car all day just for this, he wondered. Might as well carry on a bit longer, though. Seeing as he was here, after all.

'No confidants in the whole prison?'

'No,' said Joppens.

'None at all,' confirmed Bortschmaa.

'Any letters?' said Rooth.

The welfare officer thought that one over.

'He received two. Relatives, I think. And he sent a postcard a few weeks before he was released.'

'And he was inside for twelve years?'

'Yes. The card was to his sister.'

'Any visits at all?'

'Two,' said Joppens. 'His brother came once, right at the start. Verhaven refused to meet him. Wouldn't even go to the interview room . . . I hadn't taken up my appointment then, but my predecessor told me about it. The brother sat waiting for him for a whole day . . .'

'And the other?' said Rooth.

'Excuse me?'

'The other visit. You said he had two.'

'A woman,' said Joppens. 'Last year, I think . . . No, it must have been the year before.'

'Who was the woman?'

'I've no idea.'

'But he received her?'

'Yes.'

Rooth contemplated the diplomas and tennis racquets for a while.

'That all sounds a bit odd to me,' he said. 'Have you many prisoners like that?'

'None,' said the governor. 'I've never come across anything like it before.'

'Formidable self-control,' said the welfare officer. 'I've talked to my colleagues about him and everybody agrees. About what he was like on the surface, that is. What was underneath is a mystery, of course.'

Rooth nodded.

'Why are you so interested in him?' the governor wondered. 'Or is that classified information?'

'No,' said Rooth. 'It will come out sooner or later. We've found him murdered.'

The silence that fell in the room felt almost like a power cut, it seemed to Rooth.

'That really is . . .' said the welfare officer.

'But what the . . .' said the prison governor.

'You don't need to tell all and sundry about this,' said

Rooth. 'We'd be grateful to have a few days of peace and quiet before the newspapers get on our backs.'

'Of course,' said Bortschmaa. 'How did he die?'

'We don't know,' said Rooth. 'We don't have his head, his hands or his feet as yet. Somebody butchered him.'

'Oh my God,' said Bortschmaa, and Rooth had the impression that his tan faded noticeably. 'Don't say this is what the papers have been writing about?'

'Yes, it is,' said Rooth.

'When do you think he died, then?' wondered Joppens.

'Quite a long time ago,' said Rooth. 'He was dead for eight months before he was found.'

'Eight months?' Joppens exclaimed, frowning. 'That must have been shortly after we released him?'

'The same day, we think.'

'You mean he was murdered the very same day?'

'It looks like it.'

'Hmm,' said Bortschmaa.

'Being locked up seems to mean being safe, at least,' said Joppens.

There was a pause, and Rooth was starting to feel hungry. He wondered why on earth nobody had offered him anything to eat.

'Was he ever let out on parole?' he asked.

'Never wanted to be,' said Bortschmaa. 'And we don't normally press people.'

Rooth nodded. What else should he ask about?

'And so you haven't any suspicions at all,' he said as he thought feverishly, 'no idea about who might have wanted to kill him?'

'Do you?' asked the welfare officer.

'No,' admitted Rooth.

'Nor do we,' said the governor. 'Not the least idea. He didn't have any contacts at all while he was in here. Good ones or bad ones. Somebody must have been lying in wait.'

Rooth sighed.

'Yes, that's what it looks like.'

He thought for a moment.

'That woman,' he said, 'the one who came to visit him . . . last year, or whenever it was . . . Who was she?'

Bortschmaa turned to the welfare officer.

'I've no idea,' he said.

'Me neither,' said Joppens. 'We'd better go and have a look at the record books, if you really want to know.'

'Why don't we do that?' said Rooth.

It took some time for the two women in the archives to pin down the reference, but they eventually came up with the date.

June 5, 1992. A Friday.

Her name was Anna Schmidt.

'Address?' Rooth asked.

'We don't have that,' said the older of the two women. 'It's not required.'

'Only the name?'

'Yes.'

Rooth sighed.

'What did she look like?'

They both shrugged.

'You'd better ask the warder.'

'Is it possible to find out who was on duty then and who might have . . . might have seen her?'

'Of course.'

That also took some time, but at least it gave Rooth the opportunity to visit the canteen and buy a couple of cheese sandwiches while the duty officers on the day in question were traced.

'You are Emmeline Weigers?'

'Yes.'

'And you were supervising the interview room on June fifth, 1992?'

'Yes, it seems so.'

'That was the day Leopold Verhaven had a visitor. That was most unusual, I gather.'

'Yes.'

'Do you remember it?'

'Fairly well, yes.'

'But it's almost two years ago.'

'I remember it because it was him. We talked about it among the staff. He was a bit . . . special, we'd heard.'

'Did he often have visitors?'

'Never.'

'Can you describe the woman?'

'Not very well, I'm afraid. I can't really remember. She was getting on a bit. About sixty, I'd say. A bit sickly, I think. Used a walking stick.'

'Would you recognize her if you saw her again?'

She thought for a while.

'No, I don't think I would. No.'

'How long did they talk?'

'I'm not sure. Fifteen or twenty minutes, if I remember rightly. Not the full time anyway.'

'The full time?'

'The rules allow half an hour.'

'Is there anything special you remember, now that you think back about it? Any particular detail?'

She pondered for about ten seconds.

'No,' she said. 'There was nothing.'

Rooth thanked her and stood up.

*

It took another hour to complete the formalities in the prison and then find Number 4 Ruitens Allé in the village of Ulmentahl itself. He parked outside the white house. Recited a silent prayer and walked up the paved drive. Rang the doorbell.

'Hello?'

'Mr Chervouz?'

'Yes.'

'My name's Rooth. Detective Inspector Rooth. I was the one who phoned you not long ago.'

'Come in. Or would you prefer to sit in the garden? It's quite nice weather.'

'Outdoors would be fine,' said Rooth.

'It's pretty when the chestnuts are in blossom,' said Mr Chervouz as he filled two tall glasses with beer.

'Yes,' said Rooth. 'Very.'

They drank.

'What do you want to know about Verhaven?'

'You were on duty, so-called gate duty, on June fifth, 1992. Verhaven had a visitor that day. I know it's nearly two years ago now, but I wonder if you can remember anything about the woman you let in?'

Chervouz took another swig of beer.

'I've been thinking about it since you called. She came

by cab, I think. An oldish woman. Had trouble walking, used a pair of walking sticks, in any case. But Christ, it's just what I think I remember. I could be mixing her up with somebody quite different. I might be thinking of the wrong person.'

'Why do you remember the visit at all?'

'Because the visitor was for him, of course.'

'I see,' said Rooth. 'Had you ever seen her before?'

'No.'

'Was there anything else you noticed?'

'No . . . No, I don't think so.'

'Were you still on duty when she left?'

'No, it must have been somebody else. I don't remember her leaving, in any case.'

'Would you recognize her again?'

'No, certainly not.'

A few seconds passed. Then it came, and there was no mistaking the undertone of curiosity.

'What's he done?'

'Nothing,' said Rooth. 'He's dead.'

He had a moderately exciting dinner at the railway station restaurant, and it was already getting dusk when he returned to his car.

What a productive day this has been, he thought. Most impressive.

And when he started working out how much taxpayers' money had been spent – and would continue to be spent in future – on this dodgy investigation, he could feel himself growing angry.

Especially when you consider what Leopold Verhaven had already cost the state. While he was still alive, that is.

He had murdered two women. Been at the centre of two protracted trials and found guilty and spent almost a quarter of a century in jail. And now somebody had put a full stop behind him.

Wouldn't it be as well for the police to do the same?

Full stop. Draw a line and act as if they'd never stumbled upon that butchered body wrapped up in a piece of carpet. Who would benefit from the police putting vast amounts of time and energy into finding whoever it was that for whatever reason had decided to put an end to that solitary criminal's existence?

Who the hell cared if Leopold Verhaven was dead?

Was there any single person?

Apart from the one who killed him, of course.

Rooth doubted it.

But somewhere deep down at the back of his mind he could hear the echo of some guidelines, taken from the Rules and Regulations for Criminal Investigations, if he remembered rightly. He couldn't recall the precise wording, but the meaning could be expressed just as well by one of Van Veeteren's favourite sayings.

If the murderer is holed up in Timbuktu, stop the first cab that comes along and go there. We're not a profit-making company, for Christ's sake!

'Where is Timbuktu?' somebody had asked.

'The cab driver will know,' Van Veeteren had replied.

Better stick with that spirit, I suppose, Rooth thought. It's hard to judge the consequences of any other approach.

17

Van Veeteren picked up the bundle of photocopies and leafed through it.

Münster hadn't been twiddling his thumbs, he had to admit. Forty to fifty pages as least; from several newspapers, but naturally enough mainly *Neuwe Blatt* and *Telegraaf*. Arranged in chronological order with the athletics business first and comments on the judgment in the Marlene trial last. Precise dates supplied.

He wondered if it really had been Münster himself who had made all this effort to satisfy his superior's curiosity, or if it had been some assiduous librarian in the periodicals archives who had done the donkey work. He tended towards the latter explanation, but you never knew, of course.

Münster is Münster, Van Veeteren thought.

He started with the background details. Verhaven's brilliant but short career on the cinder running track. It couldn't have lasted for more than two years, if you worked it out. Two successful years before everything changed key.

'New Record by Verhaven!' was the headline of an article over four columns, dated August 20, 1958, incorporating a blurred photograph of a young man looking straight at the camera in close-up, making the V sign.

He didn't look particularly overwhelmed, Van Veeteren thought. Nor overwhelming. But it had to be said that there were clear traces of seriousness and determination in that resolute mouth, and his dark eyes seemed full of implicit faith in future triumphs and even faster times.

He contemplated that twenty-four-year-old face for a while, wondering if it was possible to read anything into it – if he could discern anything of the future in those steely features . . . Any signs of predestination, the embryo of the older man of violence, a double murderer.

Needless to say it was impossible.

He couldn't blot out the key he was holding in his hands. He knew what he was looking for, and hence it was possible to find it. No, those eyes revealed nothing; only the usual, slightly pompous self-confidence, Van Veeteren decided. The quality that is considered to indicate strength and manliness and God only knows what else that you can generally find in all modern heroes. Perhaps in the classical ones as well. Van Veeteren had never been much of a sports fan, and fooling oneself into believing that there was a qualitative difference between a Greek discus thrower and a Russian ice-hockey back was nothing more than an expression of our constant need of self-delusion. Sport is sport.

Having established that, he started reading instead:

> It has been obvious all this year to the general public with an interest in sport that Leopold Verhaven is one of our biggest stars on the track. But few people can have expected this incredibly talented athlete from Obern, still only 22 years old, to start breaking records as early as this summer.
>
> But he fooled us all, and how pleased we are to be fooled! Sunday's brilliant performance in the Verhejm stadium and the impressive new record for the 1,500 metres was followed last night, a marvellous evening of sport at Willemsroo, by a further reduction to an excellent 3 minutes 41.5 seconds, and it should be stressed that Verhaven was forced to run the last 600 metres out on his own, in solitary majesty.
>
> None of the others in the high-quality field was able to keep up when he turned on the heat after about half the race. His easy, lightning-fast stride, the apparently effortless grace and flow characteristic of his style, the rhythm and his masterly tactical brain . . .

Van Veeteren skipped the rest. Tried to go back in his memory and find himself during that August more than thirty-five years ago. But the best he could do was to establish that it must have been the summer vacation in between two of those easily confused university terms. Before he burned his bridges and threw himself wholeheartedly into police college. Probably a summer job at Kummermann's, that damn and dusty warehouse, or – much preferably – a week spent by the sea with his uncles.

Ah well. He moved on to the next clip. Almost a year later. May 18, 1959. Three columns in *Telegraaf* with a picture of the winner crossing the line in another fifteen-hundred-metre race. Obviously his favourite distance – the 'blue riband', isn't that what they called it? Chest thrust forward to break the tape as soon as possible, longish hair fluttering in the wind, mouth open and eyes more or less unseeing . . .

'Verhaven Heading for the European Record?' was the headline this time. Van Veeteren read:

> 3 minutes 40.5 seconds! That is Verhaven's new record for the 1,500 metres, set last night after a brilliant race at the international meeting at the Künderplatz. Shortly after the 800-metre mark our new king of the middle distance waved goodbye to the rest of the field, and after two magnificent solo laps posted a time that has only been bettered this year by the Frenchman Jazy and the Hungarian Rozsavölgy. Verhaven's time is the sixth best ever, and there is no doubt that the incredibly

> talented 23-year-old from Obern will be one of our strongest cards at the Rome Olympics next year. At least, as far as track events are concerned, where our national team seems to be lagging way behind the British, the French and the outstanding Americans. At yesterday's meeting no fewer than . . .

May 1959, Van Veeteren thought, putting the page to one side. Three months before the bubble burst, that is.

He took the next article, and there he was already. The scandal had happened, and this time it was also front-page news:

'Verhaven – a Cheat!' Large bold type over four columns; underneath it a blurred picture that, on closer inspection, appeared to be a man being carried away on a stretcher. In rather tumultuous circumstances, judging by appearances.

Van Veeteren read the indignant article on the five-thousand-metre race in the middle of August 1959, in which Verhaven was well in the lead with only just over two laps to go – and a probable European record – but he suddenly collapsed as he emerged from the southern bend at the Richter Stadium in Maardam.

He checked the date: yes, the article was written two days after the race. When everything had been revealed.

When the doping and the illegal payments had all come to light.

When the fairy tale was over.

Verhaven – the cheat.

Was this the background to Verhaven – the murderer? wondered Van Veeteren.

And to Verhaven – the double murderer?

Was there a link, a connection, with one thing leading to another? Not automatically, of course, but nevertheless a sort of cause and effect. Was the murderer already there as a seed, an embryo, in the cheat? Was it even legitimate to ask such questions?

He could feel weariness creeping up on him again. He smoothed out the slightly wavy sheets of paper and put them back in the envelope.

What was the point of thinking along these lines? he asked himself. Why was his brain following up these dark ideas? Whether he wanted to or not. Was there really nothing more reliable that he could turn his attention to?

If he wanted to claim that he was now in charge of this investigation?

He listened for a while to the pigeons cooing away somewhere outside the window. His thoughts wandered off on their own for a few minutes and contemplated rather vaguely peace symbols, the disintegration of Europe and ambiguous nationalism, before coming back to the matter at hand again. For – the bottom line was, what to do about the suspicion he had?

The persistent idea that kept on nagging away.

Wasn't that what he really ought to be trying to find evidence for?

How easy and simple it was for a distant observer to draw the same would-be-wise conclusions. Cheat – murderer. Build these putative bridges over imagined chasms. Look for connections where no connections exist or are needed. And come to that, one could ask just how serious the cheating had been. Did it really carry the weight and significance given to it by the gods and gurus of sports at the time, the innocent 1950s? Or budding 1960s. He found it hard to believe. Did the guy run any faster because he was being paid? The amphetamine and whatever else probably gave him a bit of a boost, one can assume, but would that kind of thing nowadays lead to a life ban?

He didn't know. It was not his field, certainly not, but Rooth or Heinemann would be bound to know about such things.

Whatever, the question remained: how much had 'Verhaven the cheat' weighed against him when he progressed to being 'Verhaven the murderer'?

In other people's eyes, that is. Journalists'. The man in the street's. The police's, the judiciary's and the jury members'. The eyes of those who condemned him.

Judge Heidelbluum's?

That was a question worth thinking about, yes, indeed.

He clasped his hands over his tender wound, closed his eyes and decided to let his dreams take care of it for the time being.

18

After a certain amount of lobbying, deBries had been allocated Detective Constable Ewa Moreno as a partner. For the forthcoming fieldwork, at least, and when they set off for Kaustin in the late afternoon, taking the pretty, meandering route by the lake, he had the impression that she was not too displeased by the arrangement.

And she could certainly have done worse. Surely it was permissible to allow oneself that degree of self-esteem? DeBries came to a halt outside the school and they stayed in the car for a while, comparing the hand-drawn map with reality.

'Gellnacht first?' Moreno suggested, nodding in the direction of a house. 'It's over there.'

'Your wish is my command,' said deBries, engaging first gear.

*

Irmgaard Gellnacht had laid a table for coffee in the arbour behind her large clapboard house. She beckoned them to sit down on a yellow porch swing, and she took one of the two old easy chairs.

'The evenings are lovely at this time of year,' she said. 'You have to try to be outside as much as possible.'

'Early summer is the prettiest time,' said Ewa Moreno. 'All these flowers.'

'Do you have a garden?' wondered Mrs Gellnacht.

'I'm afraid not. But I hope to have one eventually.'

DeBries cleared his throat discreetly.

'Ah, forgive me,' said Mrs Gellnacht. 'That wasn't what we're supposed to talk about, of course. Do help yourselves, by the way.'

'Thank you,' said Moreno. 'Did you grow the rhubarb for this pie yourself?'

'So you were the same age, in other words?' said deBries.

'Not quite. I'm one year older. Born in thirty-five. Leopold in thirty-six. But we were in the same class even so. The village school combined three age streams per class in those days – I think they still do, in fact – so I remember him all right. You don't forget five years in the same school so easily.'

'What impression did you have of him?'

'A loner,' said Irmgaard Gellnacht, without hesitation. 'Why are you so interested in him? Is it true what they are saying, that he's dead?'

No doubt it will be in tomorrow's papers anyway, deBries thought.

'We'd prefer not to comment on that, Mrs Gellnacht,' he explained, holding a finger to his lips. 'And we'd be grateful if you are discreet about our little chat.'

He thought that sounded a bit like a veiled threat, which was exactly what he had intended.

'No doubt he had some friends?' said Moreno.

Mrs Gellnacht thought that over.

'No, I don't think he did. Well, in the first year or two, perhaps. He used to go around a little with Pieter Wolenz, if I'm not mistaken, but then they moved. To Linzhuisen. I don't think there was anybody after that.'

'Was he teased at all?' asked Moreno. 'Bullied, as they say nowadays.'

She thought again.

'No,' she said eventually. 'Not really. We had a sort of respect for him, despite everything, all of us. You tried not to fall out with him, in any case. He could get very angry, I recall. He had a fiery temperament underneath that silent and sullen surface.'

'How did it make itself felt?'

'Excuse me?'

'This fiery temperament. What did he do?'

'Oh, I don't really know,' she said hesitantly. 'Some pupils were a bit afraid of him, there were a few fights, and he was strong, really strong, even though he certainly wasn't especially big or powerful.'

'Can you remember any particular occasion?'

'No . . . Wait a moment, yes, in fact. I remember he once threw a boy out of a window when he lost his temper.'

'Out of a window?'

'Yes, but it wasn't as dangerous as it sounds. It was the ground floor, so it turned out all right.'

'I see.'

'Mind you, there was a bicycle rack outside, so he did injure himself slightly even so . . .'

DeBries nodded.

'What was the boy's name?' asked Moreno.

'I can't remember,' said Irmgaard Gellnacht. 'Maybe it was one of the Leisse brothers. Or Kollerin, he's the local butcher now. Yes, I think it was him.'

DeBries changed tack.

'Beatrice Holden, do you remember her?'

'Yes, of course,' said Mrs Gellnacht, sitting bolt upright in the easy chair.

'And how would you describe her?'

'I'd rather not. Don't speak ill of the dead, as they say.'

'But if we were to lean on you a little?'

She gave a quick smile.

'Well, in that case,' she said. 'Beatrice Holden was a slut. I think that description fits her rather well.'

'Was she a slut even when she was at school?' wondered Moreno.

'From the very start. Don't think I'm an old prude just because I'm saying this. Beatrice was a terribly vulgar person. The cheapest kind. She had the looks, and she used them to wrap men round her little finger. Or boys, in those days.'

'They were in love with her?'

'The whole lot. Teachers as well, I think. She was young and unmarried. It was really awful, in fact.'

'She moved away from here later, didn't she?'

Mrs Gellnacht nodded.

'Ran off with a man when she was barely seventeen. Lived in two or three different places, I think. Came back with a child a few years later.'

'A baby?'

'Yes. A girl. Her mother looked after it. Beatrice's mother, that is.'

'When? Was that a long time before she was mixed up with Verhaven?'

'No, not all that long. I'd say it was round about 1960, that was roughly the same time as he moved back here. She and the girl moved in with her mother, in any case, only for about six months, or thereabouts. The father had gone to sea, people said, but nobody has ever seen him. Not then, not later. Well, after a few months she moved in with Verhaven, up at the Big Shadow.'

'The Big Shadow?'

'Yes, that's what it's usually called. The Big Shadow. Don't ask me why.'

DeBries made a note.

'What about the daughter?' asked Moreno. 'Did she take the girl with her?'

'Oh no,' replied Mrs Gellnacht firmly. 'Certainly not. The girl stayed with Grandma. Perhaps that was best, in view of what happened. She turned out all right.'

'What was the relationship like?' asked deBries. 'Verhaven and Beatrice, I mean.'

Mrs Gellnacht hesitated before answering.

'I don't know,' she said. 'There was an awful lot of gossip about it afterwards, of course. Some people reckoned it was inevitable from the start that it would end up like it did. Or that it would go wrong, at least; but I don't know. It's always so easy for people to understand everything when they have the key in their hands and know what actually happened. Don't you think?'

'No doubt about it,' said deBries.

'Quite a few things happened, in fact, before he killed her. I think they drank pretty heavily, but there again he was a good worker. Worked hard, and no doubt earned quite a bit from his chickens. But they certainly used to fight. Nobody can deny that.'

'Yes, so we understand,' said Moreno.

There was a pause while Mrs Gellnacht served more coffee. Then deBries leaned forward and asked the most important question of all.

'What was it like during the time before Verhaven was arrested? After they'd found Beatrice's body, that is. Those ten days, or however long it was? Can you remember anything about that?'

'Well . . .' Mrs Gellnacht began. 'I'm not sure I quite understand what you are getting at.'

'What did people think?' explained Moreno. 'Who did people suspect when they talked about it here in the village? Before they knew.'

She sat silently for a moment, her cup half-raised to her lips.

'Well,' she said. 'I suppose that's the way people were talking.'

'What way?' asked deBries.

'That it was Verhaven himself who'd done it, of course. I don't think anybody here in Kaustin was especially surprised when he was arrested. Nor when he was found guilty either.'

DeBries wrote something in his notebook again.

'And what about now?' he asked. 'Is everybody still sure that he was the one who did it?'

'Absolutely,' she replied. 'No doubt about it. Who else could it have been?'

Something to consider in a little more detail perhaps, he thought when they were back in the car.

As it couldn't very well have been anybody else, it must have been Verhaven!

One could only hope that Mrs Gellnacht's reasoning hadn't been copied to too great an extent by the police and the prosecuting authorities. No doubt it would be a good idea to look into that question. What about the forensic evidence, by the way? What exactly was it that had got him convicted, if he really had denied everything so vehemently right to the very end?

DeBries had no idea.

'What do you think?' he asked.

'Seems to be an open-and-shut case,' said Ewa Moreno. 'Possibly too open and shut. Shall we take Moltke now?'

19

'Verhaven Arrested! Sensational Development in Beatrice Case!'

The headline ran across the whole of *Neuwe Blatt*'s front page on April 30, 1962. Van Veeteren drank half a mug of water and started reading.

> Was it Leopold Verhaven who murdered his own fiancée, Beatrice Holden?
>
> In any case the police officer in charge of the notorious Kaustin murder, Detective Chief Inspector Mort, and also the public prosecutor, Mr Hagendeck, have good reason to think so. Such good reason that the former international athlete was taken into custody yesterday. At the press conference Hagendeck was very careful not to reveal the grounds for the arrest, but thought that charges would be made within the twelve-day period stipulated by law.
>
> Precisely how new evidence or proof that would throw light on this sinister business had emerged was

something neither the police nor the prosecutor were prepared to discuss at the press conference in the Maardam police station. Nor does it seem that Leopold Verhaven has made a confession. His lawyer, Pierre Quenterran, was adamant that his client had nothing whatsoever to do with the murder, and claimed that the arrest was a consequence of, and a reaction to, all that had been written about the case.

'The police are desperate,' Quenterran insisted to assembled reporters. 'The general public with its ingrained sense of justice has demanded results, and rather than admit to their incompetence, those in charge of the case have conjured up a scapegoat . . .'

Detective Chief Inspector Mort dismissed Mr Quenterran's statement as 'utter rubbish'.

Well, he would, wouldn't he? Van Veeteren thought and turned to the next photocopy, which was from the same issue of *Neuwe Blatt*, but an inside page. It comprised a short summary of the background, a résumé of developments from the time when 'this sombre and depressing course of events first began', as the reporter put it.

April 6:

A Saturday, sunny with a warm breeze. Early in the morning Leopold Verhaven sets off, as is his wont, for the towns of Linzhuisen and Maardam on business, and does not return home until late afternoon.

> Beatrice Holden has vanished by then, according to Verhaven's own testimony, but he assumes that 'she's just gone off somewhere'. However, nobody has seen Beatrice Holden from that moment on. Some neighbours noticed her on her way home on Saturday morning, several hours after Verhaven had left. She spent the morning visiting her mother and daughter in the village. There is no evidence to suggest that she left home again on business of her own, and of her own free will.

On business of her own, and of her own free will! Van Veeteren thought. What a wordsmith! He continued reading:

> April 16:
> Verhaven reports to the police that his fiancée has been missing for over a week. He declines to comment on why he left it so long before informing the police. He does not believe, however, that 'anything serious can have happened to her'.
>
> April 22:
> Beatrice Holden's dead body is found by an elderly couple in some woods only a mile or so away from Verhaven's house. She is naked and has been strangled, probably not at the place where her body was found.

April 22–29:
A major police investigation examines the circumstances of the murder. Meticulous forensic procedures are followed, and a hundred or so people, most of them from the village of Kaustin, are interviewed.

April 30:
Leopold Verhaven is arrested on suspicion of having murdered his 23-year-old fiancée, or alternatively committed manslaughter.

That was all. Van Veeteren put the photocopy at the bottom of the pile and checked the time. Half past eleven. Shouldn't lunch be served about now? For the first time since he came to after the operation, he could feel a little pang of hunger. That must surely be a sign that he was on the mend?

In any case, everything seemed to have gone according to plan. That is what the young surgeon with the cherubic cheeks had stressed enthusiastically that very morning, when he had called in to prod at Van Veeteren's stomach with his pale, cocktail-sausage fingers. A mere six to eight days' convalescence, then the chief inspector would be able to return to his usual routines, more energetic than ever.

Energetic? Van Veeteren thought. How can he know that I have any particular desire to be energetic?

He turned his head to look at the display of flowers.

Three bouquets, no more, no less, were squeezed onto the bedside table. His colleagues'. Renate's. Jess and Erich's. And this afternoon Jess was due to visit him with the twins. What more could he ask for?

Now he could hear the food trolley approaching down the corridor. Presumably he would only be allowed a few morsels of dietary fare, but perhaps that was just as well. Maybe he was not yet ready for rare steak.

He yawned and turned his thoughts back to Verhaven. Tried to imagine that little village off the beaten track around the beginning of the 1960s.

What components would have been there?

The usual ones? Presumably.

Narrowness of outlook. Suspicions. Envy. Wagging tongues.

Yes, that was about it, generally speaking.

Verhaven's outsider status?

He seems to have been an odd character, and an odd character was what was needed. The ideal murderer? Perhaps that is what it looked like.

How about proof? He tried to recall the circumstances, but he couldn't remember much more than a series of question marks that he hadn't been able to sort out.

Had they managed to resist all the half-truths that must have emerged? There had been a bit of a manhunt, he remembered. Quite a lot of insinuations in the media about the competence of the police and the courts. Or rather, incompetence. The police had been under pressure. If they didn't find a murderer, they were condemning themselves . . .

What about the forensic proof? It had been a case of circumstantial evidence, hadn't it? He must get down to the court records that Münster had brought him, that was obvious. If only he could get something nutritious down himself first. Certainly there had been one or two shaky points. He had only talked about the case once with Mort after it was all over, and it had been obvious that his predecessor had not been too happy about discussing it.

He was slightly better informed about the other business, the Marlene case. Hadn't that investigation left quite a lot to be desired as well? Van Veeteren had actually been involved in it, but only on the periphery. He'd never been in the courtroom. Mort had been in charge on that occasion as well.

Leopold Verhaven? Surely this was a chapter in legal history that would not stand up to meticulous rescrutiny?

Or was he merely imagining things? Was it just a matter of him needing something more or less perverse to occupy his mind as he lay here flat on his back, waiting for his intestine to heal properly again? Screened off and isolated from the outside world, where the only thing demanded of him was to lie still and not get excited.

Something really messy. An old legal scandal, like the one in that crime novel by Josephine Tey, whatever it was called.

Why was it so difficult to let your mind lie fallow?

What was it that Pascal had said? Something about all the evil in the world being caused by our inability to sit still in an empty room?

Shit, what an existence, he thought. Hurry up and wheel in the food trolley, so that I can get my teeth into a good old spinach soup!

20

'Quite a few stories were circulating about him,' said Bernard Moltke, lighting another cigarette.

'You don't say,' said deBries. 'What kind of stories?'

'Various kinds. It's hard to tell which ones dated from before Beatrice and which ones came afterwards. Which ones are authentic, if you like. It was mainly during the trial that gossip was rife. We'd never met up so much in the village as we did during those months. Afterwards, things quietened down, somehow. As if it were all over. Which it no doubt was.'

'Can you give us an example of the kind of story you are talking about?' asked Moreno. 'Preferably an authentic one.'

Bernard Moltke thought for a moment.

'The one about the cat,' he said. 'I certainly heard that one much earlier, in any case. They say he strangled a cat with his bare hands.'

DeBries could feel a shudder shooting down his spine, and he saw Constable Moreno give a start.

'Why?' he asked.

'I don't know,' said Moltke. 'But anyway, he's supposed to have wrung its neck. When he was ten or twelve years old.'

'Ugh,' said Moreno.

'Yes. Maybe somebody dared him to do it. I have an idea that was it.'

'Was that supposed to be a sufficient reason?'

'Don't ask me,' said Moltke. 'Lots of people say that's what he was like.'

'What do you have to say about Beatrice Holden, then?'

Moltke drew deeply on his cigarette, seemingly searching through his memory.

'A damned good-looking woman,' he said. 'A bit on the wild side, that's true, but Good Lord . . . Ah well. Same colour hair as you, miss.'

He winked at Moreno, who remained stony-faced, to deBries's great satisfaction.

'Why was she in with Verhaven, then?' she asked instead. 'He can't have been very attractive to women, surely?'

'Don't say that,' protested Moltke, poking his index

finger into his double chins. 'Don't say that. You never know what's going on inside a woman. Isn't that right, Inspector?'

'Absolutely,' said deBries.

'What about Marlene?' asked Moreno, totally unmoved. 'The same type of thoroughbred, I take it?'

Moltke burst out laughing, but soon turned serious.

'You bet your sweet life she was,' he said. 'A bit older, that's all. A goddamned scandal that he killed the pair of them.'

'You saw Marlene Nietsch as well, then?' asked deBries.

'Only the once. They hadn't met all that much before . . . it was all over.'

'I see,' said deBries. 'I understand you were a witness at the first trial?'

'Yes, sir.'

'What was your testimony about?'

Moltke thought for a while.

'I'm damned if I know,' he said. 'I was up at Verhaven's quite a bit around the time it happened, that's all really. Helped him with the lighting inside the chicken sheds. He was experimenting with daily rhythms and there was some wiring job he wasn't up to.'

'So that's it,' said deBries. 'Were you there on the Saturday she disappeared? Well, if you believe what he said, that is.'

Moltke nodded solemnly.

'Yes, I put in a few hours that Saturday. Finished about one, roughly. I was the last person to see her alive, I suppose. Apart from the murderer, of course.'

'The murderer?' said Moreno. 'You mean Verhaven?'

'Yes,' said Moltke. 'I suppose I do.'

'You don't sound too convinced,' said deBries.

A brief silence again.

'Oh yes,' he said. 'I've become convinced as the years have passed. After the Marlene murder, and then . . .'

'But you were a witness for the defence at the trial, isn't that right?'

'Yes.'

'What did you have to say?'

'Well,' said Moltke. He shook another cigarette from the pack on the table in front of him, but didn't light it. 'I worked for him the following week as well. Monday to Thursday, and they thought I would have noticed something if there was anything wrong.'

'And did you?'

'No. He was exactly the same as usual.'

'As usual?' said Moreno. 'Surely he must have reacted to her disappearance?'

'No. He said she'd gone off somewhere, but he didn't know where.'

'Didn't you think that was odd?'

Moltke shrugged.

'People were asking me that ten times a day around then. I can't remember what I thought, but I don't suppose I thought much about it. They were a bit unusual, both him and Beatrice. Everybody knew that, and it was hardly surprising that she went off for a few days.'

Nobody spoke for a few seconds. Moltke lit his cigarette. DeBries stubbed his out.

'That Saturday, the last time you saw her. What was he like?' Moreno asked.

'Same as usual, her as well,' said Moltke without hesitation. 'A touch more sulky, perhaps. They'd been fighting the previous week. She still had a bit of a bruise under one eye, but apart from that there was nothing special. I didn't see much of her, come to that. She called in at the chicken shed for a little chat, that's all. On her way back from the village.'

'What time was that?'

'Twelve, round about.'

'And you went home at about one?'

'Yes. A minute or two past.'

'What did you talk about?'

'The weather and the wind. Nothing special. She offered me coffee, but I was about to pack up and so I said no thank you.'

'Nothing else?'

'No.'

'And she was still there when you left?'

'Of course. Standing in the kitchen, busy with something or other. I just put my head round the door and wished her a good weekend.'

DeBries nodded.

'But when you gave your testimony, if I can come back to that, you didn't think Verhaven was guilty?'

Moltke drew deeply on his cigarette and exhaled before replying.

'No,' he said. 'I suppose I didn't, in fact.'

'And you still don't?' asked deBries. 'In fact?'

'I don't know. It's easier to live in this village if you think it was him, if you follow me. Is he really dead, like they say?'

'Who do you mean by they?'

'The folks in the village, of course.'

'Yes,' said deBries. 'He's dead.'

'Ah well,' said Moltke with a sigh. 'It comes to us all eventually.'

'What do we do now?' wondered Moreno. 'Time to go back to town, perhaps?'

DeBries checked his watch.

'Half past six. Shouldn't we take a look at the house, seeing as we're here? You've never been there.'

'OK,' said Moreno. 'I have a date at nine, though, and I'd like to have time to powder my nose first.'

'You'd be all right for me with no powder at all,' said deBries.

'Thank you,' said Moreno. 'It's good to know that you don't ask too much of people.'

'You learn to make the most of whatever you get,' said deBries.

'A gloomy place,' she said as they were driving back through the trees. 'Although it would have looked better in those days, no doubt.'

'Sure,' said deBries. 'It's been standing empty for twelve or thirteen years. That leaves its mark . . . What's all this! Have we time for another little chat?'

'A short one,' said Moreno.

DeBries slowed down and stopped beside a man bending down by the side of the road, painting a fence.

'Good evening,' said deBries through the open window. 'Do you mind if we ask you a few questions?'

The man straightened his back.

'Good evening,' he said. 'Please do. It will be a pleasure to stand upright for a bit.'

DeBries and Moreno got out of the car and shook hands. Claus Czermak had only been living in the blue house for just over a year, it transpired, and he was also too young to have any personal memories of the Verhaven trials. But it was always worthwhile spending a few minutes, just in case.

'We moved here when we had our third son,' he said, gesturing towards the house and garden, where a couple of toddlers were steering a pedal car down a wheelchair ramp built into the steps leading up to the front door. 'We thought it was a bit stifling in town. The country air and all that, you know . . .'

Moreno nodded.

'You don't work here in the village?'

Czermak shook his head.

'No,' he said. 'I have a post at the university. History, the Middle Ages and Byzantium.'

'I see. We're interested in Leopold Verhaven and his house up there in the forest,' said deBries. 'You are his nearest neighbours, so to speak. You and the people opposite . . .'

'The Wilkersons, yes. We had gathered there was something going on.'

'Exactly,' said deBries. 'But I don't suppose you have anything that could be of interest to us?'

Czermak shook his head.

'I wouldn't have thought so. We were still on vacation when he came back here last August. We've only heard people talking about him. What's happened?'

'He's dead,' said deBries. 'Mysterious circumstances. But don't call the newspapers tonight, if you wouldn't mind.'

'Oh dear,' said Czermak. 'No, you have my word on that.'

'Thank you for your efforts today,' said deBries as he pulled up outside Constable Moreno's apartment in Keymer Plejn. 'A pity you don't have time for a glass of something. It's often productive to sit down in peace and quiet for a while and chew over the impressions we've had.'

'Sorry about that,' said Moreno. 'I promise to plan things a bit better next time. Aren't you married, by the way?'

'A little bit,' deBries admitted.

'I thought so. Goodnight!'

She scrambled out of the car. Slammed the door and waved to him from the pavement. DeBries sat there for a while, watching her. It's Saturday tomorrow, he thought. A day off. Damn!

21

Van Veeteren snorted as he finished reading C. P. Jacoby's summary and analysis of the Beatrice case in the issue of *Allgemejne* dated Sunday, June 22, 1962. He stabbed angrily at the white button on his bedside table, and after half a minute the night nurse appeared in the doorway.

'I want a beer,' said Van Veeteren.

'This isn't a restaurant,' said the woman wearily, brushing a strand of hair from her face.

'So I've noticed,' said Van Veeteren. 'But the fact is that Dr Boegenmutter, or whatever the hell his name is, has told me to drink a beer or two. It assists the healing process. Stop being awkward and fetch me a bottle.'

'It's turned midnight. Shouldn't you go to sleep instead?'

'Sleep? I'm busy with a criminal investigation. You should be damned grateful. I'm after somebody who murdered women. And right now you are obstructing the investigation. Well?'

She sighed and went off, returning after a couple of minutes with a bottle and a glass.

'There's a good girl,' said Van Veeteren.

She yawned.

'Do you think you can manage to pour it out yourself?'

'I'll do my best,' Van Veeteren promised. 'I'll ring if I spill anything.'

The cold beer trickling down his throat was most invigorating. He had lain in bed thinking about this moment, trying to imagine the taste and indeed the whole experience, while reading through the last four or five newspaper cuttings, and now that it had come, there was no doubt that the actual enjoyment lived up to expectations.

He belched contentedly. Divine nectar, he thought. Let's see now, what do I know?

Not a lot. A fair amount from the quantative point of view. The newspaper coverage of the first trial had been comprehensive, to say the least. He had only read a small portion, but Münster's selection seemed to have been well chosen and representative: a wide range of speculation and guesses regarding Verhaven's character coupled with fairly detailed accounts of court proceedings. And the longer it went on, the more specific the conclusions drawn about the impending verdict.

Guilty. Verhaven must be guilty.

There were not many facts available. Just as he had suspected, the technical proof was rudimentary. Non-existent, to put it bluntly. The case ought to have depended mainly on circumstantial evidence, but there wasn't much of that either. Strictly speaking, there was a gaping void in both those areas.

No concrete proof.

Not much in the way of circumstantial evidence pointing towards Verhaven.

Nothing.

But he had been found guilty even so.

After discreet legal proceedings behind the scenes, no doubt, Van Veeteren thought, raising the bottle to his lips. I'd give a lot to have taken part in those.

But what the hell was it that got him convicted? Obviously, the media and vociferous public opinion had created a certain amount of pressure, but surely the machinery didn't usually succumb so readily to that?

No, there must have been some other reason.

His character.

The kind of man that Leopold Verhaven was. His past. His behaviour in court. The overall impression he had made on the jury and the legal bigwigs. That's what it was all about.

That's what got him convicted.

Verhaven was an eccentric. Having scrutinized him through the eyes and magnifying glasses of all these journalists, Van Veeteren could hardly come to any other conclusion. He was very much a loner, a man from whom it was the easiest thing in the world to disassociate oneself.

An odd man out.

A murderer? It was not difficult to take the short step from the former judgment to the latter, that was something Van Veeteren had learned over many long years; and once you had taken that step, it was not easy to retract it.

And the role?

Was that the key? The strange circumstance that practically every journalist had homed in on. The fact that Verhaven didn't seem uncomfortable with the role of accused. On the contrary. He seemed to enjoy sitting in the dock with all that attention focused on him. Not that he had strutted or swaggered, but nevertheless: there was something about the way he conducted himself, a solitary and forceful actor playing the role of the tragic hero. That was how he was perceived, and that was how he had wanted to be perceived.

Something of that sort, in any case.

Was that the reason he was convicted?

If only I'd been there and seen him, I would have had no doubt, Van Veeteren thought as he emptied the bottle.

*

What actually happened was apparently simple and beyond argument.

Verhaven had returned home that Saturday, at about five o'clock, according to what he and others said. Beatrice had gone off somewhere, and that's all there was to it. But that was his version. Nobody else had set eyes on either of them later that day. The electrician, Moltke, had left Beatrice at about one o'clock in the afternoon, and Verhaven had been seen in the village the next day, shortly after six on Sunday evening. That was all. The period between those two sightings was a blank.

He would have had plenty of time. For all sorts of things. One of the medical examiners had been in no doubt that Beatrice had confronted her killer at some point on Saturday or Sunday. She had been strangled and raped. Or the other way around, presumably? Raped and strangled. She was naked; intercourse had taken place, but there was no trace of sperm.

But, thought Van Veeteren, if the killer had been somebody else, that meant it was definite that the murder had taken place on Saturday afternoon – between one o'clock and five o'clock, or thereabouts. Between the moment Moltke had set off for home and Verhaven's return.

Or at least that she had been abducted during that time.

Irrefutable?

Certainly, he decided. He glared mournfully at the

empty bottle, then turned to the transcript from the court proceedings. Day two of the trial. The prosecutor, Hagendeck, cross-questioned the accused, Leopold Verhaven.

May twenty-fourth. Half past ten in the morning.

H: You have pleaded not guilty to killing your fiancée, Beatrice Holden. Is that correct?
V: Yes.
H: Can you tell us a little about your relationship?
V: What do you want to know?
H: How you met, for instance.
V: We bumped into each other in Linzhuisen. We were at school together. She came home with me.
H: That first time? You started a relationship right away?
V: We knew each other previously. She needed a man.
H: When did she move in with you?
V: A week later.
H: So that would be . . .
V: November 1960.
H: And she has been living with you ever since?
V: Yes, of course.
H: All the time?
V: She visited her mother and her daughter

occasionally. Stopped over in Elming for the odd night. But more or less all the time, yes.

H: Were you engaged?

V: No.

H: You didn't intend to get married?

V: No.

H: Why not?

V: That wasn't why we lived together.

H: Why did you live together, then?

[*Verhaven's reply erased*]

H: I see. Did you fall out at all?

V: Sometimes.

H: Did you fight?

V: Now and again, I suppose.

H: Did you beat her at all?

V: Yes. She liked it.

H: She liked you beating her?

V: Yes.

H: How do you know? Did she say so?

V: No, but I know she liked it.

H: How can you know that if she never said anything?

V: You can tell. They show it.

H: What do you mean by 'they'?

V: Women.

H: Did she hit you as well?

V: She tried, but I was stronger than she was.
H: Did you drink a lot of hard liquor together?
V: No, not all that much.
H: But it did happen?
V: Yes. We used to have a few drinks on a Saturday, seeing as I had Sunday off.
H: Off? Didn't you have to look after the hens?
V: Yes, of course; but I didn't have to go to market.
H: I see. Can you tell us what happened on Saturday, March thirtieth? The week before Beatrice disappeared, that is.
V: We drank a bit. Fell out. I hit her.
H: Why?
V: She annoyed me. I think she wanted a bit of a beating.
H: How did she annoy you?
V: She was being difficult.
H: You beat her so badly that she had to take refuge with a neighbour. It was three in the morning. She had no clothes on. What do you say to that?
V: She was drunk.
H: But that doesn't mean she wanted a bit of a beating, does it?
[*No reply from Verhaven*]
H: Don't you think that was overstepping the mark,

beating your fiancée so violently that she had to flee to a neighbour for safety?
V: She didn't need to go. She was drunk and hysterical. She came back again later, after all.
H: What about the following week? Did you beat her several times?
V: No, not that I recall.
H: Not that you recall?
V: No.
H: Why should you forget something like that?
V: I've no idea.
H: What did you do when you got back home on Saturday, April sixth?
V: Made a meal and ate it.
H: Nothing else?
V: Saw to the hens.
H: Where was Beatrice when you got home?
V: I don't know.
H: What do you mean by that?
V: That I don't know.
H: Shouldn't she have been at home?
V: Maybe.
H: Had you arranged anything?
V: No.
H: She hadn't planned to go anywhere?
V: No.

H: To visit her mother and daughter, for instance?
V: No.
H: Were you surprised that she wasn't at home when you returned?
V: Not especially.
H: Why?
V: Nothing much surprises me.
H: Tell us what you did the rest of the day.
V: Nothing much.
H: What, exactly?
V: I sat around at home. Watched television. Went to bed.
H: And you still didn't wonder where your fiancée was?
V: No.
H: Why didn't you wonder?
V: They come and go.
H: What do you mean?
V: Women. They come and go.
H: Tell us what you did on Sunday.
V: I was at home. I didn't do anything much. Saw to the hens.
H: And where did you think Beatrice was?
V: I don't know.
H: It wasn't that you knew where she was?
V: No.

H: It wasn't that you knew she was lying dead in the forest, murdered? Nearly a mile into the forest?

V: No.

H: So you didn't kill her, which would explain why you didn't wonder where she was?

V: No, that's not how it was. It wasn't me who killed her.

H: But you didn't miss her on Sunday?

V: No.

H: You didn't check to see if she'd gone to her mother's, for instance?

V: No.

H: Do you have a telephone, Mr Verhaven?

V: No.

H: So you weren't the least bit worried about Beatrice?

V: No.

H: And what about the following week? Didn't you miss her then, either?

V: No.

H: You never wondered where she might have gone to?

V: No.

H: Did you think it was a relief, not to have her around?

[*No reply from Verhaven*]

H: I repeat: Did you think it was a relief not to have her around?
V: At first, perhaps.
H: Did your fiancée have a job at that time?
V: Not just then.
H: Where did she work when she was employed?
V: At Kaunitz's. The garden centre in Linzhuisen. But only occasionally.
H: When did you tell the police that your fiancée, Beatrice Holden, was missing?
V: On Tuesday, the sixteenth.
H: Where?
V: In Maardam, of course.
H: And what made you report her missing on that particular day? If you weren't worried?
V: It just occurred to me. As I was driving past the police station.
H: So you still didn't think something might have happened to her?
V: No. Why should I?
H: Don't you think it would be natural to think that?
V: No. She usually got by.
H: But she didn't on this occasion.
V: No, not on this occasion.
H: How did you hear that she'd been found dead?
V: The police came and told me.

H: How did you react to that?
V: I was sorry.
H: Sorry? Sergeant Weiss maintains that you didn't react at all. That you simply thanked him and asked him to go away.
V: Why should I cry on his shoulder? I can get by.
H: Don't you think you've been acting rather strangely since Beatrice Holden disappeared?
V: No, I don't think so.
H: Do you understand that other people might think so?
V: I don't know what other people think. They can think whatever they like as far as I'm concerned.
H: Really? And you are absolutely certain that it wasn't you who killed your fiancée?
V: It wasn't me.
H: Did you often go to the part of the forest where her body was found?
V: No.
H: Have you ever been there?
V: I might have been.
H: But not that weekend when she disappeared?
V: No.
H: What do you think about her death, Mr Verhaven?
V: Nothing.
H: You must have some idea about how she died?

V: Some man or other, of course. Some sick type who can't find himself a woman.
H: You don't regard yourself as somebody like that?
V: I have no difficulty in finding myself women.
H: Thank you. No further questions at present.

Van Veeteren stuffed the bundle of papers into the narrow space under the top of his bedside table. It was very nearly one o'clock.

I'd better get some sleep, he thought.

Verhaven?

If only he'd been present at the trials! At the very least he could have spent an hour or two in court in connection with the Marlene case, when he'd played a minor role in the investigation. It might have been enough, actually seeing him in the flesh.

A few minutes watching him in the dock and he'd have known. Known if the nagging worry at the back of his mind was something to follow up. If there was any justification for it at all, or if Verhaven really was the primitive man of violence he'd been portrayed as being.

Guilty or not guilty, then?

It was impossible to say. Impossible then, impossible now.

But no matter what, there was no getting away from

one fact: somebody had been lying in wait for him when he was released from prison.

Somebody had killed him and butchered his body. Somebody had tried to ensure that they wouldn't be able to identify him. That must surely have been the intention?

And finally: somebody must have had a reason.

What?

That was another question that still remained. Untouched and unanswered.

He switched off the light. Closed his eyes, and before he knew it, he had started dreaming about Jess and the twins. In French.

It was astonishing what his mind was capable of in the early hours of the morning . . .

Mind you, their visit to the ward the previous afternoon had hardly passed unnoticed.

A cracked windowpane, a split cuticle, a demolished infusion stand and other minor calamities. He had noticed that the smiles on the faces of the staff had become somewhat strained as time went by. As the noise level increased and accidents became more frequent.

How the hell does she manage? he wondered, allowing himself a faint smile as he slept. She must have inherited some of her father's mental strength, presumably.

Sans doute, oui.

22

'Gossec's Requiem?' said the young man with dark curly hair, pushing his glasses up onto his forehead. 'Did you say Gossec's Requiem?'

'Yes,' said Münster. 'Is there such a thing?'

'Oh yes, there certainly is.' He nodded assiduously and leafed through a folder. 'It's just that we don't have it. There is a recording with the French Radio Choir from 1959, I think; but there's nothing on CD. Your best bet would be to ask at Laudener's.'

'Laudener's?'

'Yes, at Karlsplatsen. If they don't have it we could always try to get it second-hand. The label is Vertique.'

'Thank you very much,' said Münster, and left the store.

He glanced at his watch and saw that he wouldn't have time to go to Karlsplatsen. He was due to meet Judge Heidelbluum at six o'clock, and he had the feeling the old gentleman would not be best pleased if he arrived late.

I wish the chief inspector could stick with Bach or Mozart, he thought as he got into his car. Why the hell does he want to lie in a hospital bed listening to this particular requiem?

He parked in Guyderstraat, in the Wooshejm suburb, a considerable distance away from Heidelbluum's house. No doubt the old gentleman wouldn't be best pleased if he arrived too soon, either. He decided to take the opportunity of having a stroll around this exclusive district, where he didn't normally set foot.

There never seemed to be a reason to do so. Insofar as there was any crime at all in Wooshejm, it was the more sophisticated, financial kind, not the sort of thing an ordinary, simple detective inspector would get involved in.

The houses skirted the western edge of the municipal forest; a lot of the sizeable plots backed directly up to the trees, so the owners could enjoy a very pleasant combination of town and countryside. There were about sixty or seventy houses in all, built at the beginning of this century or the end of the last; nowadays you could be sure that three or four times as many villas would be built in the same area. Münster knew that the wealth and fortunes concealed behind these flowering hedges and copper-topped walls accounted for most of the town's tax income. This was where the cream lived, you could say. Retired surgeons and professors, elderly generals and district judges, the occasional former government minister and industrial magnate of the old school. Newly arrived aristocratic families, perhaps, who had tired of the family seat and life in the country. There was no doubt that the average age of the gentlefolk living in this neighbourhood was much closer to a hundred than fifty. And Heidelbluum was far from being a youngster, even in this exalted company.

A dying race, thought Münster as he sauntered slowly along the quiet street, the air laden with the scent of jasmine; and when he heard the cries of children and the splashing of water behind one of the hedges, he knew that those responsible were great-grandchildren rather than grandchildren.

Ah well, some of it will be handed on to the next generation, it seemed reasonable to assume.

He came to the Heidelbluum residence and rang the bell by the gate in the high wall. After a while he heard footsteps on the gravel path on the other side and a maid appeared, wearing a black skirt and blouse, an apron and a white hat.

'Yes?'

'Detective Inspector Münster. I have an appointment with the judge.'

'Please come this way,' she said, opening the gate a little wider.

She was buxom, with pretty red hair. She couldn't be more than nineteen or twenty, Münster thought.

What strange worlds there were in existence.

Judge Heidelbluum received visitors in his library, but the French doors were open, leading out to a newly mown lawn and fruit trees in blossom. The contrast between inside and outside was so marked, it almost seemed to be a parody of the situation, Münster thought. Outside, it was early summer, new life stirring and sprouting, fresh scents and birdsong; inside, it was predominantly dark oak, leather, damask and old books. And a rather pungent smell from the blackish-green cigarillos that Heidelbluum insisted on smoking one puff at a time, before depositing them in an ashtray of oxblood-coloured porphyry on the desk in front of him.

A bit reminiscent of the thin cigars Van Veeteren occasionally felt like smoking, Münster noted. Both in looks and smell.

He was ushered into a leather armchair in classical Anglo-Saxon style; it had obviously been placed in front of the desk specifically for this occasion, and as Münster settled down into it, he noticed that the old judge's bald and bird-like head was swaying back and forth a couple of feet higher than his own.

That was no coincidence, of course.

'Thank you for agreeing to see me and to let me ask you some questions,' he began.

Heidelbluum nodded. In fact he had been negative about the request until Hiller and Van Veeteren intervened and persuaded him to see reason.

He's not quite all there, Van Veeteren had warned Münster. Not all the time, at least. Handle him carefully.

'As things stand,' Münster continued, 'we would be most grateful if you would kindly give us the benefit of your views. There doesn't seem to be anybody who knows more about the case of Leopold Verhaven than you.'

'Quite right,' said Heidelbluum, lighting the cigarillo.

'You know that we found him murdered, I take it?'

'The chief of police mentioned that.'

'To tell you the truth, we're groping around in the dark as far as a motive is concerned,' said Münster. 'One theory we are working on is that it must be connected in some way with the Beatrice and Marlene cases.'

'In what way?' asked Heidelbluum. His tone was sharper now.

'We don't know,' said Münster.

There was a pause. Heidelbluum drew on the cigarillo, then put it down. Münster drank a little soda water from the glass he had been given. Van Veeteren had advised him to allow the old judge plenty of time; not to put him under pressure, but give him lots of time to think and reflect. There's no point in cross-questioning an eighty-two-year-old, he had maintained.

'It was my last case,' said Heidelbluum, clearing his throat. 'The Marlene trial, that is. Hmm. My very last.'

Was there a trace of regret in his voice, or was Münster only imagining it?

'So I understand.'

'Hmm,' said Heidelbluum again.

'It would be interesting to hear what you thought of him.'

Heidelbluum ran his index and middle fingers along the inside of his shirt collar, and slightly loosened the dark blue cravat he was wearing around his neck.

'I'm an old man,' he said. 'I might last for another summer, perhaps. A couple more at most.'

He paused for a moment, as if feeling for the thread. Münster eyed the rows of dark, leather-bound books behind the judge's back. I wonder how many of them he's read, he wondered, and how many he can remember.

'I'm not bothered about it any more.'

'What are you not bothered about?'

'Leopold Verhaven. You're too young to understand. He has worried me quite a lot . . . Both those damned affairs. I wish I'd been able to get out of that second trial, but there again, it wouldn't have been fair to pass it on to some other poor soul . . .'

'What do you mean?'

'I thought it would give me an opportunity to be sure about it all. Draw a line under all the doubt raised by the first tribunal.'

'Tribunal?'

'Call it whatever you like. It was a devil of a business, no matter how you look at it. Don't quote me on that.'

'I'm not a journalist,' said Münster.

'No, of course not,' said Heidelbluum, picking up the cigarillo again.

'Am I right in thinking that you believe Verhaven was innocent?'

Heidelbluum shook his head.

'Oh no. Good Lord, no. I've never found anybody guilty when I didn't think they were guilty. Good heavens no! But he was . . . a mystery. Yes, a mystery. You and your colleagues won't be able to make sense of it; you needed to be there and see the man. Everything about him was a mystery. I was on the bench for over thirty years, and I've seen it all, but I've never come across anything like Leopold Verhaven. Nothing.'

He lit the cigarillo and took a drag.

'Could you elaborate on that a little?'

'Hmm. Well, no, you don't understand this. The most remarkable thing about it is that he was found to be sane enough to plead. It would have explained a lot if they'd found some kind of derangement or mental disorder, but there was never any question of that.'

'What was so remarkable about him, then?' Münster asked.

Heidelbluum thought for a while.

'There were lots of things. He didn't care about the verdict, for instance. I've thought a lot about that, and my lasting impression is that Leopold Verhaven was totally indifferent about being found guilty or not. Totally indifferent.'

'That sounds odd,' said Münster.

'You bet it's odd, damned odd. That's what I'm saying.'

'I have the impression that he enjoyed being accused,' said Münster.

'No doubt about it,' said Heidelbluum. 'He was very happy to sit there like the spider at the centre of a legal web, playing what everybody thought was the leading role. He didn't make it obvious, of course, but I could see it in him. He longed to be in the centre of things, and now he'd got what he wanted.'

'Did he enjoy it so much that he was prepared to crawl into prison for twelve years? Twice, in fact?'

Heidelbluum sighed.

'Hmm,' he said. 'That's precisely the point at the centre of it all.'

Münster sat for some time without speaking, listening to the water sprinkler being used somewhere in the garden.

'When he heard the verdict, I'll be damned if he didn't give a little smile. Both times. What do you say to that?'

'What about the submission of evidence and the court findings, that kind of thing?' Münster asked cautiously.

'Weak,' said Heidelbluum. 'But sufficient, as I said. I've found prisoners guilty on weaker grounds.'

'And sentenced them to twelve years?'

Heidelbluum made no reply.

'Was it the same in both trials?' Münster asked.

Heidelbluum shrugged.

'In a way,' he said. 'Both were based on circumstantial evidence. Strong prosecuting counsels, Hagendeck and Kiesling. The defending counsels did their duty, but not much more. The Marlene case had a bit more meat to it, as it were. Lots of witnesses, meetings, precise timings – even reconstructions. A real puzzle, in fact. The first time, there was hardly anything to go on.'

'But still he was found guilty. Isn't that a bit strange?'

asked Münster, wondering as he spoke if he was going too far.

But Heidelbluum seemed not to have noticed the insinuation. He was bent over his desk, gazing out into the garden, and seemed to be lost in thought. Half a minute passed.

'Two of them wanted to let him go,' he said suddenly.

'Excuse me?'

'Mrs Paneva and that factory owner wanted to set him free. Two out of a jury of five wanted a not-guilty verdict, but we talked them round.'

'Really?' said Münster. 'Which of the trials was this?'

But Heidelbluum ignored the question.

'You have to accept the responsibility,' he said, scratching nervously at his temple and cheek. 'That's what some people find hard to understand.'

'But nobody abstained?' Münster asked.

'I have never accepted abstentions in any of my cases,' said Heidelbluum. 'The verdict must be unanimous. Especially when it's first degree.'

Münster nodded. A reasonable stand to take, he thought. What would it look like if somebody was condemned to ten or twelve years in jail by a majority verdict of three to two? Hardly likely to uphold people's respect for the law and justice.

'Were there any other suspects at all?' Münster wondered.

'No,' said Heidelbluum. 'That would have changed everything, if there had been.'

'How?' Münster asked.

But Heidelbluum didn't seem to have heard the question.

Either that or he's just ignoring anything he doesn't want to hear, thought Münster. He decided to put a bit more pressure on the judge. Presumably it was best to strike before the iron cooled down completely. It wouldn't be possible to go on questioning him for much longer, in any case.

'But in spite of everything,' he said, 'you don't think it is impossible that Verhaven was in fact innocent?'

Silence again. Then Heidelbluum sighed deeply, and when he responded, Münster had the impression that it had been formulated in advance – possibly a long time in advance, long before there had been any mention of a visit by the police. A statement, a final, well-thought-out judgement in the case of Leopold Verhaven.

'I thought he was a murderer,' he said. 'When there are no clear indications, you have to make up your mind. That goes with the job. I still think Verhaven was guilty. Of both murders. But to say I was certain would be to tell a lie. Such a long time has gone by, and I'm so close to death that I dare to tell it as it is. I don't know. I don't know if it really was Leopold Verhaven who killed Beatrice Holden and Marlene Nietsch. But I think it was him.'

He paused and took the cigarillo butt from the porphyry ashtray. Looked up and gazed out of the open French doors again.

'And I hope it was him. Because if it wasn't, he's been an innocent man in jail for a quarter of a century. And a double murderer has gone free.'

The last words were laden with exhaustion, but even so, Münster dared to ask one more question.

'You are assuming that no matter what else, both murders were committed by the same person?'

'Yes,' said Heidelbluum. 'I'm quite certain of that.'

'In that case,' said Münster, 'I would suggest that we are in fact dealing with a triple murderer, not just a double one.'

But Heidelbluum no longer appeared to be interested, and Münster realized that it was time to leave him in peace.

When the children were in bed at last, and Münster and his wife were drinking tea in the kitchen, he took out two photographs of Verhaven – one taken at some athletics meeting before the drugs scandal, the other taken a few years later, the afternoon at the end of April 1962 when he was arrested by two plainclothes police officers.

In both pictures the sun was shining into Verhaven's face from the side, and in both he looked guileless, squinting straight at the camera. And there was a slight trace of a smile on his lips. An air of mischievous seriousness.

'What's your impression of this man?' he asked his wife. 'You're usually good at reading faces.'

Synn put the two pictures side by side on the table and pondered them for a moment.

'Who is it?' she asked. 'He seems familiar, somehow. He's an actor, isn't he?'

'Well, I don't know about that,' said Münster. 'But there again, yes, I think you're right. Maybe that's exactly what he was – an actor.'

FIVE

24 AUGUST 1993

23

It took some time to get the stove going, but once he'd shifted a few large chunks of soot from the flue, it took hold. Some smoke belched into the room to start with, but it soon cleared. He tried the taps, but no water appeared: he had to fetch some buckets from the spring in the woods instead. He put a large cauldron on the burner, and a smaller pot next to it, for the coffee. The refrigerator merely needed switching on. The electricity was on, as he had requested. She had taken care of that.

When the water was sufficiently hot, he filled a bowl, carried it out to the rickety table at the gable end and had a good wash. The sun hadn't yet sunk below the trees, and it made him feel pleasantly warm as he stood there in nothing but his underpants. Late-summer bumblebees buzzed around in the mignonette standing three feet tall against the house wall; there was a smell of ripe apples, which had already started falling, and he had the feeling that everything was beginning again.

Life. The world.

Once he'd done what he had to do, he would be able to start living up here again; he'd had his doubts, but this afternoon and evening filled with gentle movement and a spirit of welcome could hardly be mere coincidence.

It was a sign. One of those signs.

He poured the last of the water over his head. Didn't bother about his underpants getting wet, took them off and went back into the house naked.

He put on a completely new set of clothes. The stuff he'd left in his study and in the wardrobe were pristine; maybe they smelled a little bit odd – a trace of jute or horsehair, perhaps – but what the hell? They'd been untouched for twelve years, after all.

Just like him. The same period of waiting, of being shut in.

He made his evening meal at about seven. Sausage and egg, bread, onion and beer. He ate it on the steps outside the front door, with the plate on his knee and the bottle on the rail, just like he always did. He washed up, lit a fire in the living room and tried to make the television work. There was a loud buzzing noise to accompany silent pictures from some foreign channel. He switched it off and tried the radio instead. That was better. He sat in the basket chair in front of the fire and listened to the eight o'clock news while drinking another beer and smoking a cigarette. He found it difficult to grasp that so much time had passed since he last sat here; it felt like just a few weeks, a couple of months at most, but he knew of course that this was how life stuttered along. No regular progression, nothing continuous. Ups and downs, to-ing and fro-ing. But all the same, the passage of time was inscribed in one's body: in the weariness one felt, all those increasingly sluggish movements.

And the anger in the soul. The flame refusing to die down. He understood that he needed to do what he had to do as quickly as possible. Within the next few days, preferably. He knew what he needed to know, after all. There was no reason to put it off any longer.

He waited until there was only the faintest of glows from the fire. Darkness had set in. It was time for bed, but he needed to pay a visit to the henhouse before going to sleep, just to see what it looked like. He had no intention of starting it all up again, certainly not, but he wouldn't be able to sleep a wink if he didn't take a quick look at least.

He took the lantern and went outside. He shivered a little when the cold evening air crept up on him, wondered whether to fetch a pullover, but couldn't be bothered. It was only forty yards at most and he'd soon be back by the warm fire again.

He was only halfway there when it struck him that he wasn't alone in the darkness.

SIX

11–15 MAY 1994

24

'What's this thing for?' asked deBries, pointing at the tape recorder.

'It's the chief inspector,' sighed Münster.

'What do you mean?'

'Well, he claims he's leading the investigation and he doesn't want to miss a word of this run-through. I tried to stop him, but you know what he's like . . .'

'How is he?' asked Moreno.

'He's on the mend, much better,' said Münster. 'But he'll have to stay in hospital for another three or four days at least. According to the doctors, that is. I expect the nurses on the ward would throw him out today if it was up to them.'

'Oh dear,' said Rooth, scratching at his beard. 'He ought to keep his thoughts to himself, is that it?'

'Probably,' said Münster, switching on the tape recorder. 'General update, Wednesday, May eleventh. Present: Münster, Rooth, deBries, Jung and Moreno . . .'

There was a knock and Reinhart stuck his head round the door.

'Is there room for one more?'

'. . . and Reinhart,' said Münster.

'What are you doing here?' asked Rooth. 'Have all the racists gone away?'

Reinhart shook his head.

'I'm afraid not,' he said. 'It's just that I'm a bit interested in Leopold Verhaven. I've read a bit about him. So if you don't mind . . . ?'

'No problem,' said deBries. 'Sit next to the chief inspector.'

'The chief inspector?' wondered Reinhart.

'That's him, whirring round and round.'

'I see,' said Reinhart, sitting down. 'Absent but with us all the same.'

'Let's start with the identification,' said Münster. 'I'll leave that to Rooth.'

Rooth cleared his throat.

'OK,' he said. 'It's all centred on the testicle business. Verhaven had an accident when he was about ten. He cycled into a stone wall and got the handlebar between his legs.'

'Ouch,' said deBries.

'One testicle was injured and eventually had to be removed. Meusse established that the body we found in the carpet was missing a testicle, and that fact together with all the other circumstances means that we can be pretty sure it's him. Verhaven, that is.'

'A circumstantial identification?' said Reinhart.

'You could call it that, yes,' said Rooth, 'if you can get your tongue round it. His sister couldn't say for sure if it was him – probably nobody could. But everything fits. All known factors point to him – being released from jail, witnesses in the village, traces in the house, the fact that nobody's seen him since then. But, of course, there is a slight possibility that it could be somebody else. The question is who, and where Verhaven has disappeared to, in that case.'

There was silence for a few seconds.

'If Verhaven isn't the victim,' said Jung, 'presumably he must be the one who did it.'

Münster nodded.

'That has to be right,' he said. 'But what are the odds of him finding some other poor bastard with only one testicle and then bumping him off? And why? No, I think we can forget that possibility. It's Leopold Verhaven who's dead, let's agree on that. So somebody murdered him, on August twenty-fourth last year, the day he got back home after twelve years in prison. Or shortly after, in any case.'

'Were there any signs of violence in the house?' asked Reinhart.

'No,' said Rooth. 'Nothing at all. We know nothing about how it was done, either. He could have been killed there, then taken somewhere else. The clothes he wore to come home in are still in the house. He could have changed, of course, but it looks as if he'd gone to bed.'

'The murderer could have arrived during the night carrying a blunt instrument,' said Münster. 'That's pretty plausible.'

'Mind you, the neighbours on the other side of the woods didn't see anything,' said Rooth. 'There again, even Mrs Wilkerson must presumably be off guard occasionally.'

'Unless she and her husband take it in turns at the kitchen window,' said Münster. 'That's also plausible.'

'Motive,' said Münster, when everybody had served themselves from the coffee trolley. 'That's the big question mark, needless to say. As far as the technical evidence is concerned, we don't even know what questions to ask. It might help if we found a few more body parts, but as things stand we have no alternative to a spot of speculation. So what do you think? Rooth?'

Rooth quickly swallowed half a KitKat.

'I think we have to assume that somebody was waiting

for him to be released,' he said. 'Somebody who was in a hurry as well, and had a pretty good reason for doing it pretty damn quick.'

'Hmm,' said Reinhart. 'What kind of reason might that be?'

'I don't know,' said Rooth. 'But let me develop this a bit further. There are two things that suggest it's like I said. One is the obvious fact that Verhaven was murdered so quickly. The same day that he got home, presumably. The other is that somebody phoned the prison in Ulmentahl last winter and asked when he was going to be let out. Rang again in July to check. The sleepwalkers running the jail only unearthed those facts yesterday. When I went to talk to them some time ago, they didn't even mention it.'

'The same person?' asked Reinhart.

'They're not sure, and we can't really expect them to be. Still, it was a man both times. He claimed to be a journalist.'

Nobody spoke for a few seconds.

'And why should this man want to get Verhaven out of the way?' asked Moreno.

'Hmm,' said Rooth. 'I've no idea. The most spectacular reason would be that it was something to do with the Beatrice and Marlene cases in some way. But that needn't be the reason, of course.'

'Crap,' said Reinhart.

'What do you mean, crap?' asked Rooth indignantly, scratching at his beard.

'It's plain as a pikestaff that it's to do with the other business,' said Reinhart. 'The only question is, how?'

Münster looked at the officers assembled around the oval table. There was no doubt it would make a difference if Reinhart decided to join the investigation.

DeBries lit a cigarette.

'Can't we press on a bit faster?' he said. 'I mean, there are only two alternatives, as far as I can see. I thought we all agreed on that.'

'OK,' said Rooth. 'Forgive my scientific scruples. Whoever killed Leopold Verhaven must have done it either because he couldn't stand the man, hated him, wanted to punish him even more. Somebody who thought that twenty-four years wasn't long enough. The final solution, as it were . . . Or somebody who had something to hide.'

'What?' asked Reinhart.

'Something that Verhaven knew about,' said Rooth, 'and intended to do something about the moment he was released from prison. Or, at least, the murderer thought he was intending to do something about it.'

'What?' asked Reinhart again.

Rooth shrugged.

'We don't know,' he said. 'But in any case, it must have been pretty vital for the murderer that it didn't come out.'

'If we assume that it was connected with the two earlier cases, there's really only one possibility,' said Münster.

'You mean . . . ?' said Reinhart.

'Yes,' said Rooth. 'We do. If all we've said is in fact true, it could well mean that Verhaven was not guilty of the murders he was sentenced and punished for. And that somehow he managed to find out who really did it. That's what we mean. But it's a damn fine thread, of course.'

Nobody spoke. The only sounds to be heard were the whirring of the tape recorder and the crackling in Reinhart's pipe.

'How?' said Münster after half a minute. 'How could Verhaven have found out who really did it?'

There was a strong feeling of reluctance, in himself and the others, to accept this reasoning. And thank God for that. Even if none of them had been directly involved and responsible, the twenty-four years Verhaven spent in prison were largely the fruit of work done by their predecessors and other older police officers. It was only natural.

Collective guilt? An inherited feeling of failure? Was it something like that making itself clearly felt in the smoke-filled conference room? In any case, Münster could sense the ingredients of resistance in the silence that had once again descended over them.

'Well,' said Rooth in the end, 'we have that woman.'

'What woman?' asked Reinhart.

'He was visited by a woman. An old woman who walked with sticks, it seems. It was a year or so before he came out, roughly speaking. They remember her because it was the only visitor he ever met with in all the time he was inside.'

'Twelve years,' said deBries.

'Who was it?' asked Moreno.

'We don't know,' said Rooth. 'We haven't managed to find her. But she rang the jail, in any case, and made an appointment a few weeks in advance. In May 1992. She said her name was Anna Schmidt, but that seems to have been made up. We've spoken to a dozen Anna Schmidts, and it seems pretty pointless, to tell you the truth.'

Münster nodded.

'That's right,' he said. 'But Verhaven seems to be the type who can sit brooding about what he knows for as long as you like. It's not surprising in the least that he didn't say anything to the prison governor or the police. He seems to have hardly spoken to anybody at all while he was inside.'

'Correct,' said Rooth. 'An odd bastard, but we knew that already.'

'Relatives and friends?' said Münster. 'The victims', that is.'

Jung opened his notebook.

'There's not much of interest, I'm afraid,' he began. 'Stauff and I have tracked down most of them. As far as Beatrice Holden is concerned, there's really only the daughter left. Apart from the shopkeeper, of course, but they are only half cousins anyway, or something like that, and they were barely in touch with each other. The daughter's thirty-five now, with a husband and four children of her own. They don't seem to have a clue who their grandmother was. I don't think there's any good reason for telling them, either.'

'What about the other one?' said Münster. 'Marlene Nietsch?'

'She has a brother and an ex who don't seem to have much time for Verhaven. Dodgy types, both of them. Carlo Nietsch has been inside several times – receiving and a few burglaries. Martin Kuntze, her ex-fiancé, spends half his life as an alcoholic, and the other half in early retirement.'

Reinhart grunted.

'I know who he is,' he said. 'I tried to use him as an informant in a drug case a few years ago. I can't say I got very far.'

'They live here in Maardam anyway,' said Jung, 'but I very much doubt if they've got anything to do with this. Marlene Nietsch had lots of affairs, but it was only Kuntze and one other guy that she actually lived with. The other one is called Pedlecki. He lives in Linzhuisen and doesn't seem to care much about her. He wasn't too worried when she was murdered, and the same applies now.'

He turned over a few pages.

'That seems to apply to most of the others we spoke to as well, come to that,' he added. 'Marlene Nietsch had her weaknesses, obviously.'

'No other relatives?' asked Reinhart.

'Yes,' said Jung. 'A sister in Odessa, of all places.'

Münster sighed.

'Does anybody fancy a dip in the Black Sea?' he asked. 'Shall we have a break now and stretch our legs a bit? I need to change cassettes, in any case.'

'Only a short one, if you don't mind,' said Reinhart. 'I have to see Hiller and get some authorizations from him before he goes home.'

'Five minutes,' said Münster.

25

'This village, then?' said Münster. 'What do you think about it?'

'Introverted,' said deBries. 'Constable Moreno and I have spent two whole days there now, and we both agree that it's your archetypal rural backwater.'

'I was born in a place very similar to it,' said Moreno. 'Bossenwühle, just outside Rheinau. I have to say that I recognize the atmosphere. Everybody knows everybody else. Everybody knows what everybody else is up to. No integrity. You are who you are; it's best to be on your guard and lie low, never step out of line, as it were. It's hard to put your finger on it, but no doubt you recognize the syndrome?'

'Of course,' said Münster. 'I was also born out in the sticks. It's OK while you're a kid, but when you're grown up, the social network sometimes feels like barbed wire. Are you saying there's nothing extra as far as Kaustin's concerned? Something that would distinguish it from other similar places in some way?'

Moreno hesitated.

'Hmm,' she said, biting her lower lip. 'I don't know. The shadow of Verhaven is lurking over them all, but that's scarcely surprising. I gather a delegation of locals actually wanted to change the place's name after the second murder.'

'Change its name?' said Rooth.

'Yes. They wanted to get rid of the name Kaustin. Presumably they thought everybody associated it with Verhaven and the trials. They felt they were living in a village known only for the murders. There was a petition you could sign in the village shop, but it all petered out in the end.'

'I suppose you can understand them,' said Münster. 'Anyway, can you be a bit more specific? What have you managed to find out?'

'Well,' said deBries, 'we've spoken to about twenty people, most of them old, who've lived there all their lives and remembered both cases very clearly. There's not much in the way of movement in and out of the village, and the population is only some six hundred inhabitants in all. The setting is very pretty, no arguing with that. A lake and some woodland and some open countryside, that kind of thing.'

'Many people were unwilling to talk about Verhaven,'

said Moreno. 'They seemed to want to forget all about it, as if it were something shameful for everybody who lives there. Maybe it is, in a way.'

'Isn't there more than that?' interrupted Reinhart.

'Meaning what?' said deBries.

Reinhart was poking around with a match in the bowl of his pipe.

'Did you get the feeling that they were . . . hiding something, so to speak? Damn it all, surely I don't need to spell it out? It's a matter of mood, pure and simple, that's all. A woman ought to notice it anyway.'

'Thank you,' said deBries.

For God's sake, don't start fighting now, Münster thought. I don't want to have to spend ages editing the tape.

'Maybe,' said Moreno after a little pause. 'But it's only a very faint suspicion at most. Perhaps they all have a skeleton or two in their cupboard – metaphorically speaking, naturally – and they're a bit scared of one another. That's another aspect of the syndrome, isn't it? No, I don't know.'

Münster sighed.

'But you must have put them under a little bit of pressure, surely?'

'Obviously,' said deBries. 'The butcher's a bit of a shady type, for instance. He has at least two mistresses in the village. Or has had, rather. Perhaps he had it off with

Beatrice Holden now and again, before she made a pitch at Verhaven, but that's not certain. She was a bit of a dolly, it seems. Not too difficult to persuade.'

'Her relationship with Verhaven was a stormy one, if I'm not much mistaken?' said Reinhart.

'You can say that again,' said Moreno. 'A bit of a cat-and-dog relationship, apparently. Sparks would fly now and then. Only a week before she was murdered, she knocked on the door of her neighbours' house in the middle of the night, looking for refuge. He'd given her a good beating, evidently. She was naked, just wrapped up in a blanket.'

'Did they let her in?'

'They certainly did. They let her sleep on a sofa. She was pretty drunk, but insisted she was going to report Verhaven to the police the next day. Grievous bodily harm, that kind of thing.'

'But when she woke up the next morning,' said deBries, 'she just wrapped the blanket around her and went back to him.'

'For Christ's sake!' said Reinhart. 'The faded embers of second thoughts.'

'Frailty, thy name is woman,' said Moreno, with a quick smile.

'Hmm,' said Münster. 'Anything else of interest?'

'Quite a bit about his childhood and school days,' said Moreno. 'The former janitor at the village school is still alive. He's nearly ninety, but unusually clear in the head and not unwilling to talk. Verhaven was a bit of an odd bird from the start, it appears. A loner. Introverted. But strong. His fellow pupils respected him. There's plenty of evidence for that.'

Münster nodded.

'There were a few who thought he was innocent,' said deBries. 'Of the Beatrice murder, at least. But that's no longer an opinion people are willing to shout in the streets.'

'Why not?' asked Jung.

'Same boat,' muttered Reinhart.

'Yes, that's about it,' said deBries. 'Standing in the village shop in Kaustin and maintaining that Verhaven is innocent is a bit like going to Tehran and claiming that the ayatollah has shit his trousers.'

'Ayatollahs don't wear trousers,' said Jung. 'They wear those black dresses, whatever they're called.'

'All right, all right,' said Münster.

'Maintaining that Verhaven is innocent implies something else as well,' said Reinhart.

'What?' wondered Rooth.

'You're accusing somebody else in the village of murder.'

Nobody spoke, and Münster could see exactly how long it took for Reinhart's words to sink into each one of them.

'But that's not certain,' said Rooth.

'No,' said Reinhart. 'Of course it's not certain that there's another murderer in the village, but it's shit-hot certain that the thought will occur to people. Suspicion. If you keep your mouth shut, you're not going to put your foot in it.'

'Very true,' said Moreno.

'Well,' said Münster when he had switched off the tape recorder and the others had left them alone. 'What do you think?'

'I don't think anything,' sighed Rooth. 'Or rather, I think anything's possible. I'd give a lot for a couple of hot tips at this stage. What the hell should we be concentrating on?'

'I don't know,' said Münster. 'I have the feeling Hiller will want to take several officers off the case. It'll probably be just you and me from now on. And the boss, of course.'

He nodded towards the tape recorder.

'Unless we come across something vital,' said Rooth.

'Unless the newspapers decide to make a meal of it, more likely,' said Münster. 'They'll have the story tomorrow, in any case. Maybe that's just as well. We need all the help we can get.'

*

'What do you really think yourself?' said Rooth before they went their separate ways in the underground car park. 'Do you really think there's a triple murderer on the loose in this backwater? That sounds to me like a damn awful film.'

'It wouldn't be a better film even if the locals knew who it is,' said Münster. 'No, I think I'd switch it off right away.'

Rooth pondered.

'Maybe we are sort of sitting in a movie theatre, as well,' he said. 'It can be damn hard getting out if you're stuck in the middle of a row.'

'Dead right,' said Münster.

They stood in silence for a while.

'How about a beer?' said Rooth.

Münster checked his watch.

'No time,' he said. 'I have to visit the patient. They won't let me in after eight.'

'Pity,' said Rooth, and shrugged. 'Pass on greetings. I reckon we could do with him around.'

'I couldn't agree more,' said Münster.

Why do I keep lying? Münster asked himself as he sat in the car on the way to his suburb. Why couldn't I have simply told him straight up that I wanted to go home to Synn and the kids? Why did I have to drag in the chief inspector?

Van Veeteren would get his tape after breakfast the next morning, as they had agreed. But if he didn't want to offend Rooth by turning down his offer of a drink, why should some old cop recovering from an operation be a better excuse than his wife and children?

A good question, no doubt about it.

He decided to think about something else instead.

26

Van Veeteren folded up the *Allgemenje* and dropped it on the concrete floor. Then he inserted the cassette, adjusted the earphones and leaned back against the pillow.

Elgar's cello concerto. The sun in his face and a warm breeze. Could be worse.

It wasn't exactly normal routine to allow patients to lie out on the balcony and enjoy themselves, he had realized that. On the other hand, it was hardly the only rule the hospital staff had broken during the five days he'd been in their care. The hospital rules left a great deal to be desired in every respect, but at least the staff had begun to grasp who they were dealing with. Modified rapture.

'But no more than half an hour at most,' Sister Terhovian had insisted, and for some reason held up four fingers close to his face.

'We'll see about that,' he'd responded.

Getting on for three-quarters of an hour must have

passed by now. Presumably they'd discovered that it was less trouble to let him be outside.

He called up from his memory the stuff he'd just been reading. There wasn't a lot to say about it, in fact. Bold headlines on the front page, of course, and two columns summarizing the case on an inside page, but surprisingly little in the way of speculation. Nothing at all, to be honest.

So this was the fourth time. No getting away from it. Since Verhaven had launched his career as an athlete in his early twenties, he'd taken over the headlines on four different occasions.

As king of the middle distances at the end of the fifties. King, and then cheat.

As a murderer at the beginning of the sixties.

As a murderer once again about twenty years later.

And now, in the middle of the nineties, as a victim. The last time, it seemed reasonable to assume.

Was this a logical development and an expected conclusion? Van Veeteren wondered as he turned up the volume to exclude the noise of the buses in Palitzerlaan down below.

The logical conclusion of a wasted life?

Hard to say.

What pattern could be applied to Leopold Verhaven's time on earth? Was there any pattern behind this bizarre and complicated human destiny?

Would it be possible, Van Veeteren asked himself, to make a film about his life, and thereby say something fundamental about his existence? About everybody's existence? That was a good question, in any case. A good yardstick.

Or was it just a matter of unfortunate circumstances piling up, one on top of the other? A dismal and ill-starred destiny of an unusual person under pressure, whose mutilated end was just as pointless as the rest of his days in this world?

Not the sort of life to make a film about?

He bit a toothpick and continued his line of thought.

Shouldn't it be possible to recreate any given life in some artistic form or other, if a big enough effort was made? Perhaps there was a specific genre for every individual. What about his own life, for instance? What could be made of that? A sinfonietta, perhaps? A concrete sculpture? Could Strindberg have turned it into half a sheet of paper?

Who knows, he thought.

And now here he was, lying on the balcony, asking these pointless questions again. Pretentious and incomprehensible questions that seemed to be whirring around inside his head only in order to mount a vain and idiotic struggle with the aggressive cello.

Much better would be a beer and a cigarette, he

thought, and pressed the white button. A damn sight better.

But instead of Sister Terhovian, it was Münster who appeared in the doorway. Van Veeteren switched off the cassette and removed the earphones.

'Everything OK?' asked Münster.

'What the devil do you mean? Isn't it obvious that everything isn't OK? I'm lying here miles from civilization, and I can't do anything about it. Have you made any progress?'

'Not really,' said Münster. 'It seems pretty good out here in the sunshine, no matter what.'

'Hot and sweaty,' said Van Veeteren. 'I could do with a beer. Well?'

'What do you mean by 'well'?'

'Have you brought the cassettes, for instance?'

'Of course. Both of them. I had a bit of trouble in finding the Gossec, needless to say, but they had it at Laudener's.'

He produced the two cassettes from a plastic carrier bag and handed them to the chief inspector.

'The red one is from our update meeting.'

'Are you suggesting that I can't tell the difference between a requiem and a gang of cops droning on and on?'

'No, I take it for granted that you can.'

'I've read what the *Allgemenje* has to say. What's in the other rags?'

'The same, more or less,' said Münster.

'No speculation about motives?'

'No, not in the ones I've read, in any case.'

'Odd,' said Van Veeteren.

'Why?' said Münster.

'Ah well, it'll come, no doubt. Anyway, I'm quite clear about the matter now. I read through the Marlene papers last night. I'll wager he's innocent on both counts. Do you disagree?'

'No,' said Münster. 'We've been coming round to that view as well. We're just a bit doubtful about what to do next . . .'

'Of course you are, damn it,' growled Van Veeteren. 'I haven't issued any orders yet. Wheel me back into the ward, and we can get down to business. It's disgraceful that they send patients into exile on the balcony and just leave them lying there. It's like an oven here . . .'

Münster opened the doors as wide as they would go and started to shove the steel-framed bed back into the ward.

'Where shall we start?' he asked when Van Veeteren was back in his usual place.

'How the hell do I know?' said the chief inspector. 'Let me listen to the tapes, and come back two hours from now. I'll be able to give you clear instructions then.'

'All right,' said Münster.

'Meanwhile, you can try to locate this person.'

He handed over a sheet of paper folded twice.

'Leonore Conchis,' Münster read. 'Who's she?'

'A woman Verhaven had a relationship with in the seventies,' said Van Veeteren.

'Is she still alive?' Münster asked automatically.

'You can start off by finding the answer to that question,' said Van Veeteren.

SEVEN

24 APRIL 1962

27

She wakes up yet again.

She can feel the darkness and his heavy presence like pressure on her chest. She cautiously heaves herself up on an elbow and tries to make out the faint phosphorescent glow of the alarm clock's hands.

Half past three. Very nearly. As far as she can see. The air in the bedroom is compact and stuffy, despite the window standing ajar. She raises herself into a sitting position and gropes around with her feet on the uneven floor until she finds her slippers.

She stands up and tiptoes cautiously out of the room, picking up her thin and worn terry-cloth robe on the way. She closes the door and puts her ear against the cool wood. She can hear his heavy, occasionally rattling breathing even at this distance.

She shivers and puts on her robe, then slowly makes her way down the stairs.

Down. That's the worst. The pain in her hips sends

red-hot needles up and down through her body. Along her spine and up into the back of her head, down to the arch of her foot and into her toes. It's remarkable how mobile this pain can be.

It gets worse with every step she takes.

With every day. More and more acute. It becomes more and more difficult not to turn her feet inwards and hunch her back.

It becomes harder and harder to walk.

She slumps down at the kitchen table, rests her head in her hands and feels the throbbing pain slowly receding. Waits until it has faded away completely before turning her thoughts to that other business.

That other matter.

Three times tonight she has been jettisoned by that dream. Three times.

The same ghastly idea. The same unbearable image.

Whenever he's come upstairs and plummeted down beside her, she's pretended to be asleep. He hasn't touched her. Not even placed a hand on her hip or shoulder. She's got him as far as that. He never touches her now, and she knows this is a victory she has achieved, despite everything. She has come this far thanks to her own efforts.

Beyond reach. Her body is beyond reach. Now and for evermore.

She need never be taken advantage of again.

The unspoken agreement is a sort of murky bond between them, but it is only now that she has begun to appreciate the price. The counterbalance. The incomprehensible horror on the other side of the scales.

Everything has its price, but she has not had any choice. There can be no question of guilt regarding her decision and her action – she knows all too well what would be the outcome of giving herself again to this man, even though he is her husband and the father of her child. There is medical advice as well; it's not just her. It would have a detrimental effect on her physical and mental health, and what ability to move around she still retains. If she were to become pregnant, that is. She must not give birth again. Must never give herself to him again. The hub of her life is in her pelvis. Ever since that terrible night when she gave birth, it has to be protected and made as inaccessible as a hallowed room.

A hallowed room?

This really is the way her thoughts are tending. Can anybody understand why?

God or her mother or any other woman?

No, nobody. She is on her own in this matter. A barren woman with a husband and a child. At long last she has learned how to accept the inevitable. He must never again be allowed inside her, and now his hands and the whole of his body have given up their vain attempts to plead and grope around. At long last he has resigned himself to the inevitable.

But the price?

Perhaps she did realize early on that there would be a price to pay. But now? Did she realize this would be the price?

The thought is horrific. Not even a thought; no more than the fragment of a dream. An image that has raced through her consciousness at such a dizzy speed and with such incomprehensible clarity that she has been unable to understand it.

Perceive, yes. Comprehend, no.

She has seen it, but not taken it in.

She stands up and makes her way to the stove. Switches on the light over the sink and fills a pan with water.

As it comes to a boil and she stands watching the bubbles break loose and rise to the surface, she thinks about Andrea.

Andrea, who is lying in bed on the other side of the wall behind the stove, sleeping the sleep of the innocent. Two years old – two years and two months, to be precise, and she wants to be precise tonight – and lying there underneath Grandma's crocheted quilt, sucking away at two fingers. She doesn't need to see in order to know. The image of her daughter is everywhere; she can summon it up in her mind's eye whenever she needs to, without any effort at all.

Andrea. The only child she will ever have. It is a miracle that she is alive, and all other considerations are as nothing, compared with that.

All others? she asks herself. But she already knows the answer.

Yes, all others. She takes the pan off the stove.

She sips her tea and opens the cotton curtains slightly. All she can see is the reflection of her own face and a strip of the interior of the kitchen. She closes them again.

I dare not think, she admits to herself. I dare not think clearly. I must keep it at a distance. When the images crop up inside my head, I must learn to close the eyes of my soul.

Must.

They've found her now. That's what she said in the shop, Mrs Malinska, and there was both controlled and hysterical triumph in her deep voice.

They've found her over at Goldemaars swamp.

Dead.

Strangled.

Naked.

And suddenly, in this lonely kitchen, at this lonely hour, she shudders so violently that she spills her cup of tea over the table. The hot tea runs over the checked oilcloth cover and drips onto her right thigh, but several seconds pass before she is able to stop the flow.

It was that Saturday. Eighteen days ago, or however long it was. There's been no sign of her since then, the slut; that's when it must have happened.

That Saturday, in the afternoon. She can see so clearly in her mind's eye as well. I'll go and clear some brushwood, he'd said, and there was something in his voice and his obstinate look that she recognized and might well have been able to understand, if only she'd tried hard enough.

But why should she? Andrea was the important thing, and it's Andrea that's important now. Why should she have to understand what she doesn't want to understand?

It was late when he came back home, and she knew something had happened. Not what, but something.

She could see it in his big hands as he wrung them, not knowing what to do with himself. In the blood throbbing guiltily through the veins in his temples. In his eyes, crying for help and a reduction in the pain.

In the horror that filled his body.

She had seen it, but not grasped what.

But now she is sitting here, and she knows. Dries her

thigh with her hand and feels the pain come creeping back. She knows the girl must not be allowed to know.

Nobody must know. Least of all her. The image of Andrea floats back into her mind and covers all the burning and black knowledge she possesses with a protective balm.

The comforting angel.

The child of oblivion.

Nothing has happened. She has no suspicions.

Only that one.

She stands up once more and pads over to the cupboard; she shakes out two pills from the brown glass jar. Washes them down with a mouthful of water direct from her cupped hand.

For the pain.

For the sleeplessness.

For the dreams and suspicions and knowledge.

Why? she asks herself as she makes her way slowly back up the stairs.

I am so young. My life is close to its beginning, but already I'm bound hand and foot.

To this husband.

To this daughter.

To this aching body.

To this resolve to be forever silent?

EIGHT

16–22 MAY 1994

28

From a distance, Münster estimated Leonore Conchis's age to be somewhere between thirty and thirty-five.

When he came nearer and they shook hands over the smoked-glass counter, it was clear that he would have to add at least twenty years in order to get a little closer to the truth.

Perhaps it was this illusory circumstance that led her to submit to Münster's questions in the rather dimly lit office; they sat back at opposite ends of a sofa that was so long, they had to raise their voices in order to converse.

So much for youth, Münster thought. A shadowy concept.

It had taken some considerable time to find her. She had changed her address more than ten times since living with Leopold Verhaven for a few months at the end of the seventies. And she had also changed her name.

But only once. She was now called di Goacchi, and for the last eighteen months she and her ancient Corsican husband had been running a boutique selling garish ladies' clothing in the centre of Groenstadt.

'Leopold Verhaven?' she said, crossing one black-nylon-clad leg over the other. 'Why do you want to interrogate me about Leopold Verhaven?'

'This isn't an interrogation,' Münster explained. 'I'd simply like to ask you a few questions.'

She lit a cigarette and adjusted her blood-red leather skirt.

'Fire away, then,' she said. 'What do you want to know?'

I've no idea, Münster thought. It's just that Van Veeteren instructed me to find you.

'Tell me about your relationship with him,' he said.

She exhaled smoke through her nostrils and looked bored to tears. Evidently she was not excessively positive towards the police in general, and it was clear to Münster that there was no point in trying to change that attitude.

'I don't think it's much fun either, having to root about in this kind of business,' he said. 'Can we get it out of the way pretty quickly, so that I can leave you in peace again?'

That did the trick, it seemed. She nodded and wet her lips with an exaggerated and well-practised movement of the tongue.

'All right. You want to know if he qualifies as a murderer of women. I've been asked that before.'

Münster nodded.

'So I gather.'

'I don't know,' she said. 'We were only together for a few months. I bumped into him by accident just as my second marriage hit the rocks. I was shattered and needed a man to look after me. To bring me back to life, you might say.'

'Could he do that, then?'

She shrugged.

'Are you married, Inspector?'

'Yes.'

'So I don't need to mince words?'

'Not in the least,' Münster assured her.

'OK.' She pulled a face that might have been a smile. 'He was a brutal lover. I enjoyed that at first, it was more or less what I needed, I suppose; but it became wearing in the long run. All that frantic fucking is only good for the first few times, and then you want to take things a bit more calmly, a bit more sensitively and more sophisticated – you know what I mean. Obviously, a really rough screw can ginger up an ageing relationship; but having that all the time isn't much good, no thank you.'

'Exactly,' said Münster, with a gulp. 'But he went at it like a bull all the time, did he?'

'Yes,' she said. 'It became too much like hard work. I left him after a few months. It was a hell of a dump to live in as well, in the middle of the woods and all that. But maybe that's also what I needed just then . . . Trees and nature and so on.'

I find it a bit hard to imagine you in his henhouse, Münster thought, and found that he was having trouble keeping his face straight.

'So he was a bit rough, but he didn't display any serious violence, did he?'

'No,' she said firmly. 'He was an introverted and uncultured person, but I never felt frightened of him, or anything like that.'

'You knew he'd been found guilty of murder?'

She nodded.

'He told me after our first night. And explained that he didn't do it.'

'Did you believe him?'

She hesitated, but only for a second.

'Yes,' she said. 'I don't believe Leopold Verhaven would kill a woman like that. He was an oddball, that's for sure, but he wasn't a murderer. I explained that during the second trial as well, but nobody paid any attention, of course. He was condemned in advance.'

Münster nodded.

'You haven't been in contact with him since your relationship came to an end?'

'No,' she said. 'Who killed him? That's what you're trying to find out, isn't it?'

'Yes,' said Münster, 'that's exactly it. Have you any idea?'

She shook her head.

'Not the slightest,' she said, stubbing out her cigarette. 'Will that be all, Inspector? I have a business to attend to.'

'Yes, I think that's all,' said Münster, handing her his card. 'Give me a call if you remember anything that could be of significance.'

'What might that be?' she asked.

I've no idea, thought Münster as he dragged himself up off the sofa.

It had started raining by the time he emerged into the square. A thin and warm early summer drizzle that felt like a cleansing bath, almost. And a rather pleasant contrast to Leonore di Goacchi. He stood for a moment and let the gentle drops rinse his face, before unlocking the car and clambering in.

A two-hour drive back.

Not an especially productive afternoon, it had to be admitted. But that was how things usually went. In every single case, more or less. Questions, questions and more questions. A never-ending procession of conversations and interviews and interrogations, every one of them at first glance just as pointless and unproductive as the last, until that important detail emerged. Most often when one least expected it. That link, that little unexpected reply . . . That sudden but faintly glowing sign in the darkness that one couldn't afford to overlook. It was important not to rush past it in this overgrown thicket of irrelevant and tiresome details.

He yawned and drove out of the square.

But surely what he had just been through couldn't have contained anything important?

Apart from another little support for the theory that Verhaven was innocent, that is. And we'd come to that conclusion already, in any case. Or had we?

He concentrated on the future instead.

Two days ahead, to be precise. That was when Van Veeteren would be released from hospital, if the predictions were to be believed; and even if Münster and Rooth had hoped to clear up this case on their own, by this stage they had waved goodbye to any such aspirations. More or less, at least.

We might as well let time take its course and leave it to the chief inspector to take the case by the scruff of the neck, Münster thought. From Friday onwards, that is. It was hard to predict precisely what that would involve, although there had been a few hints. Certain observations he hadn't been able to avoid making during that last visit.

Only little things, it was true, but clear nevertheless. Also, a sort of glow in the darkness, come to think of it . . . The silly and annoying air of mystery Van Veeteren always adopted, for instance. The irritation and touchiness. The humming and hawing and muttering.

The usual signals, in fact.

Only faint indications, but clearly audible and visible to anybody who'd been associated with him for a while.

The chief inspector was at the incubation stage, as Reinhart had put it on one occasion, quite independently of Verhaven and his chicken shed and all that.

Perhaps they should place him under a light? Münster couldn't help smiling to himself as he drove.

To speed things up. Wasn't that what Verhaven had done with his hens, after all?

Or was it simply that being cooped up in the ward was driving him round the bend? Münster wondered. In any case, the staff at the hospital deserved a medal – for putting up with him. For not having thrown him out or dumped him in the dirty-linen basket. He must remember to give them a bunch of flowers when he collected Van Veeteren on Friday. No harm in improving the image of the forces of law and order . . .

But then he abandoned all thought about work. Thought about Synn and the evening off that lay in store. That was a much more pleasant topic.

A visit to the theatre and a candlelit dinner at Le Canaille. Grandma and Grandad doing the babysitting. Their little flat in the town centre afterwards. Oh, life had its golden moments now and again.

29

Kiesling's case for the prosecution at the Marlene Nietsch trial occupied eighteen closely typed photocopied sheets. Van Veeteren read through them all, sighed deeply and then returned to the reconstruction – the attempt to convince the judge, the members of the jury and anybody else who might be interested in what had happened that fatal afternoon in September 1981.

> . . . and so let me instead move on to describe what happened that Friday almost three months ago, September 11.
>
> At about 7:30 in the morning Leopold Verhaven leaves his home in Kaustin, driving his van, a green Trotta, 1960 vintage, and sets off on his usual round delivering eggs to his customers – a total of ten stores in Linzhuisen and Maardam. His last delivery this morning, also as usual, is the Covered Market in Kreuger Plejn here in Maardam.
>
> As we have heard, Verhaven is very well known to

everybody who works at or is otherwise connected with the Covered Market. According to him and several other witnesses, he leaves the market a few minutes after half past nine, when he has seen to everything he needs to do. His van is parked at the back of the hall, in Kreugerlaan, where he had earlier unloaded today's delivery of eggs, but he doesn't go straight back to his van, which is his usual practice: instead he leaves through the main entrance, emerging into the square. He goes to the news-stand outside Goldmann's, buys a newspaper and starts walking back towards Zwille. When he gets to the fountain, he meets a business acquaintance, Aaron Katz, and they exchange a few words. He then continues across the square, and at the corner of Kreuger Plejn and Zwille he bumps into Marlene Nietsch. They have been conducting a sexual relationship for some six weeks; they have met and spent the night together, both at Verhaven's house in Kaustin and in Miss Nietsch's apartment in central Maardam.

They stand talking for several minutes, according to Verhaven himself and also several other witnesses, including Aaron Katz. Eventually they set off in a southerly direction along Zwille, then turn into Kreugerlaan where Verhaven's van is parked. The witness, Elena Klimenska, attests that they were standing beside the van, talking, at some point between ten and five minutes to ten. This is denied by the accused, who also denies that Marlene Nietsch got into the van with him. However, no less than three other witnesses – independently of one another – have noticed Verhaven's unmistakable van passing through Maardam. Two of them have stated under oath that there was a woman in the passenger seat beside Verhaven, a woman whose description is very similar to that of the murdered Miss Nietsch. The third witness, Mrs Bossens from Karnach, has declined to swear under oath that she saw them together, for deeply felt religious reasons, but has nevertheless indicated that she is 95 per cent certain that Verhaven was not alone in the van, as he claims.

We have no witnesses of what happened next on that tragic Friday, but it is not difficult to reconstruct the probable course of events. We cannot know, of course, what Leopold Verhaven and Marlene Nietsch talked about in Maardam, or what they say to each other in the van, but we can be quite sure that it is something of a sexual nature. Perhaps the accused tries to persuade Miss Nietsch to agree to some activity she has no desire to indulge in, that she doesn't feel in the mood for. But that is mere speculation and is in no way relevant to the question of guilt as such.

As usual Verhaven takes the route home via Bossingen and Löhr. That is unquestionably the obvious route to take from Maardam to Kaustin, but instead of actually driving home, on this day of all days, Verhaven decides to travel south towards Wurms, presumably by taking a right at the crossroads in the village of Korrim. About halfway between Korrim and Wurms, he then turns onto a narrow and rarely used road that leads into the trees and peters out after only a hundred yards or so. This is the same stretch of woodland, ladies and gentlemen, in which the body of Beatrice Holden was discovered in 1962, the woman whom Leopold Verhaven was found guilty of murdering, and for which crime he served twelve years in prison.

Verhaven parks his van beside a stack of logs, and a cyclist passing by on the main road glimpses the vehicle through the trees at half past ten or shortly afterwards. Verhaven forces Marlene Nietsch to have sexual intercourse and strangles her, either during or after the sexual act. He hides the body under a pile of twigs and branches, where it is discovered four days later by the owner of the woods, Mr Nimmerlet.

After killing her, Verhaven drives straight back home. He is seen in his van by a neighbour shortly after eleven o'clock. The accused has been unable to give a satisfactory explanation for why on this particular morning, unlike all other days, it has taken him more than half an hour longer to get from the

Covered Market in Maardam to his home in Kaustin. As far as Miss Nietsch is concerned, the only witnesses to have seen her alive after Elena Klimenska saw her talking to Verhaven behind the market are the ones who saw her in the green van. It must therefore be considered beyond a shadow of a doubt that she really did accompany her murderer in the van. The accused maintains that he and Miss Nietsch parted company in Zwille, which only goes to show that in the depths of his depraved, criminal mind [Sic! *wrote Detective Chief Inspector Van Veeteren in the margin and underscored it twice*] he is well aware that this is his only chance of being found not guilty as charged. As we have heard, Marlene Nietsch had arranged to meet a friend, Renate Koblenz, at the Rote Moor café in Kreuger Plejn at 10:15 this Friday. She never appeared.

The reason is that at the time her friend was sitting at the table they had agreed upon, waiting for her and beginning to wonder what was the matter, Marlene Nietsch was in the van with her murderer, driving out of Maardam. And this murderer, my Lord and honourable members of the jury, can in no circumstances be anybody other than the accused, Leopold Verhaven.

If we leave these incontestable facts to one side for the moment and instead turn our attention to a number of psychological questions . . .

A very neatly constructed jigsaw puzzle, Van Veeteren thought as he put the papers down. Damned neat. Ominously neat, in fact? What was required for Verhaven to have been found not guilty?

He stuck a toothpick into the front teeth in his lower jaw and folded his hands behind his neck.

In the first place: Marlene Nietsch must have met her real murderer during that short period around ten o'clock. It had to be assumed that Verhaven had never taken her in his van, although there was of course a slight chance that he could have done so and still be innocent . . . That, just as prosecuting counsel Kiesling had pointed out, he'd known he was finished if he'd admitted that he did give her a lift.

Although it would become clear that he was finished, in any case, no matter what he said or did.

Second: the murderer must somehow have persuaded Marlene Nietsch not to turn up for her meeting at the café.

Would it have been enough, perhaps, for a prospective customer simply to have handed over a bundle of cash and invited her to perform for him? Van Veeteren wondered. That couldn't be excluded as a possibility. Marlene Nietsch was hardly one of God's blameless children, after all.

Third: at least three witnesses must have been mistaken. Or lied. The woman who saw them standing by the van. The man and the woman who saw Miss Nietsch in the cab of the van. Plus the one who didn't want to swear under oath.

Three or four witnesses all in agreement? Wasn't that damning enough? Conclusive, in fact?

No, thought Van Veeteren in annoyance and bit off the end of the toothpick. During the morning, he had ploughed through more than fifty pages of interrogation minutes, only to discover that they made unusually deplorable reading. The male witness in particular had given the strongest impression of partaking in a parody. And left a very unpleasant taste in the mouth, if one happened to be even vaguely interested in the fairness of the judicial system. By all accounts, Necker had turned up four weeks after Verhaven had been charged, gone to the police of his own accord and claimed suddenly to have remembered noticing a fair-haired woman in the accused's well-known Trotta. In court he had got days wrong, places wrong, people wrong, and it wasn't until Kiesling had put all the right words into his mouth that he had managed to produce a reasonably coherent story.

And that Denbourke was certainly not the ideal lawyer to conduct your defence; but that wasn't exactly news.

Moreover – and at this point Van Veeteren had been forced to grab hold of the bed frame in order not to hit the roof – there had been no fewer than three other witnesses who claimed to have seen Verhaven's van on its way from the Covered Market, but none of them had seen a woman inside it. What had happened to these witnesses in the final summing-up was a mystery.

Deplorable! muttered Van Veeteren, and spat out the rest of the toothpick onto the quilt. Had Mort really been involved in this? And Heidelbluum?

He knew from bitter experience that the others, the laymen, the semi-educated servants of the law, could turn a blind eye to practically anything; but that the judge and the chief inspector could allow something like this to happen, that was a rude awakening. Difficult to digest, to say the least. It was true of course that it was no longer Mort's responsibility once the case reached the courtroom – but even so?

Then again, Mort hadn't been his old self during his last years in harness. Perhaps that was it; perhaps he ought to make some allowances.

And Heidelbluum had been nearly seventy at the time.

I hope they get rid of me before I lose as much sting as that, he thought. But maybe I'll die before I get that gaga? A blessing devoutly to be wished, I suppose.

But what could one say about this case as a whole? The bottom line was that he'd sat there in the dock and acted like the guiltiest of the guilty, that damned Verhaven.

Apart from denying that he'd done it, of course.

Incomprehensible, decided Detective Chief Inspector

Van Veeteren. And there's nothing I hate as much as things I don't understand!

He swung one leg over the side of the bed and sat up. After a moment of dizziness he found himself standing on the cold floor. It felt good to be able to move under one's own steam again. No denying that.

Even if his frailty and tendency to grow dizzy still scared him a bit. No denying that either.

Still, I'm going home tomorrow, no matter what, he thought as he closed the bathroom door. Then sure as hell I'll soon sort out this mess!

But when he had flopped down onto the cold seat, it dawned on him that it might not be all that easy.

The fact was, he already had all the known facts with him here in hospital. Bundle after bundle of newspaper reports. Trial transcripts. Tape recordings of the investigation updates, and detailed reports from Münster.

Surely things couldn't look all that different out there in the real world?

Another good question.

30

'Let's go and sit in the café instead,' David Cupperman had whispered, ushering him out through the door.

Now that they were sitting in a secluded corner of the bar, enveloped in the smell of cooking fat, he looked much calmer, Jung felt. It didn't take very long to explain why.

'I didn't want the wife to get involved,' explained Cupperman. 'She's a bit sensitive, and she knows nothing about this business.'

Jung nodded and held out his pack of cigarettes.

'No thanks. I've given up. Thanks to the missus,' he added, with a slightly apologetic smile.

Jung lit a cigarette.

'You don't need to worry,' he said. 'We're just calling on a few people and asking a couple of routine questions, that's all. Maybe you've seen in the papers that Leopold Verhaven has been murdered?'

'Yes.'

Cupperman nodded and contemplated his coffee cup.

'We understand you lived with Beatrice Holden for some time in Ulming. When was that? The end of the fifties, was it?'

Cupperman sighed. It seemed quite obvious that if there was anything in his life that this worryingly prim and proper man regretted, it was that unfortunate affair in his youth.

'Nineteen fifty-eight,' he said. 'We met in '57, and moved in together a few months later. She was pregnant . . . Well, then we lived together until February the following year. It wasn't my child.'

'Really?' said Jung, trying to sound as surprised as he could.

'We . . . she had a daughter, Christine, we called her; she had a daughter in August 1958; but as I said, the father was another man.'

'When did you find that out?'

'When she was five months old. He came to visit, and when he'd left, she told me the whole story.'

'Oh, shit,' Jung said before he could stop himself. 'Excuse me, but it can't have been very pleasant for you?'

'No,' said Cupperman. 'It wasn't exactly amusing. I left her that same evening.'

'That same evening?' Jung asked.

'I just threw a few things into a bag. Took the train.'

He fell silent. Jung thought for a while. Where did you

go? was the obvious question, but perhaps that wasn't so important.

'What about your daughter?' he asked instead. 'Her daughter, that is. It must have been hard to leave a child you had thought was your own?'

But Cupperman didn't reply. He just stared down at the table, biting his lip.

'You hadn't had any suspicions at all?'

Cupperman shook his head.

'No,' he said. 'I ought to have done, of course. But I was young and inexperienced. That was the top and bottom of it.'

'Did you ever meet her again? Afterwards, that is?'

'No.'

'Not Christine either?'

'I went to visit her in Kaustin. After the murder. But only once. She was four, living with her grandmother. Beatrice's mother. She didn't seem to want anything to do with me, the grandmother I mean, so there didn't seem to be much point.'

'I see,' said Jung. 'And the father? The real father, that is? Do you know anything about him?'

Cupperman shook his head again.

'He went to sea, I think. I never saw him again.'

'And Beatrice didn't meet him, after you'd left her?'

'How should I know?'

No, thought Jung after he'd taken leave of David Cupperman. If the police haven't managed to track down Claus Fritze after thirty years, it would be a bit much to expect his poor cuckolded rival to have done so.

Rooth rang the bell and the door opened so fast that he had to jump backwards to avoid being hit by it. Arnold Jahrens had been expecting him, that was obvious.

'Mr Jahrens?'

'Come in.'

He was tall and powerful and looked at least ten years younger than the sixty-five he was. Or was it sixty? It doesn't matter anyway, he decided and sat down on the chair provided at the kitchen table.

'Well,' said Jahrens. 'I expect it's about Verhaven again. And Miss Holden.'

'Exactly,' said Rooth. 'I take it you know what's happened?'

'I've read about it in the papers,' said Jahrens, gesturing towards a corner where he evidently collected them in a pile. Both *Neuwe Blatt* and *Telegraaf,* as far as Rooth could see.

'I bet you have,' said Rooth. 'To be honest with you, we're groping around in the dark; and so we're doing a bit of stocktaking, you might say. Having a chat with everybody who's been in contact with them and the case, in one way or another.'

'I'm with you,' said Jahrens, serving coffee. 'Sugar?'

'Three spoons,' said Rooth.

'Three?'

'Did I say three? I meant one and a half.'

Jahrens burst out laughing.

'I've plenty of sugar,' he explained. 'You can have three damned spoonfuls if you like.'

'Thanks,' said Rooth. 'Anyway, I don't want to keep you longer than necessary, so I'll come straight to the point. You used to be a neighbour of Verhaven's. When did you move away from there, by the way?'

'Nineteen eighty-five,' said Jahrens. 'We didn't have anybody who could take over the farm, and rather than wear ourselves out we decided to spend our twilight years in town. It's made quite a difference, in fact.'

'Your wife . . . ?' asked Rooth.

'She died two years ago.'

'I'm sorry about that. Anyway, down to business. I'd like you to tell me what you made of the pair Leopold Verhaven and Beatrice Holden. You must have seen quite a bit of them, and it was you she came to the night before she was murdered, is that right?'

'Yes, of course. You couldn't avoid noticing a few things,' said Jahrens. 'And yes, she came to us all right.

Why are you asking, by the way? Surely you don't think he was innocent? They seem to be hinting at that in the *Telegraaf* . . .'

'We don't know,' Rooth admitted. 'What we do know is that somebody's killed him. There must be a reason, and until we know what it is, we have to take every possibility into account.'

'I follow you,' said Jahrens, fishing a cookie out of his cup with the aid of a spoon. 'You could say they were at each other's throats, all the time. Not many people were surprised by what happened . . . of us in the village, I mean. I'm not saying we thought he'd do her in; but they weren't especially nice to each other.'

'We've gathered that,' said Rooth. 'What happened that night when she came and knocked on your door?'

'I must have described that at least fifty times,' said Jahrens.

'But not recently, I don't think,' said Rooth. 'Just one more time; I expect you know it off by heart anyway.'

Jahrens laughed again.

'All right,' he said. 'There's not much to tell. I was woken up by somebody knocking on the glass panel of the front door. I put on a pair of trousers and went downstairs to open up, and there she was. She could have just come in and bedded down on the sofa without waking us up, in fact – we never locked the front door. It was the same all over the village, come to that: nobody bothered to lock themselves in. It's a bit different here in town, I can tell you. Anyway, she was standing there, shivering, and she asked if she could come in and sleep on our sofa. That damn bastard Verhaven had beaten her up, she said, and she was going to report him to the police next morning.'

'Was she drunk?'

'Fairly, but I've seen worse. Obviously, I asked if we could do anything for her – she had a black eye, all swollen, and a few other bruises; but she wouldn't hear of it. All she wanted was to sleep, she said, so I let her go and lie down on the sofa. I fetched a blanket and a pillow, that's all. And poured her a glass of water. Then I went back to bed. It was gone three.'

'Hmm,' said Rooth. 'Was that all?'

'Yes,' said Jahrens. 'She woke up at about nine the next morning, but when I reminded her that she was going to call the police she turned all insolent and told me to mind my own business. And then she left. Didn't even say thank you.'

'A well-brought-up lady,' said Rooth.

'Very,' said Jahrens. 'Would you like some more cookies? I see they're all gone.'

'No thanks,' said Rooth, and thought for a few seconds. 'I can't really think of any more questions to ask you,' he said. 'Is there anything else you can add, that might be of use to us?'

Jahrens leaned back on his chair and gazed up at the ceiling.

'No,' he said. 'Not a thing.'

'But you think it was Verhaven who killed her?'

'Absolutely,' said Jahrens. 'There are a lot of things in this life that I'm doubtful about, but not that.'

'No, when all's said and done, it could well be as you say,' said Rooth, getting to his feet. 'Many thanks.'

We're all mad, no doubt about it, he thought when he emerged into the courtyard.

Who the hell was it who'd written that?

After another day in Kaustin, deBries and Moreno turned up at Krause's so late that they couldn't find a quiet corner in the bar. DeBries tried to do a quick calculation of how much cash he had in his wallet – yet again cursing his obstinate refusal to get himself a credit card – and decided he wasn't too badly off.

'Let's go to the restaurant instead,' he suggested. 'Can I treat you to a bite to eat?'

'All right,' said Moreno, taking another look around. 'I don't think we'd be able to do much in the way of chewing over our impressions in here. But if you treat me, I'll treat you – that's a condition.'

Excellent, thought deBries.

'We'll see about that,' he said, opening the glass door leading to the more substantial area.

'Well,' said Moreno when they'd had their bite to eat and ordered another bottle and the cheese board. 'What do you reckon about today, then?'

'Nice weather,' said deBries. 'You look a bit more tanned, I think.'

'Every little bit helps,' said Moreno, taking her notebook from her purse. 'Shall we take them in order? We ought to form some sort of judgements, after all.'

She looked at the names:

Uleczka Willmot
Katrina Berenskaya
Maria Hess

'Three old women,' said deBries. 'With walking sticks. Well, I'd say the odds against were a thousand to one, roughly; but I suppose we can't write any of them off until we've checked their alibis. Mind you, it's a long way to Ulmentahl. That visitor must have taken all day to get there and back. If she came from Kaustin, that is.'

'If she did, yes.'

'Hard to say,' said deBries.

'Very,' said Moreno. 'A thousand to one? Yes, I suppose that's about right.'

The waiter brought the cheese board, and deBries topped up their glasses.

'What about a motive?' he said after a while. 'Can you see any of these old dears having the slightest whiff of a motive? If there's any point in all this, the visitor must have known the identity of the real murderer. I don't think our three seemed to be particularly well informed on that matter.'

'I can't understand why she should want to keep it to herself,' said Moreno. 'If she really wanted to tell Verhaven who the murderer was, there's surely no sensible reason for being unwilling to admit to it afterwards. Or is there?'

'God only knows,' said deBries, polishing a grape on the tablecloth. 'No, I can't make head nor tail of this, swear to God.'

Moreno sighed.

'Nor can I,' she said. 'It all seems a bit odd, as far as I can see. All we know for a fact is that Verhaven was visited by a woman calling herself Anna Schmidt on June fifth, 1992. We've no idea who she really was or what they talked about. We're jumping to quite a few conclusions if we think along these lines. First we claim that the visit had to do with the murder. Then we say the reason was that she wanted to tell Verhaven who the real murderer was. Then we assume she lives in Kaustin . . . There are some weak links in that chain.'

'Besides,' said deBries, 'we're not even a hundred per cent certain that it's Verhaven who's dead. And we're definitely not sure that he was actually innocent of the crimes he's been in prison for. No, if we took this to the public prosecutor, he'd no doubt laugh us out of court.'

Moreno nodded.

'But it's not our problem, of course,' said deBries. 'We're only obeying orders: get over there and seek out all women who use a walking stick in that dump! Or all men with false teeth in Aarlach! All left-handed whores in Hamburg! Ask them what they were doing between three and four o'clock in the afternoon on the day before Christmas Eve 1973, and most important – write down every single word they say! It's great fun, this sleuthing: this is exactly what I dreamed about when I made up my mind to become a detective.'

'I get the feeling you're a little bit disillusioned this evening,' said Moreno with a benign smile.

'Not in the least,' said deBries. 'You totally misjudge my motives. I would be more than happy to go to Spetsbergen and interview every damned penguin about their views on the greenhouse effect . . . As long as I could do it alongside you. Cheers!'

'Cheers,' said Moreno. 'But I don't think there are any penguins at Spetsbergen. Anyway, I suppose we'll be given new assignments tomorrow no matter what?'

DeBries nodded.

'I assume so,' he said. 'Münster and Van Veeteren will be able to steer this ship home without our help. But they won't find it all that easy, I suspect.'

'Probably not. What do you really think? Will they be able to solve this case, full stop?'

DeBries crunched away at the last cracker and thought for a while.

'I've no idea,' he said. 'Strangely enough, I get the feeling that they will crack it eventually. VV will be in a hell of a bloodhound humour when they eventually let him out. He's not easy to put up with now, according to Münster.'

'Is he ever?'

'No,' sighed deBries. 'You're right there, of course. I wouldn't like to be married to him, I know that much.'

'What do you mean by that?'

'Nothing,' said deBries.

Moreno looked at her watch.

'Speaking of that, I suppose it's time to call it a day.'

'You're right,' said deBries. 'Thank you for a very

pleasant day. The bottle's empty, I'm afraid . . . Otherwise I'd propose a toast to you.'

'You've already done that twice,' Moreno pointed out. 'That's quite enough. There's a limit to the amount of flattery I can take.'

'Same here,' said deBries. 'Time to go home.'

31

At first sight, for the first tenth of a second after opening the door, he had no idea where he was. The thought that he might have got the wrong room after twelve long days of absence did occur to him, but then he realized that it was the same old office as usual. Perhaps it was the strong afternoon sun slanting in through the dirty windows that confused him. The whole of the far wall, behind the desk, was bathed in generous but blinding sunlight. Dust was dancing. It was as hot as in an oven.

He opened the window. Lowered the blinds and succeeded in protecting himself to some extent from the early summer. When he looked round, he found that the changes were not in fact as great as he had at first thought.

There were three of them, to be precise.

First of all, somebody had tidied up his desk. All his papers were in neat piles instead of being splayed out like a fan. Not a bad idea, he could see that immediately. Odd that it had never occurred to him before.

In the second place, a vase with yellow and mauve flowers had been placed next to his telephone. I am obviously an outstandingly popular and well-liked person, Van Veeteren thought. Hard but fair under the rough surface.

In the third and last place, he had received a new desk chair. It was turquoise in colour; he thought he could recall the shade from a coat Renate had once bought while on a catastrophic holiday in France. Provence blue, if he remembered rightly, but that was irrelevant. It had soft armrests in any case – the chair, that is – a curved back and headrest, and was vaguely reminiscent of seats in the first-class compartments of trains in one of the neighbouring countries, he couldn't remember which.

He sat down tentatively. The seat was just as soft as the armrests. He sank back into the backrest and noticed that under the seat was a selection of wheels and levers that evidently enabled him to adjust every possible feature – height, angle, headrest angle, elasticity coefficient, you name it. On the desk in front of him was a brochure in full colour with precise instructions in eight languages.

Wow! Van Veeteren thought and began fiddling with the controls in accordance with the instructions. I can snooze the time away in this chair until they start paying my pension.

*

Twenty minutes later he had finished, and just as he had started wondering how he could most easily and smartly procure a beer, the duty operator rang to inform him that a lady was in reception, asking for Van Veeteren.

'Send her up,' he said. 'I'll meet her by the elevator.'

It was Saturday, and the building was practically empty. He would prefer to avoid the blunder made by Reinhart a year or so ago when his instructions resulted in a prospective narc with a bad sense of direction ending up fast asleep on the sofa in the chief of police's office. Hiller himself had discovered the intruder early on Monday morning, and not even Reinhart's tactful reminder that it was possible to lock doors with the aid of something known as a key had persuaded the authorities that there were extenuating circumstances.

'Your name is Elena Klimenska, is that right?' he began when she had settled down on the visitor's chair.

'Yes.'

She was a rather elegant woman, he had to admit. Somewhere between forty and fifty, he would guess, with dark, dyed hair and strong features, discreetly brought out by carefully applied make-up and sophisticated perfume. As far as he could judge, that is.

'I am Detective Chief Inspector Van Veeteren,' he said. 'As I explained, it's to do with your testimony in connection with the trial of Leopold Verhaven here in Maardam in November 1981.'

'So I gather,' she said, folding her hands over her black patent-leather handbag.

'Can you tell me what your testimony comprised?'

'Er . . . I don't understand what you mean.'

She hesitated. Van Veeteren took a toothpick from his breast pocket and studied it carefully before making a cautious attempt to adjust the angle of his chair backwards. Hmm, not bad, he thought. This must be the perfect chair for interrogations.

Although the victim should ideally be sitting on a three-legged stool. Or a wooden packing case.

'Well?' he said.

'My testimony? Er, the thing is, I happened to be walking past and I saw them, behind the Covered Market.'

'Saw who?'

'Him and her, of course. Verhaven and that woman he murdered . . . Marlene Nietsch.'

'Where did you pass?'

'Excuse me?'

'You said you happened to be walking past. I would like to know where you were when you saw them.'

She cleared her throat.

'I was walking on the pavement along Zwille. I saw them a short way up Kreugerlaan . . .'

'How did you know it was them?'

'I recognized them, of course.'

'Before or after?'

'What do you mean?'

'Did you know it was Leopold Verhaven and Marlene Nietsch when you saw them, or did it dawn on you afterwards?'

'Afterwards, of course.'

'You weren't acquainted with either of them?'

'Certainly not.'

'How far away were you?'

'Twenty yards.'

'Twenty?'

'Yes, twenty.'

'How do you know?'

'The police measured the distance.'

'What were they wearing?'

'He was in a blue shirt and jeans. She had on a brown jacket and a black skirt.'

'Not particularly conspicuous clothes.'

'No. Why should they be conspicuous?'

'Because it's easier to recognize people if there's something special about their appearance. Were there any special details?'

'No, I don't think so.'

'How did you come into contact with the legal authorities?'

'There was an appeal for witnesses in the newspapers.'

'I see. And so you responded to that appeal?'

'I thought it was my duty to do so.'

'How much time had passed by then? Roughly.'

'A month. Six weeks, perhaps.'

Van Veeteren snapped the toothpick.

'You're saying that you could remember two people standing talking beside a van after . . . six weeks?'

'Yes.'

'People you didn't know?'

'Of course.'

'Had you any special reason for noticing them and remembering them?'

'Er, no.'

'What time was it?'

'Excuse me?'

'What time was it when you were walking along Zwille and happened to see them?'

'Seven or eight minutes to ten.'

'How do you know?'

'Er, that's the time it was. What's so remarkable about that?'

'Did you check the time?'

'No.'

'Where were you going? Did you have an appointment to keep or something of that sort?'

'I was out shopping.'

'I see.'

He paused and leaned back so far that his feet left the floor. For a brief moment he felt almost weightless.

Is there a lever to pull that will bring me back into the atmosphere? he wondered, but he soon regained control of his module.

'Mrs Klimenska,' he said when he had made contact with both his desk and the floor once more. 'I would like you to explain this to me, as slowly and clearly as you can. I sometimes find it a bit hard to understand things. A man has been found guilty of first-degree murder on the basis of your evidence. He has been in prison for twelve years. Twelve years! If you hadn't come forward, it is very likely that he would have been cleared. Will you please tell me how the hell you can be certain that you saw Leopold Verhaven and Marlene Nietsch standing talking in Kreugerlaan at seven and a half minutes to ten on Friday, September the eleventh, 1981! How?'

Elena Klimenska sat up straight and met his gaze without the slightest hesitation.

'Because I saw them,' she said. 'As far as the time is concerned, that's the only possibility. He drove away from there at ten o'clock, and they were together at the corner at twelve minutes to.'

'So they weren't actually at the corner when you saw them?'

'Of course not.'

'Bravo, Mrs Klimenska. You know your stuff very well, I must say. But then, it's only thirteen years ago, after all.'

'What do you mean by that?'

'Was it the police or the prosecutor who helped you with the timing?'

'Both of them, of course. Why . . .'

'Thank you,' Van Veeteren interrupted. 'That's enough. Just one more question. Was there any other witness who could confirm your evidence?'

'I don't understand.'

'Somebody you had just left, for instance. Or bumped into five minutes later, perhaps?'

'No. How would that have helped?'

Van Veeteren didn't answer. He drummed quietly on the edge of his desk instead, gazing out through a gap in the blinds at the sunshine bathing the warm streets. Elena Klimenska adjusted a pleat in her greyish-blue dress, but didn't change her expression.

'Do you usually sleep soundly at night, Mrs Klimenska?'

Her mouth narrowed to form a thin line. He could see

that she'd had enough. That she presumably had no intention of answering any more questions or insinuations.

'I ask because I'm curious,' he said. 'It's part of my job to play the psychologist now and again. If it had been me, for instance, who had been responsible for getting another human being locked up for twelve years on the basis of totally unfounded and invented evidence, I would probably not feel too good about it. You know, the conscience thing, and all that . . .'

She stood up.

'I've had enough of your . . .'

'But maybe you had some special reason?'

'What the . . .'

'For getting him locked up, I mean. That would explain it.'

'Goodbye, Chief Inspector. You can be sure the chief of police is going to hear of this!'

She turned on her heel and managed three paces towards the door.

'You lying bitch,' he hissed.

She stopped dead.

'What did you say?'

'I merely wished you a pleasant afternoon. Can you find your own way out, or would you like me to escort you?'

Two seconds later he was alone again, but he could hear her heels tapping in irritation all the way to the elevator.

Ah well, he thought, pulling the weightlessness lever. That's the way to treat 'em.

32

'I know,' said Synn. 'You don't need to apologize.'

'He's been in the hospital and read every single word about these damned cases,' Münster said. 'He feels he simply has to go and take a look for himself, and he's not allowed to drive yet.'

'I know,' said Synn again. She turned the pages of her newspaper and blew at her coffee. It was barely half past seven, but the children had been awake since long before seven, totally oblivious to that fact that it was a summer Sunday . . . A morning with a warm breeze and cherry blossom and a deafening chorus of birdsong that floated in through the half-open balcony door and mixed with Marieke's giggles from the nursery and Bart's endless monologue about dragons and monsters and soccer players.

He stood up and positioned himself behind his wife. Caressed the back of her head. Placed his hand inside her robe and gently squeezed her breast – and he suddenly felt pain creeping up upon him: a chilling fear, but also a realization, that this moment must pass. This second of absolute and perfect happiness – one of the ten to twelve that comprised a whole life, and was possibly even the meaning of it . . .

Or so he understood it. If you have twelve treasured memories, his Uncle Arndt had once said as Münster sat on his knee, you will have led a happy life. But twelve is a high number. You'll have to wait for quite a while yet before you can start collecting them.

Perhaps Synn could sense his unrest, for she placed her hand over his and pressed it harder against her breast.

'I like it,' she said. 'I like your hands. Maybe we'll manage an afternoon outing? Lauerndamm or somewhere like that. It would be good to make love in the open air; it's been a long time . . . Or what do you say, darling?'

He swallowed the lump of ecstasy that welled up inside him.

'Of course, my darling,' he said. 'I'll be back before one. Just get yourself ready.'

'Ready?' she smiled. 'I'm ready now, if you want to.'

'Oh, hell!' said Münster. 'If it weren't for the kids and Van Veeteren, then . . .'

She let go of his hand.

'Maybe we should ask him to babysit?'

'Huh,' said Münster. 'I'm not convinced that is the best idea you've ever had.'

'All right,' said Synn. 'We'll stick to this afternoon, then.'

Van Veeteren was waiting on the pavement when Münster pulled up outside 4 Klagenburg. There was no concealing his suppressed eagerness, and when he had settled into the passenger seat, he immediately fished out two toothpicks that he proceeded to roll from one side of his mouth to the other. It was clear to Münster that this was one of those frequent occasions when any kind of conversation was, if not prohibited, at the very least pointless.

Instead he switched on the radio, and as they drove through the deserted streets that Sunday morning, they were able to listen to the eight o'clock news, which was mainly about developments in the Balkans and yet more neo-Nazi disturbances in eastern Germany.

Then came the weather forecast, promising glorious weather with cloudless skies and temperatures approaching sixty degrees.

He sighed discreetly, and it struck him that if it had been his wife in the passenger seat beside him, instead of a newly operated-on fifty-seven-year-old detective chief inspector, he would probably have placed his hand on her sun-warmed thigh at about this point.

Ah well, one o'clock would arrive sooner or later, even today.

They parked outside the overgrown opening in the lilac hedge. Münster switched off the engine and unfastened his safety belt.

'No, you stay here,' insisted Van Veeteren, shaking his head. 'I don't want you breathing down my neck. This calls for solitary reflection. Leave me in peace and wait for an hour down by the church.'

He started to wriggle his way out of the car. He was obviously hampered by his surgical wound; he was forced to cling on to the roof of the car and pull himself up by the strength of his arms, rather than straining his stomach muscles. Münster rushed round to assist him, but the chief inspector was adamant in rejecting any attempt to help.

'One hour,' he repeated, checking his watch. 'I'll walk down to the church under my own steam. The slope is in the right direction, so there shouldn't be a problem.'

'Wouldn't it be best if . . .' began Münster, but Van Veeteren interrupted him.

'Stop nannying me, damn you! I've had enough of that. If I haven't turned up at the church by half past ten, you can drive up and see where I've got to!'

'All right,' said Münster. 'But be careful.'

'Clear off,' said Van Veeteren. 'Is the door open, by the way?'

'The key's hanging from a nail under the gutter,' said Münster. 'On the right.'

'Thanks,' said Van Veeteren.

Münster got back into the car, managed to turn around in the narrow road and set off through the trees towards the village.

It's amazing, he thought. We must have spent a hundred hours sniffing around this place. But I wouldn't be at all surprised if he found something we'd missed.

Not surprised in the least.

Van Veeteren stayed by the roadside until Münster's white Audi had vanished among the trees. Then he forced his way through the hedge and took possession of the Big Shadow.

The garden was overgrown, no two ways about that. He stuck a toothpick in his mouth and looked around. He began walking around the house but was forced to give up about halfway when he found himself up to the armpits in nettles. No matter, he thought. It wasn't too difficult to get an impression of what it must have looked like once upon a time. A plot of land taken over by man around the middle of the last century, tamed by plough and harrow, a lot of hard work and tender loving care. But now well on the way back into the arms of Mother Nature. Aspen and birch saplings had eaten into large chunks of the orchard; paved areas, the cellar and outhouses were lost in undergrowth and covered in moss; and the big barn, which had presumably been the famous poultry farm, would surely not survive many more winters. It was very clear that a border had been crossed – the limit beyond which it was no longer possible to reclaim what nature had taken hold of.

Not for an old lag living on his own, at least.

The Big Shadow?

With hindsight it was obvious that the house name was prophetic. He found the key, and after considerable effort succeeded in opening the door. He had to bend down so as not to hit his head on the door frame, and inside there was only just sufficient headroom for him to stand upright. He recalled having read in the newspapers about a month ago that the average height of people had shot up remarkably over the past hundred years. His own six feet two inches would presumably have been considered abnormal when the first settlers moved into this house.

Two rooms and a kitchen on the ground floor. A narrow, creaking staircase led up from a three-foot-square hall to a loft full of old newspapers, broken furniture and other junk. A faint smell of soot and sun-warmed dust clung to the rafters. He sneezed several times, then went back down to the kitchen. He felt the big iron stove, as if expecting to find it hot. Examined the bad reproduction of an almost equally bad original landscape painting hanging over the sofa, then entered the living room. The cracked windowpanes. A sideboard. Table and four ill-matched chairs. A sofa and a typically 1950s television set. A sagging bookshelf with getting on for a hundred books, most of them cheap crime novels or adventure stories. On the wall to the right of the stove was a mirror and a framed black-and-white photograph of a runner breaking the finishing tape. His face seemed tormented, almost tortured. At first he thought it was Verhaven himself, but when he went up to it and examined it more closely, he saw the caption and recognized the man: Emil Zatopek. The Czech locomotive, as he was called. The self-torturer. The man who overcame the pain barrier.

Had he been Verhaven's ideal?

Or was it just typical of the time? Zatopek had been the

king of the track in the early fifties, if his memory served him rightly. Or one of them, at least.

He left the living room for the bedroom and stood gazing at the double bed that, despite its modest size, took up almost all the floor space.

But a double bed? Yes, of course, Verhaven had lived with a lot of women. Not all of them had been murdered. At least, he assumed not.

'Was this your bedroom, then?' muttered Van Veeteren, fumbling for a new toothpick. 'Did you get one night's sleep as a free man, or didn't he even allow you that?'

He left the bedroom.

What the hell am I doing here? he thought suddenly. What am I kidding myself that I can sort out by strutting around here? Even if I begin to form an impression of what Verhaven was really like, that's not going to get me one inch closer to the answer.

The answer to the question of who murdered him, that is.

He was overcome with exhaustion and sat down at the kitchen table. Closed his eyes and watched the flickering yellow light that floated past from right to left. Always from right to left: he wondered what that might be due to. They had warned him that he would have moments of weakness, but he hadn't fully realized that they would be as treacherous as this, practically making his legs give way under him.

He rested his head in his hands. Reinhart always said you should never try to think about anything important when your head's not right. It's better to shut down altogether, otherwise you'll only fill it with a lot of garbage.

An unusually ugly tablecloth, he thought therefore, when he had opened his eyes again. But it seems somehow familiar. Didn't Aunt K. have one like it when I visited her in summer about the beginning of the fifties? In that boathouse heated by the summer sun, where you could hear the water lapping under the floorboards. It felt a long way away from the Big Shadow in both time and space, but it must have been around the time when Verhaven left his father here in Kaustin to lead his own independent life.

Forty years ago, or thereabouts.

And then things turned out the way they did . . .

That's life, Van Veeteren thought. One big goddamn lottery!

Or wasn't it like that, in fact? Were there directions and patterns?

A determinant?

*

Münster leaned against the old gravestone and looked at the clock.

Ten minutes past ten. There were voices inside his head stubbornly urging him to go to the car and immediately drive back to the Big Shadow. The chief inspector had been on his own for more than an hour at this point – recently operated on, weak and sickly; it could be regarded as irresponsible not to keep an eye on him.

But there were other voices as well. Van Veeteren hadn't actually insisted on any more than one hour of solitary majesty, although he had set the limit at half past ten. Münster had to choose between arriving too soon and arriving too late. An awkward choice, certainly; but if he stuck to the later time, at least he would escape being told off for disturbing the chief inspector's holy thought processes. If Van Veeteren turned out to be unconscious somewhere among all the junk, that would be a serious matter, to be sure. But he'd rather turn up as an angel of mercy than as an unwelcome and premature intruder.

Münster closed his eyes. From inside the church came the muted, monotonous chanting of today's sermon. He had watched the whole flock – about twenty pious souls – come wandering at regular intervals along the newly raked gravel path to the church door, where the shepherd had greeted each one with a handshake and a watery smile. Münster had tried to remain discreetly in the background, but the prelate had naturally got wind of him and fixed him with his beckoning gaze. Who was this person remaining wilfully outside the temple gates?

But Münster had resisted. The other sheep had trotted slowly and patiently inside. The shepherd followed them in. The bells binged and bonged ten o'clock, a flock of temporarily homeless pigeons fled the steeple, and the service got under way.

The average age was unusually high, Münster noted as the doors closed behind them. It was clear to him that all the faithful would doubtless have deepened and sealed their relationship with the church within ten to fifteen years at most. By lying down to rest in the churchyard, that is.

Or being laid to rest, rather.

On a day like today he was almost inclined to envy them, just a little bit. Or at the very least to detect something serene and transfigured in this well-tended graveyard surrounding the ancient stone-built church with its recently repaired and profane red-tiled roof and black lacquered weathercock. Here, obviously, there was no cruel and avenging God. No trumpets sounding on the day of judgement. No eternal and inevitable damnation.

Only tenderness, reconciliation and the forgiveness of sins.

Mercy?

And then Synn intervened and interrupted (or joined in) his pious thoughts. The image of her naked body, curled up on her side in a summer-warm bed, her knees raised and her dark hair fanned out over the pillow and her shoulders. This image filled him with another kind of tenderness, the same uncomplicated happiness he had felt at the kitchen table a few hours ago, perhaps. And before long, he was recalling the talk about making love in the sight of God in the Garden of Eden He had created. If they could work out how to keep the children out of the way for a while, that ought not to be impossible. They had managed it before; soon he was busy recalling various moments of passion . . . Making love in the rowboat on Lake Weimar last summer. In the middle of the lake with only the sky and the gulls as witnesses. And another occasion, early one morning high up on a Greek mountain with a panoramic view over the deep blue Mediterranean Sea. Not to mention the beach at Laguna Monda – that was before Bart was born, one of the very first times . . . They had lain there in the warm, dense darkness with the breeze from the mountains caressing her body, her incredibly smooth skin and her . . .

A chord from the organ brought him back to his senses. Presumably it was intended to wake up a few other sheep dozing off in the flock inside the church. He opened his eyes and shook his head. The hymn-singing gathered strength. With the vicar's baritone, magnified by the microphone around his neck, leading the way, it floated out of the open windows and rose unshackled through the leaves of the trees, up into the heavens, where it was received and enjoyed, one can assume, by those already in residence to whom it was doubtless and unreservedly addressed.

Hallelujah, Münster thought, and yawned.

He sat up and checked his watch.

Twenty-seven minutes past. Time to act. He stood up, made his way through the graves and jumped over the wall next to where his car was parked. He had just opened the door and was about to get in when he clapped eyes on the chief inspector. He was strolling towards the churchyard, an unpleasant sight with his shirt unbuttoned down to his navel and a garishly coloured handkerchief knotted over his head. There were sweat stains under his arms, and his face was worryingly red; but amid all the wretchedness was a certain expression of satisfaction. A sort of restrained, contented grimace that could hardly be overlooked. Certainly not by somebody who had been around for as long as Münster had.

'There you are,' he said. 'I was just going to get you. How's it gone?'

'OK, thanks,' said the chief inspector, removing the handkerchief from his head. 'Damned hot, though.'

'You took your time, I reckon,' Münster ventured. 'Was there really all that much to scratch around in up there?'

Van Veeteren shrugged.

'There was a bit,' he said. 'I had a chat with the neighbours on the way down as well. Had a beer with the Czermaks. It was all go.'

He wiped his forehead. Münster waited, but the chief inspector said nothing more.

'Did you get anywhere?' Münster asked eventually.

'Hmm,' said Van Veeteren. 'I think so. Let's be off, then.'

As usual, Münster thought, slumping down behind the wheel. Just the same as ever.

'Where exactly did you get, then?' he asked once they had got under way, and the wind coming in through the windows had begun to restore the chief inspector's usual facial colour.

'I have an idea about who might have done it,' said Van Veeteren. 'An idea, remember that, Inspector! I'm not claiming that I know anything.'

'Who?' asked Münster, but he knew that he was wasting his time.

Instead of answering, the chief inspector leaned back in his seat, stuck his elbow out of the window and started to whistle *Carmen*.

Münster stepped on the accelerator and switched on the radio.

NINE

11 SEPTEMBER 1981

33

At least nobody would be able to say that she hadn't been out in good time.

Marlene started prowling around the Covered Market as early as half past eight. He didn't usually finish until about a quarter past nine or even half past, but obviously, it was best to leave a safety margin. The stakes were high, and Renate had made it clear that she wasn't prepared to wait any longer for her money.

A lousy two thousand guilders. A few years ago she'd have been able to cough up twice as much as that with no trouble at all. Simply dig down into her purse, pull out a bundle of notes and tell the dolled-up slut to shove the change up her ass.

It wouldn't really matter if Renate didn't get her money; Marlene wasn't dependent on her. But she was dependent on Raoul, and Renate happened to be Raoul's woman. For the time being, at least. Without him Marlene would soon be without an apartment and without any work, that was for sure. But what the hell, she could manage on her own account, of course she could, start again from scratch like she'd done before; but there was no denying that it was good to have everything taken care of and made easy for her. Certainly. She was living a pleasant life as middle age started to creep up on her . . .

So it was worth making an effort to scrape together the money she owed. She hadn't really understood how serious the situation was until last night, that was why she was a bit short of time now. Renate hadn't sounded the same as usual on the telephone; she wouldn't be able to get away with excuses this time, that had been very obvious.

Two thousand guilders. A quarter past ten at the Rote Moor. Otherwise, you're in the shit.

That was her problem, basically.

She'd phoned three or four friends, but it had been a waste of time, needless to say. She could have got a few hundred, maybe more, if she'd kept going a bit longer, but it was nearly midnight, and there were limits.

And then there was Leo Verhaven. He'd struck her as a possibility – perhaps the best one – the moment she'd put the receiver down after Renate's ultimatum.

Leo.

And he didn't even have a telephone.

That was somehow typical.

*

She checked that the van was parked where it usually stood. By the loading bay in Kreugerlaan. Then she wandered through the market hall and across the square, but she didn't see him anywhere. She wanted to bump into him as if by accident. A happy coincidence. Hover around like a cat faced with hot milk, perhaps.

Or would it be better to come straight to the point? Hard to say. Verhaven wasn't exactly easy to handle.

She stationed herself next to the monument in Zwille, where she could keep an eye on both the van and the lower part of the square. Sat down on one of the benches under the statue of Torres, lit a cigarette and waited. The pale autumn sun had risen over the rooftops and was spraying jets of heat onto her back and her neck, giving her a feeling of hope and well-being, despite everything. Now she was a cat in the sun again, and when she noticed the furtive looks being given her by some of the passing men, she automatically started adjusting her clothing; she took off her scarf, unfastened a couple of buttons in her blouse, opened her legs the couple of inches every man worthy of the name noticed without being aware of it . . .

This is me, she thought. I'm made for this, and I'm better at it than any other woman in the world.

That was an exaggeration; she knew it was, but just now she needed all the self-confidence she could talk herself into.

She checked her watch.

Twenty minutes to ten.

She had less than two hours left to live.

He turned up at a quarter to ten.

She stood up immediately, crossed over the street and bumped into him just as he was coming round the corner.

'Leo!' she said, and thought she'd made it sound as much of a nice surprise as she'd intended.

He stopped. Nodded in that slightly surly way of his. As if she'd interrupted him in the middle of some important calculation or fascinating line of thought. He gave her what might have been the beginnings of a smile. Perhaps there was hope after all.

She moved closer to him and placed her hand on his arm. Continued smiling. They'd had sex – she counted the occasions in a flash – six times. He was the hot type; no interest at all in foreplay or romantic stuff. Easy to start, hard to drive, as her friend Nellie usually said.

'Where are you going?' she said.

Verhaven shrugged. Nowhere, it seemed. Or at least, nowhere important.

'Could we get together, maybe?'

'Now?'

'Yes. I have to meet a friend of mine shortly, but after that if you like.'

He shrugged again. Not a good sign, she realized that, but she had no choice.

'I've got a little problem.'

'Really?' said Verhaven.

She hesitated. Looked rather worried as she stroked his arm.

'What kind of a problem?'

'Money.'

He didn't answer. Looked away and stared over her shoulder.

'Can you help me, please?'

Nicely put. Just the right pitch between pleading and pride.

'How much?'

'Two thousand guilders.'

'Go to hell.'

She ran out of steam.

'Please, Leo . . .'

'I have to go.'

She took hold of him with the other hand as well. Spoke close to his face now.

'Leo,' she said, 'it's so very, very important. I'll repay every single . . .'

'Let go!'

He tore himself free. She took a pace back. Bit her upper lip hard and managed to fill her eyes with tears in only one second.

'Leo . . .'

'Goodbye.'

He thrust her to one side and walked past her. She spun around.

'Leo!'

He didn't even stop. Kept on walking down Zwille and turned into Kreugerlaan. Oh, shit!

Fucking shit!

The tears were almost genuine now. She stamped several times and gritted her teeth. Shit!

A car pulled up beside her. The driver leaned over and rolled down the window.

'Like to come with me?'

Without hesitation she opened the door and jumped in.

When she had dried her tears with the handkerchief he held out for her, she saw who it was.

She also looked at her watch.

Ten to ten.

Maybe it would turn out OK after all.

TEN

23–28 MAY 1994

34

'Right, we're dropping this case as of now!'

The chief of police removed a dry leaf from a fig plant. Van Veeteren sighed and contemplated the blue-suited outline of his boss against the lush green background. The hell you are! he thought.

Although it didn't exactly come as a shock.

'We have more important things to do.'

Another leaf was selected for feeling and analysing. The chief inspector averted his eyes. He turned his attention instead to a half-chewed toothpick and waited for what came next, but nothing did. Not right away, at least. Hiller pushed his glasses up onto his forehead and continued fumbling with the plants. Van Veeteren sighed again; the chief of police's weakness for botanical pursuits was a constant and frequently discussed topic of conversation in the lower regions of the Maardam police station. There were a number of theories. Some considered the phenomenon to be an obvious substitute for a withered love life – elegant

Mrs Hiller was said to have put up the shutters after her fifth child – while another body of opinion supported the theory that the green panorama was in fact camouflage to conceal the secret microphones that served to record every word uttered in the sombre and solemn building that served as police headquarters. Inspector Markovic in Missing Persons generally advocated the so-called lack-of-potty-training theory, but most people, including Van Veeteren, felt it sufficient to maintain that, damn it all, the chief of police would have been much better as a head gardener.

A head gardener in a suit? he thought, stuffing the tooth-pick into the gap between the seat and the armrest of the leather armchair he was sitting in. Why not? The more time Hiller devoted to his potted plants and the less time he spent attending to his police duties, the better.

Leave the monkey to do whatever it wants in the jungle, Reinhart always said. Life is easier that way.

But at this stage the monkey had decided to interfere. Van Veeteren scratched tentatively at his scar.

'Crap,' he said.

He had evidently been expected to say something, after all. Hiller spun round.

'What do you mean by that?'

'Do I need to spell it out?' Van Veeteren asked, and blew his nose. His cold had been coming and going all day. Perhaps he was allergic to some of these weird plants; perhaps it was just returning to reality after his time in hospital that had got the better of him.

Or a combination of the two. The chief of police sat down at his desk.

'We have a dead body,' he said. 'With no head, no arms and legs . . .'

'Hands and feet,' said Van Veeteren.

'. . . nine months old by this time. After five weeks you have managed to establish that it might be Leopold Verhaven, convicted twice as a murderer of women. One of the country's most notorious criminals. And that's it.'

The chief inspector folded up his handkerchief.

'The only theory that makes sense,' Hiller went on, beginning to straighten out a yellow paper clip, 'is that it's an underworld killing. Somebody from his time in jail was waiting for him when he came out and killed him for some reason or other. Possibly after a fight, possibly by accident. Whatever, it is indefensible for us to waste any more time and money than we've already done. We have more important matters to deal with than underworld goings-on like this.'

'Crap,' said Van Veeteren again.

Hiller snapped the paper clip in two.

'Perhaps you could kindly elaborate a little on that comment.'

'By all means,' said Van Veeteren. 'You've been leaned on, haven't you?'

'What do you mean, leaned on?'

The chief of police raised his eyebrows and tried to look as if he didn't understand. Van Veeteren snorted.

'You're forgetting who you're talking to,' he said. 'Are you familiar with Klimke's razor?'

'Klimke's razor?' Hiller asked. This time the surprise was genuine.

'Yes. Simple guidelines for civilized and intelligent conversation.'

Hiller said nothing. Van Veeteren leaned back and closed his eyes for a few seconds before continuing. Might as well give him a salvo, he thought. It was some considerable time since he'd had one.

He cleared his throat and started shooting.

'The basic principle is balance. You can't demand any more of the person you're talking to than you are prepared to give of yourself. Decision-makers, persons in positions of power and careerists in general usually like to give the impression of possessing a little democratic polish – God only knows why, although it goes down well with the media, of course. They like to give the impression that they are conducting a reasoned two-way discussion or a conversation, call it what you like, when what they are really doing is giving orders. It seems to give them a mysterious feeling of satisfaction; old Nazi bigwigs used to like carrying on in a similar fashion. A mild, understanding, paternal tone of voice as they sent people off to the execution squads; don't take it personally, but . . .'

'That's enough!' snarled the chief of police. 'Explain what the hell you're talking about! In plain language, if you don't mind.'

Van Veeteren fished out another toothpick from his breast pocket.

'If you respond in plain language.'

'Of course,' said Hiller.

'All right. You only need to say yes or no, in fact. As I see it, this is how things stand: Leopold Verhaven has been murdered. For all those concerned – and I mean specifically the courts, the police, the general public and its deep-rooted respect for our more or less just legal system, and so on – for all those it would be damn convenient and satisfactory if we could decide that this case was an underworld killing and nothing more. Draw a line under it. Forget it and move on. Pay no more attention to this butchered old jailbird and concentrate instead on maintaining public order and other mythologies . . .'

'But?' interrupted Hiller.

'There's a snag,' said Van Veeteren.

'What's that?'

'It wasn't an underworld killing.'

Hiller said nothing.

'Leopold Verhaven was murdered because he was innocent of both the murders he was found guilty of, and because he knew who the real killer was.'

Ten seconds passed. The bells started ringing in the Oudeskerk. Hiller clasped his hands on the leather writing pad on the desk in front of him.

'Can you prove that?' he asked.

'No,' said Van Veeteren. 'Especially if we drop the case.'

Hiller started rubbing his thumbs together and tried to frown.

'You understand this as well as I do,' he said eventually. 'In some circumstances . . . In some circumstances we simply have to consider the public good above all else; it's as simple as that. In the unlikely event of your managing to winkle out a new murderer in this age-old business, who would get any satisfaction from that?'

'I would,' said Van Veeteren.

'You don't count,' said Hiller. 'Consider all the other interested parties and ask yourself if any of them would benefit. Let's take them one by one. The murdered women? No! Verhaven? No! The police and the courts? No! The general public and the legal system? No! . . .'

'The murderer? No?' said Van Veeteren. 'Don't forget him. He would no doubt be the happiest of all if he escaped punishment. Three murders, and he doesn't get arrested. Not bad. Not bad at all!'

Hiller put his glasses on. Leaned forward over his desk and allowed a few seconds to pass.

'There is no other murderer, only Verhaven,' he said eventually, emphatically. 'The case is dropped on the grounds of lack of evidence and concrete proof. It's dead.'

'You mean you are ordering me to allow a triple murderer to go free?'

The chief of police didn't respond. Leaned back again in his chair. Van Veeteren heaved himself out of the armchair. Stood with his hands in his pockets, swaying back and forth.

Waited.

'Are you sure about what you've said?' Hiller asked after a while.

Van Veeteren shook his head.

'I suspect it,' he said. 'I'm not sure yet.'

'And you also think you know who did it?'

Van Veeteren nodded and started to make his way slowly towards the door. The chief of police rubbed his thumbs together again and stared down at his desk.

'Wait a moment,' he said as Van Veeteren took hold of the door handle. 'If you . . . er, if you really do unearth something that will stand up in court, that changes everything, of course. The worst thing we could do is to set something in motion that we can't finish off. Put somebody in the dock, and he's discharged . . . You can imagine what that would mean, I hope. Fourteen hundred journalists, first of all, screeching on about corruption and miscarriage of justice in the Verhaven case, and then incompetence and abuse of power and God only knows what else, when we let the real murderer go because we haven't got enough convincing evidence. I assume you are clear about that? You can surely imagine what a mess we'd be in?'

Van Veeteren said nothing. The chief of police sat for some time in silence, clenching his teeth and fiddling with his watch. Then he stood up and turned his back on the chief inspector.

'You'll have to do it all yourself. As from today Münster joins Reinhart's team. I don't want to know about anything.'

'That suits me down to the ground,' said Van Veeteren. 'I'm on sick leave, in any case.'

'Yours won't be the head that rolls; I hope you can understand that as well. I don't want any unnecessary trouble right now.'

'You can trust me,' said Van Veeteren. 'You can go back to your potted plants. We must cultivate our garden.'

'Excuse me?' said the chief of police.

A waste of time, Van Veeteren thought as he left the room.

35

'Tell me about your illness,' he said.

She lifted the snotty-nosed girl onto her knee and looked somewhat doubtfully at him.

No wonder. His cover story was hardly a masterstroke – a fifty-seven-year-old university lecturer busy writing a dissertation on certain types of hip injuries contracted at birth! What a likely story! He hadn't even bothered to check any details in advance, just tried to give the impression that his method was statistical. A sociomedical approach, he'd explained. He had equipped himself with a form that wouldn't have withstood a close examination, of course, but even so – provided he kept it concealed inside the folder he had in front of him – it ought to give the suggestion of professionalism.

Or so he tried to convince himself. Who cares if she was confused, anyway? The main thing was that she answered his questions; she could have as many suspicions as she liked afterwards.

'What do you want to know?' she asked.

'When did it start?'

'When I was born, of course.'

He ticked a box on the form.

'In which year was she confined to bed?'

She thought that one over.

'Nineteen eighty-two, I think. Completely, that is. She spent most of her time in bed before that as well, but I don't remember her ever walking, or even standing up, after Christmas 1981. I left home in June 1982.'

'Did she ever use a stick?'

She shook her head.

'Never.'

'Did you have much contact with her after you'd moved out?'

'No. What does that have to do with your research?'

He bit his tongue.

'I just want to get a few things about the relationship between you pinned down,' he explained and ticked another box. 'So you are saying that she was a total invalid from 1982 until her death?'

'Yes.'

'Where did she spend her last years?'

'In Wappingen. Together with a Sister of Mercy in a little apartment. She had divorced my father – I don't think she wanted to be a burden on him any longer. Or something of that sort.'

'Did you visit her there?'

'Yes.'

'How many times?'

She thought for a moment. The girl started whimpering again. Slid down onto the floor and hid away from his gaze.

'Three,' she said. 'It's a long way.'

'And her state?'

'What do you mean?'

'How was she?'

She shrugged.

'The same as usual. A bit happier, perhaps.'

'But confined to bed?'

'Yes, of course.'

Damn, Van Veeteren thought. There's something that doesn't add up.

When he emerged into the bright sunshine, he had a short but intense dizzy spell. Was forced to hang on to the iron railing that surrounded the row of houses while he closed his eyes and recovered.

I need a beer, he thought. A beer and a cigarette.

Ten minutes later he had found a table under what

looked like a plane tree outside a café. He emptied the tall glass in two swigs and ordered another. Lit a cigarette and leaned back.

Damn! he thought again. What the hell is it that doesn't add up?

How far could it be to Wappingen?

A hundred and fifty miles? At least.

But if he went to bed early, surely he could raise the strength to drive 150 miles? With stops and rests and all that. It wouldn't matter if he had to spend the night there. It wasn't time he was short of nowadays. On the contrary.

He checked the address in his folder.

I'd better ring and arrange a meeting.

Why change my cover story when it seems to be working so well?

Beer number two arrived, and he sucked the froth off it.

What a damned awful story this is, he thought. Have I ever followed a thinner thread?

Just as well that nobody else is involved, thank God for that.

36

'What do we do in here?' wondered Jung.

'We could have a bite to eat, for instance,' said Münster. 'Sit down and try to look as if you're at home here.'

Jung sat down tentatively and looked around the austere premises.

'That won't be easy,' he said. 'But what's the point? I assume we're not being allowed to sit here in the town's most expensive restaurant as a reward for our virtue.'

'Can you see that character in the dark blue suit next to the grand piano?' Münster asked.

'Of course,' said Jung. 'I'm not blind.'

'According to Reinhart, he's one of the top brass in the neo-Nazi movement. His name's Edward Masseck, incidentally.'

'He doesn't look like the type.'

'No, he's an anonymous sort of character, Reinhart says. But he's well documented. He's the one behind an awful lot of shit, it seems. Arson in refugee hostels. Riots, desecration of graves, you name it. In any case, he's sitting there and waiting for a contact from big business, a real big shot. We don't know who, but when he turns up we're supposed to let them sit and shuffle paper for a quarter of an hour or so. Then you go and phone from the vestibule while I go and arrest them. Reinhart and a couple of other officers are in two cars just around the corner.'

'I get it,' said Jung. 'Why can't Reinhart do it himself?'

'Masseck knows him,' said Münster. 'Anyway, let's order something to eat. What do you say to some lobster mousse to start with?'

'I had that for breakfast,' said Jung. 'But I expect I can force down a bit more.'

'This Verhaven business,' said Jung as they waited for their main course. 'How's it going?'

Münster shrugged.

'I don't know. I'm also off the case. It looks as if they don't want to put any more resources into it. I suppose that's understandable.'

'Why?'

'I expect they're scared of stirring things up in the courts again. There could be one hell of a row if he should prove to be innocent, especially in the press and on television.'

Jung scratched the back of his neck.

'What does the chief inspector have to say about it?'

Münster hesitated.

'I don't know. He's still on sick leave. But it's obvious that he's not sitting at home, twiddling his thumbs.'

'Is it true that he's got somebody on the hook? There was some talk about that in the canteen yesterday afternoon. Somebody who might have done it, that is?'

There was no doubting Jung's curiosity, and it was obvious to Münster that he must have been aching to ask that question from the moment they'd sat down.

'I don't know, to be honest,' he said. 'I was out at Kaustin with him the day after they released him from the hospital. He pottered around at the house for an hour or so, and then he appeared with that look . . . you know what he's like.'

Jung nodded.

'It's damned amazing,' he said. 'We spend several weeks going through that village with a fine-tooth comb – four or five of us – without finding anything of interest at all. Then he drives out there and picks up the trail inside an hour. Astonishing. Do you think it really is possible?'

Münster thought for a few seconds.

'What do you think?' he said.

'No idea,' said Jung. 'You're the one who knows him best.'

That's true, I suppose, Münster thought. Although he sometimes had the feeling that the closer to Van Veeteren you got, the more unfathomable he became.

'It's hard to say,' he said. 'He's certainly on to something, though, no doubt about that. But the last time I saw him he was going on about thin threads. And how long a flabby policeman could be stuck in a spider's web, that kind of thing. He didn't sound all that enthusiastic, but you know what he's like.'

'I certainly do,' said Jung. 'He's a one-off, that's for sure.'

There was a clear tone of admiration in Jung's voice; there was no mistaking it, and Münster suddenly wished he could think of a way of conveying that to the chief inspector. Perhaps it wouldn't be completely impossible, he thought. Since the cancer operation, he'd had the impression that their cooperation and level of communication had improved noticeably. There was more of a feeling of equality and more mutual respect. Or however it ought to be expressed.

Despite Van Veeteren's unfathomability. And it was only in the early stages.

'No,' he said. 'Van Veeteren is Van Veeteren.' He glanced over at the grand piano. Why hadn't anybody appeared? Reinhart had guessed it would be one o'clock, but it was twenty past by now.

'I don't know,' said Jung. 'Anyway, here comes our sole. Yum-yum!'

Forty-five minutes later, Edward Masseck paid his bill and left. He had been all alone from start to finish. Jung had just ordered a second helping of candied walnuts, but they decided to pay and report to their colleagues.

'Hell's bells!' said Reinhart when he heard that his prey had escaped. 'How much did the meals cost?'

'It's all yours,' said Münster, handing him the bill.

Reinhart stared at the pale blue scrap of paper.

'Well I'll be damned,' he said. 'Stauff and I have been sitting in the car for two hours with half a packet of peanuts between us.'

'It was an excellent meal,' said Jung from the back seat. 'Maybe it would be a good idea to try again tomorrow?'

37

Dvořák's New World Symphony had enveloped him during the last fifty miles or so, and that had been the right choice of music. Over the years he had begun to get a feeling for this kind of thing – the relationship between the task he was involved with, the weather and time of year and music. There were rising and falling movements that needed to be followed, not resisted. Flows and analogies that worked together, harmonized and illuminated one another . . . Or however you might like to express it. It was difficult to put such things into words and explain them. Much easier to feel them.

Ah well, everything gets easier as the years go by. But as the years passed he had also become more wary of words. That wasn't exactly surprising – bearing in mind his usual working environment, in which it was more of the exception than the rule when anybody stuck to the truth.

Language is lying, as somebody said.

Anyway, the New World. And as the skies cleared and

the afternoon sun started to dry out the persistent rain that had fallen during the night and morning, he approached his goal. His fears about dizzy spells and lack of judgement in traffic had proven to be unfounded. He had also made frequent stops; sat with coffee and cake in depressing concrete-and-glass roadside cafés, gone for short walks, stretched his legs again and again and even performed gymnastic exercises as recommended in the post-operative programme he'd had thrust into his hand on being released from hospital.

He had also been careful to refrain from alcohol and tobacco. He had to get back home again. Preferably, in any case.

His stock of toothpicks had been exhausted long before the Dvořák.

He parked in a little square called Cazarros Plats, and as he looked around for a suitable place to eat, he wondered who Cazarro might have been. He sounded more like a conquistador than a north European statesman, that was for sure.

Wedged between a department store and an undistinguished 1950s local government building was a little Italian restaurant specializing in pizzas and pasta dishes. He decided to give it a try. His meeting with Sister Marianne was at five o'clock, and he didn't have all the time in the world.

But the food wasn't the main point anyway. That was a glass of red wine and that longed-for cigarette.

And also the need to concentrate before what was in store. He had made an unnecessary fuss regarding preparations many times in the past, but there was something special about this occasion that had been clear to him from the moment he set off from home. Something he wasn't able to handle and that he'd given up trying to control a long time ago.

A game in which he was much more of a chip than a punter.

It was not a new sensation, just an example of or a variation on that old deterministic principle, presumably: the unavoidable business of patterns and preordained order in the environment. Of increasing or decreasing entropy.

No, those thoughts about the arbitrary nature of life that he had flirted with the other day were something he now felt no enthusiasm for.

If there really was a creator or a force – or at the very least an all-seeing eye – it must be able to look down from its elevated position and make out the lines, the veins and arteries in time and space. The structures that seem so incomprehensible from our usual worm's-eye view.

And the mutual connections and consequences of

actions. Was there any other possibility? This must be what constituted the categories of a god.

These patterns.

But if there was no higher force – did it really make much difference?

What about Anselm and the proof of God's existence? Hadn't he always had trouble in seeing the point of it?

He fumbled in his breast pocket for a toothpick, then remembered the state of affairs and lit a cigarette instead.

Wouldn't the pattern exist even so, in the same way as DNA spirals and the crystals making up snowflakes have always existed, irrespective of whether there has been anyone or anything to observe them?

What does a fractal care about a camera? he asked himself.

Good questions. Recurring questions. He put down his cigarette, poked listlessly at his fettuccine and took a sip of wine. It was hard to feel really hungry these days, for whatever reason. Whether it was due to the missing piece of bowel or something else.

Justice was another aspect.

Simpler and easier to deal with, he had always thought, even if he had never really needed to put it to the ultimate test. Despite more than thirty years in the force.

The tool of justice. That was how he needed to regard himself, after all, if he was to be really serious about it. It sounded a little high-flown, even a little pathetic; but it wasn't something he went on about. It was merely an attitude he adopted in order to motivate himself, but it was a damned important one.

When it came to justifying his own existence and the work he did, he sometimes needed to dig deep, that was something he had learned. Deeper and deeper, perhaps – as if with every year that passed the very foundations became coated with a new and thicker layer of mud and dirt stirred up by the underworld in which he spent every working day.

Something like that anyway.

He still hadn't found an answer to the key question. He had formulated it several years ago in connection with the G file, and it wasn't especially complicated: Am I prepared to take things into my own hands when the law and the institutions fail?

If he was standing beside a murderer or some other violent criminal, and knew for certain – with 100 per cent certainty – that the person was guilty, would it be morally more correct to let him go because of lack of proof rather than ensuring that justice was done?

He inhaled on his cigarette.

There were endless special cases, of course, and it was impossible to oversee the consequences. He had been through it all many times in theory, and perhaps he ought to be grateful that he hadn't needed to put the theory to the test.

It had been a close thing at times, though. Especially then, seven years ago, in Linden.

And there was nothing to indicate that it would become relevant on this occasion, either.

Or was there?

He looked at his watch and saw that it was high time he paid and set off for her apartment, if he didn't want the nun to have to wait for him.

The apartment was painted white and tastefully appointed. There was a minimum of furniture; in the living room, which was where she took him, there was only a low couch, two floor cushions and a table, with a bookcase and a prayer bench in a corner. On the walls were a crucifix and two candles in brass holders. And a picture of a church window, probably Chartres Cathedral. That was all.

No television, no armchairs, no knick-knacks. The floor was covered by a large dark-coloured carpet.

Good, thought Van Veeteren, sitting down on the couch. Nothing but essentials. The essence.

She served tea from an earthenware teapot. Simple cups, without handles. Thin cookies. No sugar, no milk.

She didn't even ask if he wanted any, but he didn't, in any case.

She was old, at least fifteen years older than Van Veeteren, but she radiated vitality and alertness like an aura. It was clear that he was facing a person who inspired and demanded respect beyond the norm. The familiar feeling of deference came creeping up on him, the kind he sometimes felt when confronted by deeply religious and serene individuals – people who had worked out the answer to questions he himself had barely been able to formulate. A deference that was just as naturally complemented by its opposite, contempt and loathing, when he met the opposite type: submissive and loudly braying sheep, dominated by the herd instinct, the sanctimonious fellow travellers of hypocrisy.

He had sensed her qualities the moment they shook hands; she was a slim, erect woman with serious-looking brown eyes and a high forehead. She sat down opposite him, sinking onto one of the cushions with a graceful movement reminiscent of a curtsy. It struck him that as she squatted there with her legs hidden underneath her in the Asian manner, she could almost have been a twenty-five-year-old Buddhist woman. But in fact she was a Roman Catholic nun, three times as old as that.

'Help yourself,' she said.

He sipped the aromatic tea, groping for the folder he had placed on the floor beside him.

'I think I must ask you to clarify your intentions once more.'

He nodded. It was obvious that to produce the folder and the form would be an insult. Klimke's razor, that he had justifiably thrown into the face of the chief of police only the other day, now threatened to bring shame upon himself, and nobody else.

'I must apologize,' he said. 'My name is indeed Van Veeteren, but I am not who I said I was. I am a detective chief inspector, stationed in Maardam. My visit has to do with a case that I would prefer not to go into in detail. Will you be satisfied with my assurance that I have the best of intentions, but am dealing with a matter wallowing in evil?'

She smiled.

'Yes,' she said. 'It's to do with Anna, if I understood you rightly?'

Van Veeteren nodded.

'She lived here with you for a few years before she died, I think. From 1987 to 1992, is that correct?'

'Yes.'

'You cared for her and looked after her?'

'Yes.'

'Why?'

'Because that is my vocation. That's the way we work

in our order. It's a way of creating meaning. And love between people. Anna got in touch with us; there are about twenty of us sisters, and I was free at the time.'

He thought for a moment.

'I take it that you became . . . quite close to her?'

'We meant a lot to each other.'

'Confided in each other?'

'Of course.'

'Can you tell me about her illness?'

'What do you want to know?'

'Was she confined to bed all the time, for instance?'

It was clear to him that she already knew and had considered in advance what the conversation would be about, but perhaps that didn't matter.

'She improved.'

'Improved?'

She suddenly became more serious.

'Yes, Chief Inspector. She improved. You are doubtless aware that her wounds were not confined to her hips. There is such a thing as a soul as well.'

'So I've heard,' said Van Veeteren with unintentional irony. 'What on earth are you hinting at?'

She drew a deep breath and straightened her back.

'Irrespective of whether or not you are a believer,' she said, 'perhaps you can agree that many physical phenomena also have a psychological side. A spiritual dimension.'

She spoke very slowly, as if she had prepared the words in advance and wanted to be certain that none of them escaped his attention.

'Can you explain in a little more detail?' he said.

'Preferably not. It is a matter of trust as well. Not spelled out, but just as binding. I'm sure you understand what I mean.'

'You consider that you are bound by professional secrecy?'

'To some extent, yes.'

He nodded.

'But when the wounds in the soul had healed, her handicap also became less severe, is that it?'

'Yes.'

'How much better did she become? Could she move around? With the aid of a rolling walker or walking sticks, for instance?'

'Yes.'

'Did she go out?'

'I took her out in a wheelchair every day.'

'But she never went out on her own?'

'Not as far as I know.'

He looked past her and out of the window.

'Can you tell me what you were doing on June fifth, 1992?' he asked.

'No.'

'Do you know what Anna was doing that day?'

She didn't reply. Looked at him with those calm, brown eyes of hers without an ounce of worry or embarrassment.

'How far is it from here to Ulmentahl?'

'Eighteen miles,' she said with no hesitation.

He drank the rest of his tea and allowed the silence to settle on the low table. It's remarkable how information can be passed on via silence, he thought. He could have asked important questions now; that would have been the normal procedure, no doubt about that. He would have received no answers, but he was used to reading the nuances in unspoken words. But this was different. There was an infinitely wide gap between this almost stylized situation and the usual unspoken exchanges. For a moment he could feel a dizzy spell coming on again. Possibly not the kind of dizziness due to his operation, but nevertheless a feeling of weakness, a loss of strength and a feeling that he was losing his foothold . . . Or that there was something about which he was the only person to have total knowledge. And hence the total and unavoidable responsibility.

'Those wounds in her soul . . .' he said eventually. 'Have you any idea about what caused them?'

'She never told me about it.'

'I have gathered that. But I asked you if you had any idea about it.'

She smiled faintly once more.

'I can't go into this, Chief Inspector. It doesn't belong to me any more.'

He paused for a few seconds.

'Do you believe in divine justice?' he asked.

'Absolutely.'

'And earthly justice?'

'That too. I am sorry that I am inhibited with regard to what I can tell you, but I think you already know what you need to know. It is not up to me to break my confidence and to speculate. If she had wanted me to have a complete knowledge of everything, she would have told me everything, of course. But she didn't. If it had been the intention that I should take the matter further, I would have known. But that is not the case.'

'So Nemesis is my role?'

'Perhaps. A profession is also a calling, is that not the case?'

He sighed.

'May I ask you a personal question that has nothing to do with this?'

'Of course. Please do.'

'Do you believe in a God who intervenes?'

She clasped her hands over her knee.

'Certainly,' she said. 'I believe that to the greatest possible degree.'

'How does He intervene?'

'In many ways. Through people.'

'And you believe that He is careful when He selects His agents?'

'Why should He not be?'

'It was just a thought,' said Van Veeteren.

Suspicions! he thought as he sat down in the first of his stopping places on the way home. Suspicions and thin air.

He sighed. Ferrati, the prosecutor, would kill himself laughing if Van Veeteren approached him with stuff like this.

Without really thinking what he was doing, he started to draw a series of circles in the margin of the evening paper on the table in front of him. He contemplated the pattern that was emerging and at the same time tried to summarize the situation:

If Verhaven really was innocent, it *could* be that the real murderer was the person he *suspected*. Furthermore, it was *not impossible* that the invalid Anna, who had died six months before the murder, *suspected* this. In any case, he *had the feeling* that Sister Marianne *presumed* that Anna was the one who had visited Verhaven in prison . . . In which case, of course, it was *possible* that she had told him what she *thought*!

My God, Van Veeteren thought. What a deduction!

In schematic form, along the edge of the crumpled newspaper, the chain of thought looked even more dodgy, if that was possible. A series of clumsily drawn circles joined by feeble lines the size of a spider's thread. Damn it all! Solid proof, Heller had gone on about. If he saw this, he would probably accept my resignation without further ado, Van Veeteren thought.

But even so, he knew that he was right. This is how it had happened. The murderer was surrounded. Van Veeteren had no doubt. It was obvious.

He could picture Leopold Verhaven as a young man – the successful athlete. Fast, strong and vital; on his way to entering the record books . . . In the middle of the naïve, optimistic 1950s. The decade of the Cold War, but also of optimism in many respects. Wasn't that the case?

And then?

How had things turned out?

What a complete and permanent change of fortune!

Wasn't the bottom line that Verhaven's fate was symbolic? What kind of a bizarre sequence of events was this, spread out over almost half a century, that had led to the man's death, and that Van Veeteren was sitting here now trying to conjure up in his mind's eye? What was the significance of his probing into forgotten deaths from the past? That had taken place during that failed, worn-out life?

Was this really just a straightforward part of Van Veeteren's job?

As he sat there gazing out into the dusk that was descending over the edge of the forest and the featureless section of motorway, it struck him that, in fact, everything had come to an end a long time ago. That he was the last, forgotten soldier, or actor, in a play, or war, that everybody else had left years ago, and that nobody could care less about his efforts and undertakings. No matter if they were fellow actors, opponents or spectators.

Close down the case, he thought.

Close down Chief Inspector Van Veeteren. Offer a draw, or tip the board over. Stop all these pointless activities linked to his own vanity. There's a murderer on the loose; leave him alone!

He paid and went back to his car. Picked out Monteverdi from the pile of CDs, and as the first notes were released from the speakers, he knew that he had no intention of giving up. Not yet, in any case.

What the hell! he muttered. Justitia or Nemesis, same thing!

38

'Police!'

He held up his ID for half a second, and after three he was in the hall.

'I want to ask you some questions about the murders of Leopold Verhaven, Marlene Nietsch and Beatrice Holden. Can we do that here, or do you want to accompany me to the police station?'

The man hesitated, but only for a second.

'Come this way.'

They went into the living room. Münster took out his notebook with the questions.

'Can you tell me what you were doing on August twenty-fourth, last year?'

The man shrugged.

'You must be joking. How can I be expected to remember that?'

'It'll be best for you if you try. You didn't happen to be in Kaustin?'

'Certainly not.'

'Had you any reason to be hostile towards Leopold Verhaven?'

'Hostile? Of course not.'

'So it's not the case that he knew about things that could be dangerous for you?'

'What on earth could they be?'

'Were you in Maardam on September eleventh, 1981? That's the day when Marlene Nietsch was murdered.'

'No. What are you getting at?'

'Is it not the case that you were in the area around the Covered Market that morning? Kreuger Plejn and Zwille and thereabouts?'

'No.'

'At about half past nine, ten o'clock?'

'No, I've already said no.'

'How can you be so sure what you were doing and not doing one day thirteen years ago?'

No answer.

'What about Saturday April sixth, 1962, then? That was when it all started, wasn't it?'

'You are making insinuations. I would like you to go and leave me in peace now.'

'Did you not call in on Beatrice Holden that Saturday afternoon? While Verhaven was out on business?'

'I'm not going to put up with this utter rubbish.'

'When did your love life with your wife come to an end?'

'What the hell has that got to do with this business?'

'You were forced to satisfy your needs elsewhere, isn't that the case? After she was confined to bed. There must have been others as well as Beatrice Holden and Marlene Nietsch . . . Why did you kill just those two?'

He stood up.

'Or have you killed others as well?'

'Get out! If you think you can scare me into saying things that are not true, you can tell your superiors that they're wasting their time.'

Münster closed his notebook.

'Thank you,' he said. 'This has been a very enlightening conversation.'

'Yes, it could be him,' said Münster as he sat down opposite the chief inspector.

Van Veeteren parted the curtains.

'Be ready in case he comes out,' he said. 'You never know what he could get up to.'

'He won't be easy to arrest,' said Münster. 'I don't think he's the type to break down and submit.'

'Damn and blast!' said Van Veeteren. 'Although we've only given him the first warning, so to speak.'

Münster knew that was what Van Veeteren had in mind when he'd sent his assistant in advance. So that he could save himself for a more important, possibly crucial encounter.

Good thinking, of course; but there again, it must give the murderer a chance to prepare his defence. He pointed that out, but Van Veeteren merely shrugged.

'Very possible,' he said. 'But it could also be those preparations that trip him up. In any case, he's not in an enviable position. He knows that we know. Just think about that. He's a rat trapped in a corner. We are the cats waiting for him to come out.'

'We don't have any proof,' said Münster. 'We won't get any, either.'

'He doesn't know that.'

Münster thought that over.

'But he'll soon realize it, surely. If we know that he has three murders on his conscience, it must seem a bit odd that we don't arrest him.'

Van Veeteren stubbed out his cigarette in annoyance and let go of the curtains.

'I know,' he muttered. 'It's a bit of my bowels they cut out, Münster, not my brain.'

Silence. Van Veeteren heaved a sigh and put a toothpick in his mouth. Münster ordered a beer and took out his notebook.

'You only asked the questions I told you to ask, I trust?' said Van Veeteren after a while.

'Of course,' said Münster. 'There's one thing that puzzles me, though.'

'What's that?'

'How did he know that she'd told Verhaven at the prison?'

Van Veeteren snorted.

'Because she told him so, of course. Just before she died, I assume. According to Sister Marianne, he went to see her that final day at the hospital.'

'She eased her conscience in both directions?'

'That's one way of putting it, yes. You might think she ought to have kept quiet altogether instead. That would have saved one life, at least. But people tend to get a bit obsessed by the truth.'

'What do you mean?' asked Münster.

Van Veeteren downed the rest of his beer.

'The truth can be a heavy burden to bear,' he said. 'It seems impossible to bear it alone in the long run. It would be good, though, if people could learn not to pass it on any old way.'

Münster pondered for a while.

'I've never thought of it like that before,' he said, looking out of the window. 'But there's a lot of truth in it, of course. He doesn't seem to have been overcome by panic, though.'

'No,' said Van Veeteren with a sigh. 'We may need to take some special measures in this case. But you can go home now. I'll sit here for a while and do a bit of thinking.'

Münster hesitated.

'I hope you'll let me know if I can do anything else to help. I take it the case hasn't been reopened?'

'It's closed and boarded up,' said Van Veeteren. 'Anyway, thanks.'

Münster left the bar, and as he crossed the street on the way to his car, he found himself feeling sorry for the chief inspector again. That was the second time in a short period – only a month or so – so perhaps there was some truth in what people say:

The older they get, the more human they seem to appear.

Mind you, they were talking about mountain gorillas, weren't they?

39

The Club's premises were in a basement at the end of a narrow alley that started at Cronin Square and finished with a fireproof gable. On all maps of the town, and according to the filthy and barely readable nameplate above Wildt's antiquarian bookshop, it was called Zuygers Steeg. But it was always known locally as Butcher's Alley, after an unusually brutal murder at the end of the 1890s, when body parts of two prostitutes were found scattered over practically the full twenty yards comprising the stunted street. The parts were found by a young chaplain from the cathedral, who had to be locked away in the Majorna asylum in Willemsburg. The murderer was never caught, despite a large-scale hunt.

Van Veeteren seldom managed to get as far as the Club without being reminded of the story, and he didn't succeed in doing so this evening either.

Perhaps things were worse in the old days, despite

everything, he thought as he ducked to avoid hitting his head on the lintel and entered the lugubrious vault.

Mahler was sitting furthest in as usual, in the secluded corner under the Dürer print, and he had already set up the pieces. Van Veeteren sat down with a sigh.

'Oh dear,' said Mahler, digging into his tousled beard with his fingers. 'Was it as bad as that?'

'What?' said Van Veeteren.

'What! Being butchered, of course! The green men going about their bloody business.'

'Oh, that,' said Van Veeteren. 'A mere bagatelle.'

Mahler looked puzzled for a moment.

'Then what the hell's worrying you? You've been resurrected, early summer is at its colourful peak, the whole of nature is squirming with pleasure at the celebration of exuberant life that is almost upon us. What the devil do you mean by coming here and sighing?'

'I have a problem,' said Van Veeteren, opening with his queen's pawn.

'I have a thousand,' said Mahler. 'Cheers, and welcome back to the world of the living!'

They drank, and Mahler pored over the chessboard. The chief inspector lit a cigarette and waited. Of all the people he had ever played chess with since he started as a teenager, he had never come across a single opponent who played in the way Mahler did. After an introductory period of intense concentration that could last as long as ten or twelve minutes – before the first move, that is – he would then play more than thirty moves without thinking for more than a minute altogether. Then, before the endgame was embarked upon, he generally allowed himself another in-depth analysis lasting for ten minutes or a quarter of an hour, then finished off the game at breakneck speed – irrespective of whether he was playing for a win, a draw or an honourable defeat.

He could give no plausible reason for his method, apart from maintaining that it was a question of rhythm.

'Sometimes it can feel that making the move at the right time is more important than the quality of the move itself,' he had maintained. 'If you see what I mean.'

Van Veeteren hadn't the slightest idea what he meant.

'It's the same with poems,' the old poet had revealed. 'I often sit staring into space for ages, maybe half an hour or more – then I pick up my pen and write down the whole poem. As quick as a flash, there mustn't be a pause.'

'What goes on inside your head, then?' Van Veeteren wanted to know. 'While you're charging your batteries?'

Mahler had no idea either, it seemed.

'I daren't try to analyse it,' he said. 'Certain things will not tolerate introspection. That kills them off.'

Van Veeteren thought about that as he took a swig of beer and waited for Mahler's move.

Action without thinking, he thought.

Is that what it looked like?

Perhaps there are a few points of contact after all?

'Well?' said Mahler, when they had agreed on a draw after less than forty-five minutes. 'What's the matter?'

'A murderer,' said Van Veeteren.

'I thought you were on sick leave for the rest of this month?'

'I am,' said Van Veeteren. 'It's just that I find it hard to turn my back on things. And also to turn a blind eye.'

'What's the problem with this murderer, then?'

'I can't nail him.'

'Do you know who he is?'

Van Veeteren nodded.

'But you have no proof?'

'Not a thing.'

Mahler leaned back and lit a cigar.

'It can't be the first time you've been in this position?'

'I can usually manage to shoo 'em in.'

Mahler burst out laughing.

'Shoo 'em in! I like it! And why can't you do that this time, then?'

Van Veeteren sighed.

'Does the name Leopold Verhaven mean anything to you?'

Mahler turned serious.

'Verhaven? Yes, of course. A notorious murderer. Of women. Wasn't he murdered himself, or something of the sort? I read about it in the paper not long ago.'

'He was innocent,' said Van Veeteren.

'Verhaven was innocent?'

'Yes.'

'But he's been in jail for . . . God knows how long.'

'Twenty-four years,' said Van Veeteren.

'He's been in jail for that damn length of time, and you're claiming that he's innocent?'

Van Veeteren nodded.

'*Was* innocent. He's dead, as you said. And it seems that it's not only the real murderer who would like to draw a line under the whole business, if you follow me . . .'

Mahler said nothing for some seconds.

'Huh,' he said eventually. He drew on his cigar and spilled ash into his beard. 'I think I get it. The big shots?'

Van Veeteren shrugged.

'It's not all that bad, I hope, but however you look at it, there's no chance of getting proceedings under way unless we're standing on solid ground. Very solid ground.'

'But can't you dig out some proof? Isn't that what

usually happens? You know who did it, but you have to work your butts off to turn the knowledge into proof, afterwards? I thought that was how the police usually went about things.'

'Yes, you're right, of course,' said Van Veeteren. 'But it looks pretty hopeless in his case. Time has run out on the first murder; we're not allowed to open it again. And if the second one is to be reopened, we either have to produce cast-iron proof more solid than the defences at Fort Knox, or he has to confess and stick with that confession. And we're nowhere near either of those set-ups.'

'What about the murder of Verhaven? The same killer yet again?'

'Very much so. No, there's not an ounce of technical proof there either. We don't know when he died. Nor how. Nor where.'

He shrugged again.

'That's about it, all in all.'

'But you know who the murderer is?' said Mahler, raising his bushy eyebrows to register doubt.

'We're absolutely certain,' said Van Veeteren.

Mahler turned the board around and started setting up the pieces for another game.

'How can you be so certain that you won't be able to make him confess? Don't try and tell me you don't resort to third-degree stuff when you have to?'

Van Veeteren lit another cigarette.

'I've been following him for two days,' he said. 'Not furtively, of course, but making it obvious. So that he couldn't avoid noticing. That usually puts anybody you care to name out of his stride, but not this character. He seems to be enjoying it. Gives me a nod now and then. Laughs up his sleeve. He seems to be certain that we haven't got a shred of evidence that could nail him. I haven't confronted him yet, but I'd be amazed if he lost his cool. And even if he did, he'd find it again before the trial started, and we'd be back to square one, having made all that effort for nothing . . .'

'Hmm,' said Mahler. 'What are you going to do, then? It sounds a bit on the awkward side, I have to admit.'

Van Veeteren didn't answer at first, but Mahler was determined to get a response.

'Well?'

'I've given him an ultimatum,' the chief inspector said eventually. 'Would you like another beer?'

'Of course. What kind of an ultimatum?'

Van Veeteren stood up, made his way to the bar and returned after a while with two new, frothy tankards.

'What kind of an ultimatum?' asked Mahler again, after they'd drunk each other's health.

'I've given him an opportunity, that's all. To bow out like a gentleman.'

'Meaning?'

'To commit suicide.'

Mahler seemed almost moved.

'But what if he isn't a gentleman? There seems to be a lot of evidence to suggest that he isn't.'

'Then I'll make public what I know. He has a daughter and two grandchildren. If he merely shrugs and turns away, I'll tell her that her father has three murders on his conscience, and I'll make sure she's convinced that it's the truth. His wife held her tongue for the whole of her life for this very reason . . . Or so I think.'

Mahler thought it over.

'Yes, sounds good,' he said. 'Do you think it'll work?'

Van Veeteren pulled a face.

'The devil only knows,' he said. 'We'll find out tomorrow at noon. I'm going to pay him a visit then.'

'You cunning bastard!' said Mahler. 'You have your methods; I have to grant you that.'

He took another swig, then started to study the board again. After barely a moment's thought, he advanced his king's pawn two squares.

'Not much of a job, the one you've got,' he said.

'Serves me right,' said Van Veeteren.

'Yes, I expect it does,' said Mahler.

*

An hour and a half later, Mahler had turned a single-pawn advantage into a win after just over sixty moves. He bent down and produced a small, flat parcel from the briefcase he had on the floor beside him.

'You can have this as consolation,' he said. 'Hot off the press this afternoon, so it's as fresh as it comes.'

Van Veeteren tore off the wrapping paper.

Recitative from the Back of Beyond, it said.

'Many thanks,' he said. 'Just what I need, I suspect.'

'You never know,' said Mahler, looking at his watch. 'About time to call it a day, methinks. You can start with page thirty-six. I reckon you might find something there that rings a bell.'

Van Veeteren split open the pages of the thin collection of poems after taking a shower and settling into bed. The clock radio on his bedside table said a couple of minutes after half-past twelve, and he decided to make do for the time being with the author's recommendation. Poetry was not something you lapped up at any old time, especially not Mahler's fastidious verses, and he could feel slumber lurking behind his eyelashes.

The poem was called 'January Night' and was only seven lines long.

Light unborn
Lines unknown
The law as yet unwritten
In the darkness the child
In the dancing shadows the rhythms
From the rules of Chaos for the handling of heartache
And a little categorical imperative

He switched off the light, and the lines lingered on, both in the darkness of the room, or so it seemed, and in his own fading consciousness.

The inner and the outer darkness, he thought, just before succumbing to the infinite embrace of sleep.

Tomorrow at noon.

40

As he stood outside the door, his watch said 11:59, and he decided to wait for that one last minute. He had written noon, and perhaps there was a point in being precise with details. Not neglecting the apparently insignificant.

He rang the bell.

Waited for a few seconds, listening for sounds from inside. Put his finger on the button and pressed again. A long, angry ring. Then he leaned forward, listening with his ear pressed against the cool wooden door.

Nothing.

No footsteps. No voices. No human sounds.

He stood upright. Composed himself for a moment. Took a deep breath and tried the door handle.

Open.

He crossed the threshold. Left the door slightly ajar. It was the first time he had entered an apartment where he might expect to find a dead body – it was not a certainty, but there was something else this time. Something that felt both worrying and predictable at the same time.

The air was heavy in the dark, cramped hall. The kitchen was straight ahead. Sun could have been streaming in, but the blinds were drawn. On the right, a door to what looked as if it ought to be a bedroom was half open. On the left was a bathroom and double doors to the living room.

Two rooms and a kitchen, that was all. It was no bigger than that, as Münster had said.

He took the bedroom first. The bed ought to be the obvious place; that's where he'd have chosen himself, if he'd found himself in this situation.

He carefully opened the door wide.

Empty. Bed made, everything neat and tidy. Blinds drawn here as well. As if he had gone away somewhere.

Then the living room. Just as tidy and boring. An ugly suite in some sort of greyish brown, durable synthetic material. A large television set, a bookcase with ornaments. Seascapes on the walls.

The same dreary cooped-up feeling in the kitchen. A calendar and garish landscapes on the walls. Washed dishes in the drying rack, covered with a tea towel. Refrigerator almost empty. A withered potted plant on the table.

Only the bathroom left. A possibility Van Veeteren

might also have chosen. Slowly fading away in hot water. Like Seneca. Not Marat.

He switched on the light.

He could almost imagine the murderer's smile, a lingering, half-ironic reflection in the shiny, dark-blue tiles. As if he'd known that Van Veeteren would save this until last. As if he'd played with the idea of writing a message to this interfering cop and leaving it here, but then decided not to because it was so obvious who would draw the longest straw in this pointless duel.

Van Veeteren sighed and briefly studied his face in the mirror over the sink. It was not a particularly uplifting sight – something midway between Quasimodo and a mournful bloodhound. As usual, in other words; possibly even a bit worse.

He switched off the light and went back into the hall. Paused for a moment, checking that the letter basket on the inside of the door was empty. That had to suggest that he'd left not very long ago. Abandoned this gloomy but well-looked-after apartment about an hour ago, most likely.

It seemed impossible that he had just slipped out for a few minutes. Everything suggested that he had gone away. For a few days at the very least.

Forever? Perhaps that was a good sign, when all was said and done. A glimmer of hope twinkled once more. Why should he do it inside his home?

No reason at all, as far as Van Veeteren could see.

He left the apartment and closed the door behind him.

Why had he left it open?

So that Van Veeteren would be able to examine the apartment? If so, what was the point?

Or had he simply forgotten to lock it?

'Mr Van Veeteren?'

He gave a start. He hadn't noticed that one of the neighbouring doors had been cautiously opened. A woman with red frizzy hair peeked out.

'You are Mr Van Veeteren, aren't you? He said you'd come at about this time.'

Van Veeteren nodded.

'He asked me to tell you that he couldn't meet you here, unfortunately, because he'd gone to the seaside.'

'To the seaside?'

'Yes. He left you a message as well. Here you are.'

She held out an envelope.

'Thank you very much,' said Van Veeteren. 'Did he say anything else?'

She shook her head.

'No, what else was there for him to say? Excuse me, but I've got a cake in the oven.'

She closed the door.

Ah well, thought Van Veeteren, staring at the envelope.

*

He didn't open it until he'd found a table at the outdoor café a bit farther down the same street. As he sat with it in his hand, waiting for the waitress, he thought back to what Mahler had said the previous evening.

Doing something at the right time is more important than what you actually do.

A bit exaggerated, of course, but perhaps it was true that timing was the most important part of all patterns? Of all actions, of every life. In any case, it wasn't an idea to be sneered at, that was clear.

The beer arrived. He drank deeply then opened the envelope. Took out a sheet of paper folded twice and read:

Florian's Guesthouse
Behrensee.

He took another swig.

The sea? he thought. Yes, that was a possibility, of course.

ELEVEN

25 NOVEMBER 1981

41

Night once more.

Awake once more. Judgement was passed yesterday, and her last hope was blown out like a candle flame in a storm.

Guilty.

Verhaven guilty again. She fumbles for her glass. Sips at the lukewarm soda water and closes her eyes. Turns her thoughts inside and out. What is it behind this unbelievable turn of events? What is it forcing her to hang on despite everything? Instead of just letting everything go, dropping all her resistance?

Breaking this lunatic silence and sinking down into the darkness. What?

Andrea, of course.

Last time she was two years old; now she's of marriageable age. A mature woman. The woman her mother never became; there is a progression in everything, an inexorable, black logic against which she has no defences. A destiny, it seems to her.

Please, God, let her relationship with Juhanis come to something.

Please, God, make them make their minds up soon so that he can take her away from here.

Please, God.

When?

When did the first crystal-clear suspicion enter her mind this time?

The same day? That same rainy afternoon in September when the body was discovered by Mr Nimmerlet? As early as that?

Perhaps. Perhaps she knew right away. Suppressed it and slammed the door shut on it. Immediately hit upon her twisted excuse to escape and swallowed it hook, line and sinker; he hadn't been in town that day. He'd driven to Ulming with the broken chainsaw; she checked that herself in her diary. It must have been that very day . . . He stopped by at the Morrisons', on the way as well, even if they weren't at home, it seems. He said that himself, and there had been nothing unusual about what he'd done or the way he'd acted. Nothing unusual.

They couldn't do anything with the saw, but of course

he had been there, and as it's a long way between Ulming and Maardam, it can't have been him. Not this time; this time it really is Verhaven; it must be Verhaven.

Guilty!

But she knows even so.

She's lying here in her big bed in the refurbished bedroom, and knows. Is more and more convinced of this black certainty. Chained to him and to her silence, that's how it feels; more and more bitter, more and more strong, and clearer than ever during these ecstatic, sleepless hours in the early morning.

Him and her. Man and wife.

But never man and woman. Not since Andrea was born. All these years they have never come together. She has closed her legs to him and left him outside; that's what has happened. Transformed this strong and healthy man into somebody who runs after whores. A married man who every month takes his car to town in order to satisfy his tortured urges with bought love.

That's what I have turned him into.

And into a murderer.

Him and her. This unavoidable certainty. And the choice, has she ever had a choice?

No, she thinks, and swallows that as well. I have never had a choice.

She sits upright. Dries the cold sweat off her brow with the back of her hand. Tries to relax her shoulders and take slow, deep breaths while she looks out of the window. The sky in the east is defined by the dark outline of the coniferous forest.

Oh God, she thinks. Can anybody understand?

Even You?

She clasps her hands, but the words of her prayer are locked inside her.

I will take the punishment, she thinks. Punish me for my silence!

Let me remain in my bed forever! Let me . . . let me do just that. Let me cease once and for all staggering through this house, which is my home and my prison. Let me stay here.

May my wrecked pelvis split open forever!

She sinks back against the pillows and it dawns on her that this is how it must be. Exactly like this.

But may there be some kind of meaning, despite everything. At last the words find their way over her lips. May . . . may my unfathomable darkness be my daughter's light! she whispers out into the night. I do not beg for forgiveness!

I do not beg for understanding! I ask for nothing! Punish me, oh God!

Then she closes her eyes, and almost as if she has been given an answer, she can feel the shaft of pain shooting up through her body.

TWELVE

29–31 MAY 1994

42

The rain had been with him for most of the journey, but it started to ease off as he approached the coast. The setting sun broke through the clouds on the horizon, shooting jagged shafts of light over the choppy sea. The air smelled salt-laden and fresh when he got out of the car, and he paused for a few seconds to savour deep breaths of it. Seagulls were gliding over the water, filling the bay with their self-assured, drawn-out screams.

The sea, he thought once again.

People had ventured out onto the beach between the two piers after the rain – it was not a long beach, not much more than half a mile. Some dogs were chasing one another; a group of young people were playing volleyball; a fisherman was sorting out his nets. Van Veeteren couldn't remember when he had last visited this rather old-fashioned seaside resort with its olde-worlde charm; its heyday, when the Casino and Spa Hotel flourished, came to an end at some point in the twenties, unless he was much mistaken – but he had been there several times even so. With Renate and with the children as well; perhaps it was only a couple of occasions, now that he came to think about it . . . A few days each time, but Behrensee was small enough for him to remember where Florian's was located.

Strictly speaking there wasn't much more to the place than the elegant promenade, so he couldn't very well have missed the guesthouse, in any case. But he had a clear memory of it.

A high, art nouveau façade at the southernmost end of a row of hotels and boutiques, squashed between a recently built supermarket and the slightly shabby Sea Horse hotel, where he had stayed during one of his short visits.

If he remembered rightly, that is.

And he did. It was a narrow building, five storeys high, painted pink and white. The copper roof was still glowing faintly in the last rays of the setting sun, and the balconies were a deep wine-red colour. A little bit worse for wear here and there, but certainly not one of the cheaper establishments in this idyllic if crackled resort.

He went through the milky-white glass doors. Placed his briefcase carefully on the floor and rang the bell on the reception desk. After half a minute a middle-aged woman appeared with a towel in her hands. It looked as if she had been busy drying dishes. She squinted at him over the edge of her gold-framed spectacles, and hid the towel away.

'Yes?'

'I'm looking for Arnold Jahrens. If my information is correct, he is staying here.'

'Let's have a look.'

She turned some pages of the ledger.

'Yes, that's right. Room 53. It's on the top floor. You can take the elevator.'

She stood on tiptoe and pointed over his shoulder.

'Is he in now?'

She checked the key rack.

'I think so. He hasn't left his key here, in any case.'

'The top floor, you said?'

'Yes.'

'Thank you,' said Van Veeteren. 'I'll just see to a few things first; then I'll be back in a few minutes.'

'As you wish,' said the woman, picking up the towel again.

He knocked twice, but there was no sign of life.

He tried the handle, and the door swung open.

An ordinary sort of room, he decided. But with a certain traditional charm. A wide bed with an iron frame.

Quite high, dark wainscoting. A small desk. Two even smaller armchairs. A wardrobe.

To the left, just inside the door, was the bathroom. As he could see the room was empty, he opened the door and switched on the light.

Empty here as well. There was no bath, only a modern shower; there was no suitable place for somebody intending to commit suicide.

He entered the room. Put his briefcase on the desk and dug a toothpick from the supply in his breast pocket. Looked around.

'Detective Chief Inspector Van Veeteren, I presume?'

The voice came from the balcony and had just the restrained tone of mockery and self-confidence that Van Veeteren was dreading most of all.

'Mr Jahrens,' he said, going out onto the balcony. 'May I sit down?'

The powerfully built man nodded and indicated the empty basket chair on the other side of the table.

'I have to say that you seem to have a damn good imagination for a police officer. I really don't understand how anybody could cook up a story like this one.'

Van Veeteren opened his briefcase.

'Whisky or brandy?' he asked.

'If you think it will help if you make me drunk, you have another thought coming.'

'Not at all,' said Van Veeteren. 'It's just that I couldn't find any beer.'

'All right.'

Jahrens fetched two glasses from inside the room, and Van Veeteren poured.

'You don't need to play around,' he said. 'The fact is that I know you have three lives on your conscience, and I shall make sure that you don't get away with it. Cheers.'

'Cheers,' said Jahrens. 'And how do you think you are going to do that? I expect you have a little microphone or transmitter hidden away somewhere that's linked to a tape recorder somewhere else, and you're hoping that I'm going to get tipsy and let the cat out of the bag. Isn't that a cheap trick? Is that how you trap folks nowadays?'

'Not at all,' said Van Veeteren. 'It wouldn't hold up in court, anyway, but I'm sure you know that. No, I'm simply going to tell you how I see it. If you're frightened of a tape recorder or something of the sort, you can nod or shake your head as you please. I think you need to run through it all, you as well.'

'Rubbish,' said Jahrens, sipping his whisky. 'Sure as hell, you've made me curious. It's not every day you get an opportunity to study a police officer with a screw loose at close quarters.' He smiled and shook a cigarette out of the pack on the table in front of him. 'Would you like one?'

'Yes, please.'

Van Veeteren accepted both the cigarette and a light before he got under way.

'Tell me about Leopold Verhaven!'

Arnold Jahrens smiled again and drew on his cigarette. Looked up and gazed out to sea. A few seconds passed.

'It'll be fine weather tomorrow, don't you think, Chief Inspector? Will you be staying here for some days?'

'As you like,' said Van Veeteren, leaning forward over the table. 'I'll tell you what happened, and you can interrupt me if anything is unclear . . . You have murdered three people. Beatrice Holden, Marlene Nietsch and Leopold Verhaven. Verhaven has been in jail for twenty-four years, thanks to you. You are a bastard; don't be misled by my friendly tone.'

Jahrens's cheek muscle twitched several times, but he said nothing.

'The only thing I'm not a hundred per cent certain of is the motive. Although I'm pretty sure about that in outline even so. Correct me if I'm wrong, as I said. On April sixth, 1962, a Saturday, you go up to Verhaven's house in the woods because you know Beatrice Holden is alone there. Presumably you've waited until the electrician finished what he was doing, and when you've seen him walking back home to the village, you set off. You are horny. Less than a week ago you've had Beatrice lying on your sofa, naked under a blanket, and that's more than you can cope with. You've probably peeked at her under the blanket, maybe touched her as well, while she was sleeping off her intoxication and your semi-invalid wife is upstairs in the bedroom with no idea of what's going on. Your two-year-old daughter as well. Maybe you put your hands between her legs . . . between Beatrice Holden's legs; that's where you're itching to be. A hot-blooded, sexy, good-looking woman – unlike your wife, lying upstairs as cold as ice, who never lets you in.'

Arnold took a sip of his drink, but his expression didn't change.

'You arrive at the Big Shadow, and there she is. All on her own. Verhaven is in Maardam and isn't expected home for several hours. She's there for the taking. All you need to do is to go up to her, whisper a few fancy words, pull off her panties and get cracking. Why didn't she want to, Mr Jahrens? Tell me that. Why weren't you allowed in between Beatrice Holden's legs – she was generally so keen? Hadn't she already half-promised you a reward that night when you took her in? Or was it just that you'd misunderstood it?'

Jahrens coughed.

'What an imagination,' he said and emptied his glass. 'You're the one who's perverted, Chief Inspector, not me.'

'It was scandalous, wasn't it? Isn't that how it felt?'

'What was?'

'That you weren't allowed to screw Beatrice Holden. That the wretched Leopold Verhaven could have her, but not you. That stupid lump of shit that you'd looked down on ever since you'd been at school together. Leopold Verhaven! The cheat! The egg seller in the Big Shadow! A pathetic creature you've despised all your life . . . And here he is, living with this desirable woman, while you, you've married a highly desirable farm, one of the richest in the whole of Kaustin, but at what price! The price is your worn-out wife who'll never let you have her, and now you're here, this particular Saturday afternoon, and Beatrice Holden won't let you have her either. Maybe she laughs at you – yes, damn it all, I think she laughs at you, and says she'll tell Verhaven when he comes home what a useless old goat you are.'

He paused briefly. Jahrens stubbed out his cigarette and gazed out to sea again.

'Would you mind telling me if there are any details in my reconstruction that are not correct?' said Van Veeteren, leaning back in his chair.

Jahrens said nothing. Sat there without moving, but showed no sign of nervous tension or irritation.

'So I was right from start to finish? I thought as much,' said Van Veeteren with a satisfied smile. 'Maybe you'd like to continue yourself, nevertheless? How you raped her and strangled her. Or was it the other way round?'

'I shall be informing your superiors about this conversation,' said Jahrens after a few seconds. 'First thing tomorrow morning.'

'Excellent,' said Van Veeteren. 'A drop more whisky?'

Without a word, Jahrens picked up the bottle and refilled his glass. Van Veeteren raised his glass as if to toast him, but his host wasn't even looking at him. They drank in silence.

'Number two,' said Van Veeteren. 'Marlene Nietsch.'

Jahrens raised his hand.

'No, thank you,' he said. 'You've gone far enough. You can go to hell with your damned fantasies. I've better things to do than to . . .'

'That would never occur to me,' Van Veeteren cut him short. 'I'm staying where I am.'

Jahrens snorted and for the first time looked to be of two minds. About time, Van Veeteren thought.

'All right. Either you give me your word that you'll be out of here in half an hour at the most, or I'll call the police right now.'

'I *am* the police,' said Van Veeteren. 'Wouldn't it be better if you tried to contact a lawyer? A good lawyer? You still wouldn't have a chance, but it generally feels better if you've done everything in your power, believe you me.'

Jahrens lit another cigarette, but made no move to head for the telephone. Van Veeteren stood up and looked out to sea. The sun had sunk below the horizon some considerable time ago, and blue twilight hovered over the town. He stood there for about a minute with his hands on the low railing, waiting for Jahrens to make a move. But he didn't.

Just sat there in the basket chair. Took a sip of whisky now and again, apparently unconcerned by the presence of Van Veeteren.

Perhaps he had never been worried? Not even for one moment?

Better press on, thought Van Veeteren, sitting down opposite him once more.

He poured out the last drops from the whisky bottle and held it out over the table.

'It doesn't go very far,' he said, and Jahrens gave a laugh.

It was dark now. The little lamp in the corner of the balcony was not strong enough to reach very far either. For the last half-hour Arnold Jahrens had been little more than a motionless outline. A dark silhouette, with his face in shadow, making it impossible for Van Veeteren to see what effect his words and all his efforts were having. Assuming they had any at all.

'So you're not going to tell me where you interred his head? That's a little shameful, don't you think? I fear you will not end up very high in Dante's inferno, I suppose you're aware of that?'

He was expressing himself rather more formally; hard to say why, perhaps it was to do with the alcohol and the darkness.

Jahrens said nothing.

'How do you think your daughter is going to react?'

'What to? To your laughable insinuations?'

'Laughable? Do you really think she'll laugh?'

Jahrens burst out laughing again, as if he wanted to be the one who judged what was an appropriate reaction.

'Your wife was able to refrain from laughter, in any case.'

Jahrens snorted instead. There was a distinct trace of tipsiness in it, Van Veeteren thought, and he decided to pin his faith on that judgement and that circumstance. Now's the moment, he thought. Make or break. He was beginning to feel less than clear in the head himself, in fact; they had certainly drunk a great deal, and there was a limit to the time available.

'Would you like to check on that?' he asked.

'On what?'

'How your daughter reacts to all this?'

'What the hell do you mean?'

Van Veeteren pulled the little pin out of his lapel and held it up between his thumb and index finger.

'Do you know what this is?'

Jahrens shook his head.

'A transmitter. Just as you guessed at the start.'

'So what, damn it?' said Jahrens, interrupting him. 'You know very well that I haven't confirmed the tiniest detail of all this crap you've been coming out with.'

'That's what you think,' said Van Veeteren. 'Perhaps you'll change your mind when you hear the tape. That's what usually happens.'

'Crap,' said Jahrens, fumbling for another cigarette. 'What's this got to do with my daughter? Are you going to play it for her, or what the hell do you mean?'

'That won't be necessary,' said Van Veeteren, carefully replacing the pin in his lapel.

'Won't be necessary? And what's that supposed to mean?'

'She's already heard it all.'

Jahrens dropped his cigarette and gaped. Van Veeteren stood up.

'These two rooms,' he said, pointing with both hands. 'Number 52 and number 54 . . .'

Jahrens took hold of the chair arms and started to rise to his feet.

'What the devil . . . ?'

'Three police officers are sitting in room 52 with a tape recorder. They have noted every single word of our conversation. Haven't missed a detail, I can assure you. In the other room . . .'

He pointed.

'. . . in the other room are your daughter, Andrea, and her husband.'

'What the hell . . . ?'

Van Veeteren went over to the railing and pointed again.

'If you come here you can catch a glimpse of them, if you lean out a little bit . . .'

Arnold Jahrens needed no second invitation, and it was soon all over. Even so, Van Veeteren knew that those brief seconds would haunt him through all the dark nights of the rest of his life.

Perhaps even longer.

When he came out to the car, he could feel that he was much more drunk than he had thought, and there was obviously no question of him sitting behind the wheel. He took off the false beard and wig, put them in a plastic carrier bag and pushed it under the driver's seat for the time being. Then he nestled down under the blanket on the back seat and wished himself a good and dreamless night.

Five minutes later he was sleeping like a log, and by the time the ambulance and the police cars started arriving, he was beyond reach of the sirens and the raised voices.

Nobody paid any attention to the slightly battered Opel, somewhat carelessly parked in the darkness two blocks north of Florian's Guesthouse. Why should they?

43

'Have you seen this?' asked Jung, handing over the newspaper. 'Wasn't it you who interviewed him?'

Rooth looked at the photograph.

'Yes, it was. What the hell's happened to him?'

'Fell from the fifth floor. Or maybe jumped. Accident or suicide, that's the question. What was he like?'

Rooth shrugged.

'Much like everybody else. Quite pleasant, I seem to recall. Served up coffee, in any case.'

Reinhart sat down opposite Münster in the canteen.

'Good morning,' he said. 'How are you?'

'Now what are you after?' said Münster.

Reinhart tipped the contents of his pipe into the ashtray and started filling it.

'Can I ask you a simple question?' he said.

Münster put the *Neuwe Blatt* to the side.

'You can always try.'

'Hmm,' said Reinhart, leaning forward over the table. 'I don't suppose you happened to be in Behrensee the evening before last?'

'Certainly not,' said Münster.

'What about the chief inspector?'

'I can't imagine he would have been. He's still on sick leave.'

'Ah yes, so he is,' said Reinhart. 'I just thought I'd ask. An idea had occurred to me.'

'Really?' said Münster.

He went back to his newspaper, and Reinhart lit his pipe.

Hiller knocked and came straight in. DeBries and Rooth looked up from the reports they were writing.

'That was a nasty accident out at Behrensee,' said the chief of police, rubbing his chin. 'Is it something we ought to look into?'

'Surely not,' said deBries. 'The local boys can look after it.'

'OK. I just thought I'd ask. You can go back to whatever it was you were doing.'

And the same to you, deBries thought, exchanging glances with Rooth.

'You know that we've had two phone calls, I suppose?' said Rooth when the chief of police had closed the door.

'No,' said deBries. 'What kind of phone calls?'

'Anonymous. From Kaustin. They don't seem to be from the same person, either. One was a man, the other a woman, according to Krause.'

DeBries looked up and bit his pen.

'What do they say?'

'The same thing, more or less. That this Jahrens had something to do with the murders. The Verhaven murders. They've always suspected it, but didn't want to say anything, it seems. That's what they say, at least.'

DeBries thought for a while.

'Well. I'll be damned,' he said. 'So he's got his punishment after all, has he?'

'Could be,' said Rooth. 'Mind you, they are probably just a couple of nosy parkers who want to get themselves noticed. In any case, it's not something we need to worry about.'

Nobody spoke for several seconds. Then deBries shrugged.

'No, the case has been dropped, if I understand matters rightly. I think so. We've got plenty of stuff to keep our noses to the grindstone.'

'More than enough,' said Rooth.

*

'May I join you?' asked Mahler, sitting down on the empty chair. 'Why are you sitting here, by the way?'

'I sit wherever I like,' said Van Veeteren. 'I'm on sick leave, and the weather's not bad. I like watching people trudging away on the treadmill. Besides, I have a book to read.'

Mahler nodded in sympathy.

'It wouldn't be so good for you in the sun, perhaps.'

He looked out over the square and summoned one of the waitresses.

'Two dark beers,' he said.

'Thanks,' said Van Veeteren.

They waited until the beer was served, toasted each other, then leaned back in their chairs.

'Well, how did it go?' asked Mahler.

'How did what go?'

'Don't play games with me,' said Mahler. 'I've just bought you a damn beer, and given you my poems.'

Van Veeteren took another drink.

'That's true,' he said. 'Anyway, it's all over now.'

'So he succumbed to your pressure in the end?'

The chief inspector pondered on that for a while.

'Precisely,' he said. 'You couldn't put it more poetically than that.'

THIRTEEN

19 JUNE 1994

44

In the churchyard at Kaustin there were lime trees and elms, and a few horse chestnut trees, whose extensive root systems had many a time caused the verger, Maertens, to swear out loud when he encountered them with his spade. On this summer Sunday, however, he had every reason to think otherwise – as did the rest of the group standing around the newly opened family grave. They were grateful for the dense network of branches that provided shade and a degree of coolness during the simple burial ceremony.

If they had been forced to stand in the scorching sun, you could bet your life that some of them would have fainted.

There were only six of them, to be precise. And three of those were part of the team, you might say: Maertens himself, Wolff, the choirmaster and organist, and Pastor Kretsche, who conducted the service. The rest were Mrs Hoegstraa, the deceased's ancient sister who evidently didn't have many years left herself, and two of the Maardam police force. They had been here sniffing around a month or so ago, but needless to say, they hadn't achieved anything.

But that's the way it goes. Leopold Verhaven had been buried. Well, most of him; needless to say, they hadn't succeeded in finding the missing body parts. They would have to slot them in later, if they ever turned up. Sometimes you had to ask yourself what on earth the police did with their time. And what they were being paid for.

But that's the way it goes. He had no desire to ask them about it. He was just waiting for Kretsche to finish so that he could fill in the grave and go home to watch the international soccer match on the box.

The vicar was going on about inscrutability. The all-consuming love and mercy of our Lord God. Forgiveness.

Well, what the hell could he say? Maertens sighed and leaned discreetly against the trunk of an elm tree. Closed his eyes and felt a faint breeze creeping in over the churchyard, barely discernible, and not really providing any cooling effect at all. In his mind's eye he could see a large, misty beer glass in his own hand, in front of the television screen.

Ah well, would but that we were there, he thought, and wondered where on earth that expression came from. Something biblical, presumably; given the way he earned his daily bread, it was inevitable that he would pick up the odd phrase here and there.

He opened his eyes and looked at the group. Mrs Hoegstraa was wearing a veil; she looked dogged, and hadn't shed a single tear. Kretsche was going on and on as usual. Wolff was half asleep. The elder of the two police officers was sweating profusely and occasionally wiped his face with a bright-coloured handkerchief. The younger one seemed to be brooding over something or other, goodness only knows what.

Were they actually getting paid for standing here? That wouldn't surprise him in the least.

'. . . on the Day of Judgment, Amen!' said the vicar, and it was all over.

Rest in peace, Leopold Verhaven, Maertens thought, and looked around for his spade.

'I've been thinking about a few things,' said Münster as they came to the parking lot.

'Let's hear about them,' said Van Veeteren.

'Well,' said Münster, 'in the first place, how did you come to think that he was the guilty party? Jahrens, that is.'

'Hmm,' said Van Veeteren. 'The wheelchair ramp at the Czermaks' house, of course. And that woman at the prison with the walking stick. Maybe I didn't catch on right away, but there was a link, in any case. A little bell ringing somewhere in the background . . .'

'But Mrs Jahrens was an invalid. She couldn't walk, not even with walking sticks.'

Van Veeteren fanned himself with a newspaper.

'Not everything is as it seems, Münster. I thought we'd agreed on that?'

'And what might that mean?' asked Münster.

'Oh, various things,' said the chief inspector, gazing out over the churchyard. 'That the root, or source, of evil isn't always where we expect to find it, for instance. Leopold Verhaven's fate – and I really do hope we shall be able to restore his reputation one of these days – has hardly anything to do with him. Like it or not, he becomes the unwilling main character in a silent and bitter and pointless drama fought between Mr and Mrs Jahrens. He's totally innocent, but he is cast as the scapegoat and gets to spend a quarter of a century in jail. No wonder he becomes a bit odd! When Mrs Jahrens eventually decides to go to confession, all it leads to is the death of Verhaven. That is the biggest barrow-load of garbage you can ever imagine, Münster; but there again, maybe there is some kind of inverted logic behind it all. You can almost hear them roaring with laughter down there in the underworld, if you get my meaning.'

He looked up at the bright, cloud-spattered summer sky.

'Even on a day like this,' he added.

They stood in silence for a while.

'And Marlene Nietsch?' Münster asked.

'A coincidence, I reckon,' said Van Veeteren. 'He'd probably come across her in the village and recognized her, and that morning he just happened to be driving past Zwille when Verhaven left her. He most likely saw an opportunity and picked her up, no more than that, and we know what happened next. She didn't want to, and so he turned violent. That's what I think happened, but there are lots of other possibilities, of course.'

'And the missing bits? Of Verhaven, I mean.'

The chief inspector shrugged.

'No idea. I expect they're buried somewhere – I'm inclined to hope they stay wherever they are. Just think if they find them a hundred years from now and start a new investigation! I sometimes get the feeling that this is a case that could go on forever.'

Münster nodded and opened his car door.

'Anyway, that'll have to be it for now,' he said. 'I'd better get home and pack. We're off tomorrow.'

'Italy?' asked Van Veeteren.

'Yes. Two weeks in Calabria and one in Tuscany. When are you going on holiday?'

'August,' said Van Veeteren. 'I haven't really started to think about it yet, but I suppose that's not necessary. July is usually rather a good month to spend in Maardam. Calm and peaceful. All the idiots are away on holiday. Don't take that personally, by the way.'

'That would never occur to me,' said Münster. 'All the best!'

'Have a good holiday,' said Van Veeteren. 'Take good care of your lovely wife. And the kids, of course. It'll be badminton time again, come September.'

'It certainly will,' said Münster.

Once again he drove up to the Big Shadow. Never got out of the car. Merely sat there, contemplating the overgrown house and garden while smoking a cigarette and drumming his fingers on the steering wheel.

What a goddamn awful business, he thought.

And now all those involved were dead. Just as in a Shakespearean tragedy. Beatrice Holden and Marlene Nietsch. Arnold and Anna Jahrens. And Verhaven himself, of course.

But justice had been done after all. Insofar as that was possible, that is. Nemesis had claimed her due. That was the only way of looking at it.

And who were left?

Verhaven's ancient sister, who had played no part at all in the events.

Andrea Jahrens, or Välgre, as she was called nowadays. The daughter, with two children of her own.

You could say they were the only survivors, in fact; Mrs Hoegstraa would soon join the others six feet down.

Survivors, and completely ignorant of the whole business. Needless to say, there was no reason why they should be informed.

He would never dream of doing so.

Never.

And as he drove slowly back down the hill for the last time to the village, which was wallowing sleepily if misleadingly in the summer sunshine, he thought about what he had said to Münster.

Not everything is what it seems.

Kaustin – the village of murders.

Then it struck him that he hadn't really told Münster the whole truth. The real reason why he'd stopped by at the Czermaks' that morning was, of course, not because he had noticed the wheelchair ramp – that was something he'd picked up in passing. No, the real reason was more prosaic than that, and just now he was beginning to feel the same symptom.

He'd been thirsty.

Ah well, he thought, possessed by a sudden if brief

attack of cheerfulness, and an obvious risk of repeating himself: not everything is what it seems.

He sped up and started thinking instead about that borderline that he'd at long last overstepped.

If you enjoyed The Return *you'll love*

THE MIND'S EYE

the next Inspector Van Veeteren mystery

Teacher Janek Mitter wakes up one morning not remembering who he is. As he stumbles into the bathroom, he sees the body of a beautiful young woman floating dead in his bath. The woman is his wife, Eva, and she has been viciously attacked.

Even during his trial, Janek has no memory of attacking his wife, nor any idea as to who could have killed her if it wasn't him. Only when he is sentenced and locked up in an asylum for the criminally insane does he have a snatch of insight. He scribbles something in his Bible, but he is murdered before the clue can be uncovered.

Chief Inspector Van Veeteren becomes convinced that something, or someone, in the dead woman's life has caused this tragic double murder. As he delves further, Eva's tragic story begins to emerge, and Van Veeteren realizes that the past never really stops haunting the present . . .

The first chapter follows here . . .

[illegible] unable to [illegible]

[illegible]

[illegible]

[illegible] but [illegible]

1

He woke up and was unable to remember his name.

His pains were legion. Shafts of fire whirled round in his head and throat, his stomach and chest. He tried to swallow, but it remained an attempt. His tongue was glued to his soft palate. Burning, smouldering.

His eyes were throbbing. Threatening to grow out of their sockets.

It's like being born, he thought. I'm not a person. Merely a mass of suffering.

The room was in darkness. He groped round with his free hand, the one that was not numb and tingling underneath him.

Yes, there was a bedside table. A telephone and a glass. A newspaper. An alarm clock.

He picked it up, but halfway it slipped through his

fingers and fell onto the floor. He fumbled around, took hold of it again and held it up, close to his face.

The hands were slightly luminous. He recognized them.

Twenty past eight. Presumably in the morning.

He still had no idea who he was.

He didn't think this had happened before. He had certainly woken up and not known where he was. Or what day it was. But his name . . . Had he ever forgotten his name?

John? Janos?

No, but something like that.

It was there, somewhere in the background, not only his name, but everything . . . Life and lifestyle and extenuating circumstances. Lying there waiting for him. Behind a thin membrane that would have to be pierced, something that had not woken up yet. But he was not really worried. He would know soon enough.

Perhaps it was not something to look forward to.

The pain behind his eyes suddenly got worse. Possibly the strain of thinking had caused it; but it was there, whatever. White-hot and excruciating. A scream of flesh.

Nothing else mattered.

*

The kitchen was to the left and seemed familiar. He found the tube of tablets without difficulty; he was becoming increasingly sure that this was his home. No doubt everything would become clear at any moment.

He went back into the hall. Kicked against a bottle standing in the shadow cast by a bookcase. It rolled away over the parquet floor and ended up under the radiator. He shuffled to the bathroom. Pressed down the handle.

It was locked.

He leaned awkwardly forward. Put his hands on his knees to support himself, and checked the indicator.

Red. As he'd thought. It was occupied.

He could feel the bile rising.

'Open . . .' he tried to shout, but could produce no more than a croak. He leaned his forehead against the cool wood of the door.

'Open up!' he tried again, and this time managed to produce the right sounds, almost. To stress the seriousness of his situation, he banged several times with his clenched fists.

No response. Not a sound. Whoever was in there obviously had no intention of letting him in.

There was a sudden surge from his stomach. Or possibly from even lower down . . . It was obviously a matter of seconds now. He staggered back along the hall. Into the kitchen.

This time it seemed more familiar than ever.

This is definitely my home, he thought as he vomited into the sink.

With the aid of a screwdriver he succeeded in unlocking the bathroom door. He had a distinct feeling that it was not the first time he'd done this.

'I'm sorry, but I really had to . . .'

He entered the room and, just as he switched on the light, he became quite clear about who he was.

He could also identify the woman lying in the bath.

Her name was Eva Ringmar and she was his wife of three months.

Her body was strangely twisted. Her right arm hung over the edge at an unnatural angle. The well-manicured fingernails reached right down to the floor. Her dark hair was floating on the water. Her head was face-down, and as the bath was full to the brim there could be no doubt that she was dead.

His own name was Mitter. Janek Mattias Mitter. A teacher of history and philosophy at the Bunge High School in Maardam.

Known informally as JM.

After these insights he vomited again, this time into the lavatory. Whereupon he took two more tablets out of the tube and telephoned the police.

extracts reading groups
competitions books new
discounts extracts
competitions
books new
events books
extracts new reading groups
interviews
events extracts
discounts
new books events
events new
discounts extracts discounts
www.panmacmillan.com
extracts events reading groups
competitions books extracts new